# Carry Me Home

# Carry Me Home

Sandra Kring

DELTA TRADE PAPERBACKS

CARRY ME HOME
A Delta Trade Paperback / January 2005

Published by
Bantam Dell
A division of Random House, Inc.
New York, New York


Cover design by Royce Becker

Book design by Glen Edelstein



Library of Congress Cataloging in Publication Data
Kring, Sandra.
Carry me home / Sandra Kring.
p. cm.
I: Teenage boys—Fiction. II: World War, 1939–1945—Veterans—Fiction. III: Brothers—Fiction. IV: Wisconsin—Fiction. V: Genre/Form: Historical fiction. VI: Humorous fiction. VII: Domestic fiction.
ISBN: 0-385-33813-9
PS3611.R545 C37 2005
813/.6 22
2004056200

Manufactured in the United States of America
Published simultaneously in Canada

BVG 10 9 8 7 6 5 4 3 2 1

*For the soldiers of all wars,*
*and the families who waited for them to come home*

# Carry Me Home

# Chapter 1

Jimmy stands out by the oak tree next to the garage. He's turning in circles, all skittery-like. From my bedroom window I see the orange dot from his cigarette making streaks as he turns. I know if I don't hurry and get down there, he's gonna say piss on me, and leave. I walk real careful and put my ear against my door and it's cold. The door, not my ear. And I listen real good for Ma, but I don't hear nothing but for that loud whooshing you get in your ears when you're scared of getting caught climbing out your window.

I go back to the window—the one I opened while the house was still all noisy with Glenn Miller, 'cause simpleminded or not, I ain't exactly a fool—and I climb out real quiet-like.

Them shingles feel like a cat's tongue against my hands as I scoot across the rooftop on my ass.

I get to the edge of the roof and drop down, my hands squeezing real tight, then I dangle there like a string of snot 'til Jimmy comes and gets ahold of my legs. He catches me, then drops me with a thud. "Crissakes, Earwig, you get any taller and you won't need me to catch you." Jimmy calls me "Earwig." He says it's 'cause I'm like one of those bugs that crawls in a guy's ear and goes right to his brain, making him go crazy. Jimmy reaches up and rubs his knuckles over my hair that is turd-brown and grows straight up like quack grass, then he grabs our fishing gear and off we go down the sidewalk.

Jimmy whistles as we go down them empty, dark streets to get to Louie's house. Jimmy's car is in the garage, the motor all ripped to shit, so Louie's gonna drive his car to the millpond, where we're gonna spear suckers and drink beers. Jimmy's real nice to let me come along. Ain't many brothers who'd take their sixteen-year-old, dumb-as-a-stump brother to fish and drink beers with 'em. But Jimmy's always letting me tag along. He knows I ain't got friends like he's got, 'cept for Eddie, and he don't count 'cause he's only six years old, fat as a Thanksgiving turkey, and maybe even dumber than me.

Louie's coming outta the garage with his creel when we get there, his orange, frazzly hair looking like fire with the porch light shining on it. John is leaned up against Louie's car, smoking a cigarette, and Floyd, he is standing there kicking up gravel with his shoe, his shoulders all drooped forward, like they always is.

"You took long enough, Gunderman," John says, and Jimmy says to him, "Ah, give it a rest, Pissfinger." I don't call John Pissfinger like the rest of the gang does, on accounta I know if I do, he's probably gonna stick his boot so far up my ass I'll gag on his shoelaces.

We all whoop and holler as we pull outta the driveway, spitting gravel.

"Serve 'em up, Earwig," Jimmy says. I reach under the seat to fetch the bottles of Schlitz that are clinking and clanking there. I pry a cap with the opener I got dangling from my belt, slip the cap into my pocket, and hand the first bottle to Louie. It's the rule: The number-one guy gets the first beer, and usually, whoever's got a car that's running is the number-one guy.

All the way to the millpond, them guys talk about titties, beers, and whose asses they're gonna kick. Jimmy's the only one of them guys that can really kick anybody's ass. Jimmy ain't real tall, but he's got muscles pert' near as big as Captain Midnight's, and like John says, Jimmy knows how to use his fists when he's gotta. I tell 'em I know a few asses I'd like to kick, and Jimmy tells me to shut up or he's gonna fart in my face. I know he will too, so I shut up.

Them trees along the road to the millpond look like butt-naked skinny girls against the sky that's bright from a fat moon. Jimmy told me once that them fat circle moons remind him of a big, white titty. Course, he thinks everything looks like a titty.

We turn off Mill Street and head down the dirt road that goes to the millpond. Louie drives so fast over the bumps that I bang my head on the roof.

Louie jams on the brakes and we stop real fast. Beer slops down the front of John's shirt and he pisses and moans about it like he's going to the town hall for a fancy-up dance instead of grubbing for suckers at the millpond.

We stand on the bank and rip our shoes and socks off. I know damn well it's gonna be cold as shit in that rushing water, the snow here in Wisconsin not being gone all that long when them suckers start wriggling upriver looking for a place to drop their eggs. We're all laughing and joking and having a good time. Ain't nothing more fun than spearing suckers with Jimmy and the guys.

"Hey, Earwig," John says, as he balls up a sock and throws it at me. "I hear you tried choppin' off Edna Pritchard's fat leg." Floyd and Louie start to laughing. I talk real loud so John can hear me above the laughing and the whooshing of the water. "I wasn't trying to chop her leg off. That's the God's honest truth."

"That's right," Jimmy says, talking all mumbled 'cause he's got a Camel sticking outta the corner of his mouth. "He wasn't trying to cut off her leg, he was trying to measure her fat ass." This makes them laugh all the harder.

"Tell us the story, Earwig," Floyd says, so I tell 'em. I tell 'em how Dad said, right there at the table while buttering a piece of nut bread Mrs. Pritchard brought, that that Edna Pritchard has the biggest ass he ever see'd on a woman. Dad said, "That ass has got to be at least three ax handles wide."

"Well, that didn't sound right to me," I tell the guys, and it didn't. "Mrs. Pritchard has a fat ass, sure as my name's Earl Hedwig Gunderman, but three ax handles wide, that just didn't sound right to me. So I wait 'til I hear her big mouth yapping in the store, then I go out to the woodpile real fast and I fetch myself the ax. Then I go back into the store, whistling so as no one thinks I'm up to something, and I start taggin' after Mrs. Pritchard. Ma and her was talking about that Dickens girl getting polio and what a pity it will be if her legs get all crippled, and how, worse yet, if that little girl dies, her mama's heart's gonna cripple up too and she'll die right along with her. Mrs. Pritchard is looking at cans of applesauce while she talks, 'cause she's gonna make some gingerbread and Mr. Pritchard won't eat gingerbread unless it's got applesauce poured over the top."

"Crissakes," Jimmy says as he roots around in our stuff for a spear, "get to the goddamn point of the story, Earwig," but he ain't mad when he says it, 'cause he's laughing.

"Well," I tell 'em, "I go'ed up behind Mrs. Pritchard, holding that ax like this," and I show 'em how I holded it, sideways like, right behind her fat ass. "And it sure is a fat ass," I say, and Floyd holds his skinny guts that are sunk in like a bowl and asks how would I like to hose that fat ass, and I say I wouldn't like that at all. Jimmy says, "The story, Earwig, get to the point of the goddamn story."

So I go on with the story. I tell 'em how I was holding that ax up crossways, following behind her, and how when she walks, her ass under that dress looks like two bulls fighting under a sheet of mill felt.

"Then Ma looks up and sees me behind Mrs. Pritchard, who ain't so far seeing nothing but that can of applesauce in her hand, and Ma yells, 'Earl Hedwig Gunderman, what on earth are you doing with that ax?' and Mrs. Pritchard starts to turn and she sees me holding that ax, and she starts to screaming. I get all scared 'cause her scream is as big as her ass, and that ax falls right outta my hands, just as her fat legs are turning her around." Floyd is slapping the ground with his hand, laughing real hard.

I turn to Louie, who is laughing too, but not so hard he can't hear me. "You ever see an ax fall, Louie? It don't fall flat and nice at all. That cutting part, it falls first, making it look like a ghost is fixing to split a chunk of wood. And that ax come right down on Mrs. Pritchard's fat ankle."

Jimmy is laughing 'til he's choking out, "Cut through her fat almost right down to the bone!" Floyd laughs 'til his dark hair is slapping his forehead like a horse's tail. "Ol' Fat Ass starts hopping around like she's got a rat trying to crawl up the crack of her ass, and Earwig here goes nuts like he always does when he gets rattled. He starts slapping the sides of his head, almost knocking himself out. Then Pritchard really loses it." They're all in stitches now, only I'm starting to think it ain't so goddamn funny. Ain't nothing funny about blood, all red and shiny, spewing out of somebody's fat ankle.

Jimmy shakes his head. "Ma starts in with her 'Oh, good Lord! Oh, good Lord!' And she runs to fetch a towel, then gets down on all fours, trying to get that towel slung around Pritchard's ankle to stop the bleeding. That Pritchard was going nuts, yelling that Earwig had tried to kill her, and Ma was going nuts, screaming at me to go get Dr. McCormick. I had to leave then, so I missed the rest of that freak show."

Them guys start joking about how I shoulda chopped a chunk of her ass off while I was at it, but I ain't listening too hard to 'em now. I'm trying to get Mrs. Pritchard's words outta my head. Them words, "You should have locked that boy up long ago, Eileen."

Ma didn't make me mop up that blood that was already seeping into the cracks of the floor, turning it all dark by the time Dr. McCormick come and took Mrs. Pritchard back in the kitchen to stitch her fat back together. Ma, she came back into the store with a pail of soapy water and started scrubbing with a bunched rag. She made me stand right there, where she could keep an eye on me. She sounded all winded, like she'd just run all the way down Main Street and back without stopping, as she preached at me about minding my Ps and Qs and not scaring people.

"So," John asks after he lights his Lucky Strike, "how many ax handles wide is the old bag's ass, anyway, Earwig?"

"Well, I didn't exactly get to finish measuring it," I tell him, "but I got as far as knowing it's more than one ax handle wide, that's for sure."

I'm real glad when the guys get done laughing and go back to talking about titties and kicking ass.

I go to the trunk of Louie's car to get the bucket we use for keeping the beer cold. I take that bucket and dig the rest of those Schlitz bottles out from under the seat and put them in the bucket. Then I bring the bucket to the groove in the bank that Louie cut out, leaving a little ditch so the water fills up the hole some. I put water in the pail and I set the pail in that little ditch.

While I do this, Floyd and John are getting some wood for the little fire that Jimmy's leaning over, huffing into the thick smoke to get the flames sparking.

When we get everything all set up perfect-like, Jimmy hands me a spear, reminding me to stay on them flat rocks in the shallow part. Jimmy knows I can't swim for shit. The guys head upstream, laughing as they slosh through the water, their arms pumping, each of 'em taking turns bitching about how cold the water is.

The water looks like silver coins swirling in beer foam. I steady myself on a rock and stare real hard through them swirls. I wait for a dark shadow to come along, 'cause that would be one of them suckers. Suckers are ugly critters if I ever see'd one, with scales big as fingernails, and round mouths that move like an asshole trying to squeeze out a turd. Them suckers are mighty ugly, but after Louie sets 'em up in his smokehouse for a time, they end up tasting mighty damn good.

I see one, not far from my feet, and I stab my spear as hard as I can. It don't go into the fish, though. It just bangs against the rock I'm standing on, then skids sideways. I do a little dance to keep that spearhead from kicking up against my foot. Upstream, I can hear the guys and I can tell from their yelling that they're gonna come back with their creels stuffed.

I get real busy then, listening to some noise in the brush, hoping it ain't no bear. I'm scared shitless of bears 'cause I know if one starts wailing on me, there's gonna be lots of blood. And while I'm watching for bears, I'm jabbing my spear into the water any which way, and it keeps clanking against the rocks. Then, about the time Floyd calls out that it's time for a beer break before they all freeze their balls off, I stab my spear into the water and it hits something tender. That handle starts dancing all over in my hands, and I can feel that I got a pissed-off sucker stuck at the other end. "Jimmy! Jimmy!" I shout, real loud.

"You got one, Earwig?" Jimmy shouts back, all excited.

I can't talk, 'cause I'm excited as shit. I don't know what to do, so I don't do nothing 'cept keep dancing on that rock and hanging tight to the spear that's still bucking in my hands.

Jimmy kicks water up on me as he jumps to the rock I'm standing on. "Jesus Christ, Earwig, you gonna stand there pissing yourself, or are you gonna pull it up?"

I ain't gonna piss, but Louie is. He's in the water, his pecker out, and he's about to start pissing. Excited or not, I know I don't want Louie's piss getting on my fish, so I lift that spear up. And there it is, a big-ass sucker, wiggling and squirming 'cause he's got two tines stuck through his back. Even though it's mostly dark, I can see blood, black and shiny, running down the sides of that poor fish.

Jimmy takes the spear from me, clapping me so hard on the back it hurts. "You did it, Earwig! You speared yourself a sucker!" Jimmy leads me to the bank that's cold and hard on my icy feet. He pins the sucker to the ground with his bare foot and yanks the spear out like it don't even turn his stomach. He holds up my fish. "Wow, this bastard's gotta be over two feet long." He's proud of me, and, if I don't look at all that blood, I'm proud of me too.

Louie, John, and Floyd are coming outta the water. They're proud of me too. So proud that after they stoke the fire and I get the beer bucket, they tell me I get the first one. I ain't never been number one 'til now, so I get a happy feeling in my belly that gets so big it starts me to laughing.

Them guys lift their beers high in the air and give me a cheer. I take a big swig like they do, hoping my Adam's apple is bobbing like theirs, 'cause I think that looks real manly. Beer tastes like horse piss to me, but when I take that first swig, I wipe my mouth on my shirtsleeve and say, "Ahhhh," just like they do. I only get one beer 'cause if I have more, I start to puking, but them guys, they keep on drinking 'til the Schlitz caps I got in my pocket are the size of a baseball.

It's the best night ever, with that titty moon shining over us as we drink our beers and warm our naked feet close to the fire 'til it's almost morning. And, dumb as I am, I think that these good days are gonna last forever.

# Chapter 2

I wasn't always simpleminded. Ma says when I was a bitty baby, I was smart as a whip, my big brown eyes always busy. But then I got real sick with a bad fever that baked my brain and about killed me dead. Ma said after that fever was gone, my brain was like meat cooked too long, and it just fell apart whenever I tried to learn something new. "But, Earl, there's no point in crying over spilt milk," Ma said. I ain't exactly sure what spilt milk got to do with that fever, but one thing I do know for sure is that I'm glad that fever got me, and not that goddamn polio. Jimmy says that polio is some wicked shit. It freezes your whole body from your neck to your feet and leaves you either crippled or dead. The President is crippled up from the polio, so he's gotta get around in a wheelchair 'cause his legs are freezed. Dad says he knows this for a fact, even if them newspapers never show him in a chair, 'cause Dad's friend, Delbert Larson, met a big-timey reporter for *The Milwaukee Journal* who said he saw it with his own eyes. One thing I know for sure is I'd rather have my brain baked any day than have my whole body freezed. I might be dumb as a stump, and I might look sorta skinny, but I'm real strong and I'm a fast runner, 'cause I got feet that are big and straight, not all buckled up from the polio.

Fast runner that I am, there ain't no running away from Ma when Jimmy and me get back from sucker fishing. She's sitting at the kitchen table and it's dark in the room 'cause the light from the new sun ain't crawled inside the house yet. She snaps the light on and about scares the shit outta me. She is wearing her robe and she's got them pin curls stuck to her head.

She eyes up my clothes that are splotched with mud, and without even looking at Jimmy, she tells him to go up to his room so she can yell at me. Well, she don't say so she can yell at me, but I know that's what she means.

Jimmy, he holds on to the wall and he uses a heel to wedge off his shoe, 'cause he's all wobbly from beers. "Ah, Ma, don't give Earwig a hard time now. It's my fault. I took him even though I knew he wasn't supposed to go."

"Go upstairs, Jimmy, and get cleaned up before your father wakes up." There ain't no mad in Ma's voice when she talks to Jimmy. Ma never gets mad at Jimmy.

Ma tells me to sit down at the table.

"Earl, do you understand why I told you you couldn't go anyplace for a good long time?" Ma is looking at me real hard, her blue eyes skittering back and forth, looking first at one of my eyeballs, then at the other, probably on accounta my lazy eye.

"Yeah," I say. "'Cause I axed Mrs. Pritchard." I am picking at the legs of my pants like I always do when I'm scared of getting my ears boxed. Something gunky gets on my fingers, and I hope to hell it ain't sucker guts.

Ma sighs like she's just plumb tired out. She rubs the sides of her face with her fingertips. "Go wash up, Earl, and change your clothes. I don't care if you boys didn't get one minute of sleep, you're both going to work. I will not have people thinking that Eileen Gunderman raises irresponsible children. And, Earl," she says, "I've agreed to pay Mrs. Pritchard's doctor bill and the wages of a high-school girl to do her cooking and cleaning until she's back on her feet. That means you'll be working extra hard over the next few weeks to make that money back. Nothing's free in this life, Earl. We always pay for our mistakes. Remember that."

Ma sees to it that I remember too. By noon, I'm wishing she was one of those mean kinda mas, 'cause then she woulda just taked a willow stick and whipped the shit outta me and got it over with quick. Instead, she makes me work and work and work 'til I'm about ready to drop dead.

I'm on the back porch stuffing greasy work clothes into the wash machine when Eddie comes peddling his bike, all wibblety-wobblety, down the sidewalk. He's got an empty pail rocking from the handlebars. "Hey, Earlwig," he says. Eddie calls me "Earlwig" even though I've told him about a million times that it's "Earwig."

"Hey, Eddie," I say. Eddie's got sparkly cinnamon and sugar smeared across his cheek.

"The frogs been croaking, so they probably laid their eggs by now. Want to go to the swamp and get some tadpoles?"

"I know they're croaking," I say. "I was at the millpond last night spearing suckers with Jimmy and the guys, and I heared 'em. I speared myself a big-ass sucker too." I stand all big and tall when I say this, 'cause Eddie, he's just a little kid, and he can't do that grown-up guy stuff yet.

I scoop a pair of soapy pants onto the end of my stick and feed 'em into the wringer part of the washer. "Watch this, Eddie," I say. "There's a man in these pants and he's gonna get squished." I crank the handle, and those pants move between the rollers. Soap and muddy water squishes and bubbles up out of 'em. "Look, that's his blood and guts getting squished out of him!" I start screaming then, like I'm the man who's getting squished. Eddie, he don't laugh, though. He just blinks, scratches at a skeeter bite on his hand, and asks me again if I want to go fetch tadpoles.

If you turn at Sam's Barber Shop and go down that street a couple a blocks, you come to the swamp that has tadpoles in it every spring. Them little eggs are clear and all clumped together, sticking to the grass close to the bank. Inside each of them eggs is a black little dot, and that would be the tadpole, all round like a rolled booger. If that dot inside that jelly part is white, then you might as well leave them eggs right there, 'cause there ain't gonna be no tadpoles hatching outta those. Then they're gonna start to rotting and stinking and your ma is gonna yell at you to get rid of 'em.

So you get the good ones, the ones with the nice black dots inside, and you take 'em home in a pail of swamp water, and you put 'em by the shed or somewhere where the sun ain't gonna bake 'em. In time, them little tadpoles, they hatch and go skittering around in that pail. Then one day them little tadpoles grow bumps, some in the front and some outta their ass end, right close up by their tails. Then their tails just disappear. It's the damnedest thing, but I shit you not. In time, those tadpoles turn right into frogs or toads, just like magic.

"I can't go, Eddie," I say.

"How come you can't go?" Eddie asks.

" 'Cause I can't leave the yard today."

"How come you can't leave the yard today, Earlwig?"

If there's one thing that gets on my nerves about Eddie (besides that he calls me "Earlwig"), it would be that he asks too many goddamn questions.

" 'Cause I did something bad, that's why." I grab the squished man as he falls from the wringer and plop him into the clothes basket. I point and tell Eddie, "That's the squished man's casket."

"What did you do bad, Earlwig?"

"I chopped Mrs. Pritchard's leg with an ax, and I went fishing at the millpond."

"Why'd you do that, Earlwig?" The more I talk about it, the more I see that blood squirting out of Pritchard's leg, and that makes me want to scoop Eddie up with my stick and run him through the goddamn wringer so he shuts up.

"Beat it, Eddie," I say, just like Jimmy says to me when he's got his girlfriend, Molly, around and wants to kiss on her or grab her titties.

Eddie scratches at the sugar on his face like it's tickling him now, shrugs, then props his foot on the pedal of his bike. "You want me to bring you some tadpoles then, Earlwig?" When he says that, I feel kinda bad for even thinking of running little Eddie through the wringer.

"Yeah, Eddie," I say, "that would be real nice. Get the ones that are black inside." Eddie nods, then pedals away.

# Chapter 3

That store at the south end of Main Street, the one with a house stuck on the back and folded up over the top, that would be our store. Gunderman's Grocery, it's called. Out front there's tall glass windows and a wide cement porch with six steps. There's bent pipes to hold on to when you walk up 'em if you're old or crippled up from the polio. Ma's proud of our modern store, 'cause it don't got the stuff behind the counter so the customer's gotta ask you to fetch it. It's all right there on the shelves where people can grab stuff for themselves, just like at the big Piggly Wiggly stores in the city.

After Ma gets old and dead, I'm gonna take over the store, so I gotta learn how to work it. That's what Ma says. She's been teaching me how to work the store ever since that skinny-minny teacher kicked me outta school, saying I was getting too big for the third grade. Ma teached me how to stack the canned goods so they don't come crashing down on some poor little kid's head, and she teached me how many brown paper bags to stack under the counter at a time, so when she goes to grab one, the whole shitload of 'em don't fall on her feet. She showed me, too, how to line up bottles of Milk of Magnesia, Bayer aspirin, and Mother's Remedy, so the labels show toward the counter where the ladies can see 'em right off when they come in 'cause someone in their family is feeling punky or looking peaked.

I'm gonna run the store one day, and Jimmy, he's gonna take over Dad's gas station. The Skelly station is at the other end of Main Street, smack dab on the corner. It's got a big garage where him and Jimmy fix broked cars, and it's got a little room where people come in to pay at the counter. I wish I could take over the Skelly station when the folks get dead instead of Gunderman's Grocery, 'cause I sure do like the Skelly. There's tires and junk parts stacked all over the floor along the walls, and lots of greasy tools that make clinkity-clankity noises when you dig 'em out of the toolboxes. At the Skelly, them oilcans don't gotta be stacked all neat and tidy, label sides out, either. Dad stacks 'em any which way and he don't even care when one of 'em comes crashing to the floor when the door gets slammed too hard. The best thing about the Skelly, though, is that you ain't gotta mind your Ps and Qs there. If there ain't no ladies in paying for their gas, you can burp, fart, cuss, or scratch yourself wherever you gotta, and ain't nobody gonna bitch at you.

Ma says I can't inherit the garage 'cause I don't know how to fix cars. Jimmy, though, he's the best goddamn mechanic in town. That's what folks in Willowridge say, anyway, and that don't surprise me none. Jimmy is the best at everything. Well, 'cept at stocking shelves. Jimmy says he ain't never been good at that, like I am.

Even though Jimmy's good at fixing things, he tells me when we're alone that he don't wanna work in the Skelly 'til hell freezes over. Used to be, he wanted to pitch for the Chicago Cubs. Jimmy's a damn good pitcher too. Most folks in town came to see him play when he was still in high school. When he cranked that arm back and threw the ball, you didn't even see it whiz through the air. You just heared the slap noise it made in the catcher's mitt. I don't know if Jimmy still wants to play for the Cubs. All I know is that he wants to get outta this hick town.

Even though I'd rather work at the Skelly, when Ma starts heaping extra chores on me on accounta what I did to Mrs. Pritchard, working in the store don't sound so bad.

Just like on the last two Monday mornings since I axed Pritchard, Ma brings the laundry baskets to the back porch and I gotta fill up that damn wash machine and wash the clothes. This morning, it's one of them nice, sunny spring days, warm enough that my fingers don't sting when I get 'em wet, at least.

When the clothes are washed and squished, I go tell Ma like she told me to. She tells me to watch over the store while she runs out and hangs the clothes up to dry. Ma don't let me hang clothes, 'cause she says I bunch 'em up and wrinkle 'em worse, and 'cause I always hang her raggedy things on the outside lines where the ladies who come into the store can see 'em.

I wait in the store behind the counter. When Eva Leigh comes into the store, I stand real straight and say, "Morning, Mrs. Leigh," real polite, just like I will when I get the store. Eva Leigh's got her hip all poked out so Luke Junior, who she calls LJ, don't fall on the floor when she carries him. He's slobbering all over her blouse.

"Morning, Earl," she says, real nice. Eva Leigh's only about Jimmy's age, I know, 'cause once I heard her tell Ma that she woulda graduated from high school in '37 too, if she hadn't dropped out. Same age or not, she don't look young as Jimmy. She's got lines on her face that look like scars from kitty scratches, and she walks drooped over like a picked flower. Ma says that's 'cause Eva is married to Luke Leigh, who is as mean and nasty as a bull and, like the rest of the Leighs, as worthless as a three-dollar bill. Sometimes when I'm stacking shelves or dusting, Eva Leigh comes in and talks to Ma about her mean, nasty husband. Ma's face gets all droopy when she listens to Eva Leigh, then after she listens a spell, she gives Eva Leigh advice on how to keep Luke from being so ornery. She gives her little things she calls "tips" on how to get that house cleaned, lickety-split, and she tells her what time she's gotta stick the potatoes and carrots in with the pot roast so supper will be done when Luke gets home from work.

Eva Leigh don't look at me when she says, "I need a can of Copenhagen, Earl." I like how Eva Leigh don't shout when she talks to me, like a lot of people do, like they don't know the difference between simpleminded and plain-ass deaf.

I'm hoping Eva Leigh needs more than a can of snuff, 'cause if she don't, then I'm gonna have to check her out. I'm real good at pressing them numbers on the till, but I ain't so good at giving change. Ma showed me lots of times what each of them monies is called and what they're worth, but I think it's my lazy eye that keeps me from seeing it right. I don't care how many times she tells me that a dime is bigger than a nickel, it don't look that way to me.

Eva Leigh starts walking around the store, touching cans and boxes as she goes, but she don't pick nothing up. "Where's your ma, Earl?" she finally asks as she hoists LJ up higher on her poked-out hip. I tell her Ma go'ed out back to hang up laundry. Then I get to thinking maybe she's asking 'cause she's scared I'm gonna ax her like I did Mrs. Pritchard, so I hold up my hands and say, "I don't got no ax today, Mrs. Leigh."

Eva Leigh turns to me and smiles, but her smile don't look happy. When I see her whole face, I see she's got a big bruise right over her cheek. It's purple and yellow and gets me to thinking about how those ain't real pretty colors when mixed together on a lady's face. She tips her head back down, real quick, and her sand-colored hair that Luke says don't need curling slides across her cheeks and hangs there like closed curtains.

"It's all right, Earl. I know you wouldn't hurt anyone on purpose."

"No, ma'am, I sure wouldn't," I say. I can't see that ugly bruise on her cheek no more, but I can still see it in my head. "Mr. Leigh, he do that to you on purpose?" I ask. She stops and looks scared for a minute. She clears her throat, but she don't answer me. Maybe she don't know the answer to that question.

"I got hit bad like that once too, by that O'Malley kid. He had big fists just like your Mr. too, and it really hurt. Jimmy beat him up for doing that. Broke his nose even. I sure was glad when the O'Malleys moved outta town 'cause Mr. O'Malley had to find work when times was hard. Mrs. Leigh, you want Jimmy to beat up Mr. Leigh for you? I think he'd do that."

I don't see Ma come in, but I hear her. "Earl!" she yells, and I start picking at my pants 'cause I know I'm in trouble now.

Eva Leigh steps out of the aisle where Ma can see her. "It's all right, Mrs. Gunderman. He didn't mean any harm." Then she turns to me and says, "You're a good boy, Earl." I'm hoping Ma hears her, 'cause Ma ain't thinking I'm such a good boy right now.

"Earl, go in the kitchen and keep an eye on those eggs boiling on the stove."

I sit on a stool by the stove and watch them little bubbles that jiggle the eggs and rise up in little streams. I want to listen to the radio, but Ma says the radio is for after the day's work is done, not before, even though she's got a radio on in the store all the time, listening to them soap operas where all them ladies got troubles.

With nothing else to listen to, I listen to Ma and Eva Leigh. They is talking about that mean Luke again. Then I hear Betty Flannery come into the store and they hush up. Before you know it, Ma is showing off her hands, like she done at breakfast, saying that it *is* true. That that Lux dish soap does make a lady's hands softer and prettier than the other leading brands in just twenty-eight days. Ma tells the ladies that she heard about the test on *Lux Radio Theater* and thought it was just an advertising gimmick, but oh, look and feel her hands. See how soft and white-looking they are. "Even Hank noticed the difference," Ma says. Seems from what I can remember, Dad only grunted and didn't even look up from his newspaper while Ma was showing off her new hands. All this ladies-talk makes me wish to hell I knowed how to fix broked cars.

I poke my head into the store to ask Ma how long I gotta watch the eggs boil. Betty is buying two boxes of Lux soap, 'cause Betty Flannery always likes looking pretty even if she's old, but Eva Leigh ain't buying nothing but that can of Copenhagen for Luke. I don't suppose Luke cares a lick about if her hands are soft and pretty when they make his supper. Ma tells me to never mind, that she'll be in in a minute.

When them eggs get done, Ma makes 'em into egg salad sandwiches. "Can I eat lunch with Dad and Jimmy today?" I ask, and she says I can, if I don't dilly-dally there too long. She takes handfuls of oatmeal raisin cookies and drops 'em in the bag.

When I pedal my bike down to Dad's Skelly, I'm not Earl Hedwig Gunderman riding a bike. I'm Charles A. Lindbergh in my flying machine. That cold air is blowing in my face and I'm flying so high that when I pass Sam outside the barber shop and he calls hello, I can't even hear him, but I wave from the sky. Charles A. Lindbergh drove his plane, all by himself, all the way across the Atlantic Ocean. I shit you not. And he didn't crash, not even once. I don't wanna take over Gunderman's Grocery when Ma gets old and dead. I want to fly airplanes across the Atlantic Ocean.

Jimmy's outside when I pull into the parking lot, his yellow hair so lit up that I pretend it's the sun I'm circling before I cut the engine and go down for a landing. "Nrrrrrrrrrrr," my voice goes lower 'til it stops. I prop my bike up against the brick building 'cause the kickstand is broke and it tips over if I don't. Jimmy hears my plane engine kill and he grins. "Hey there, Lucky Lindy." I look but don't see Dad right off, which is a good thing, on account of Dad thinks Charles A. Lindbergh might be one of them Nazi bastards, after he saw a picture of him in the paper a couple years ago, getting some award from some Nazis in Germany. I take our lunch bag outta my basket. Jimmy holds out his hands and I toss it to him. "Hey, Jimmy," I say, "how come folks call Charles A. Lindbergh 'Lucky Lindy,' anyway? What's so goddamn lucky about your boy getting stealed and killed?"

Jimmy don't answer, 'cause he's digging in the lunch bag. He unwraps his sandwich and groans, "Ah, shit, don't tell me this is egg salad." So I don't tell him.

Dad lets me and Jimmy have a Coca-Cola with our lunch, and that's a real treat. We sell Coca-Cola at the grocery store too, but Ma hardly ever lets me have one. She says we ain't the Rockerfellers, and that if she let me take whatever I wanted from the store, whenever I wanted it, we'd still be using the outhouse, and Ted the ice man would still be delivering blocks of ice for the store coolers. Ma is all proud when she says this, 'cause ain't many in town with flushing toilets or electric coolers. If you ask me, though, I wouldn't mind pissing in the old shithouse that's still out back, long as what I'd be pissing would be Coca-Cola.

Me and Jimmy sit on the steps eating our sandwiches while Dad pumps gasoline into Delbert Larson's Oldsmobile. I take a long swig of my pop and burp real loud and Jimmy laughs. "Don't hurt yourself there, Earwig."

"I'll tell you one thing, Delbert," Dad's saying. "There's no way this country's gonna stay out of the war. I was listening to that new program on NBC's Red Network. That one Kaltenborn is hosting—you catch that last night?"

Delbert shakes his head. "Nah, I took Ethel over to her sister's."

"Well, he was telling how Roosevelt just asked Congress for 2.5 billion dollars to pump into the military. For crissakes, Dieter was in here earlier, and I was telling him about it. When I finished, Dieter said he still thinks Roosevelt will keep us out of the war. That ignorant bastard can't put two and two together for nothing." Dad shakes his head, and so does Delbert. "Of course Roosevelt knows we're headed to war. Why in the hell would he pump all that money into the military if he didn't?"

"I know it, Hank. I know it," Delbert says. "He's not building up our forces for nothing. Goddamn shame it's coming to this, though. Just when we're getting back on our feet."

Dad takes a hankie outta his pocket and wipes his forehead that always gets sweat-bubbled when he talks about the government. Dad glances up at the pump. When Delbert's car is filled up, he takes out the nozzle and hangs it back up.

"What're you gonna do, though, sit back while those Nazi bastards take over the whole goddamn world? I read a few years back that our country's army is ranked seventeenth in the world. Seventeenth, for crissakes!"

"That right?" Delbert says.

"That's what they said." Dad shakes his head, which is big and turns red when he's pissed off about something. "Right behind Romania. Behind Romania, for crisssakes!

"I'll tell ya one thing, Delbert. Hitler ain't gonna stop. Nazi bastard, attacking France like that. He'll keep going until he's got all of Europe, then he'll be heading over here for us. I don't care how much aid we give to the Brits, weapons and food aren't gonna be enough. We'll have troops over there. You wait and see."

"I know it. I know it," Delbert says. Delbert looks over to where Jimmy and me is sitting on the step eating our sandwiches. His forehead scrinches down 'til you can't even see he's got eyes under those clumpy eyebrows. "You and me remember war," he says. Dad nods. "Goddamn shame," Delbert says, and Dad says it sure is.

Delbert takes the door handle of his Oldsmobile, but Dad, he don't stop yapping. "Yeah, it is a shame, Delbert, but still, we gotta do what we gotta do. I came across some papers from that Isolationist group at home. Someone brought them in the store and left them right there on the counter. I threw them out and told Eileen I don't want to see that kind of crap in the house again. I don't like the thought of us going to war any more than the next guy, but what to hell you gonna do?"

Then Dad and Delbert talk a bit about the Japs, who Delbert says are just as power-hungry as that goddamn Hitler. Me and Jimmy just eat our lunch and we don't say nothing. Jimmy's busy downing them cookies, and I'm busy thinking about them Japs. I ain't never see'd a Jap before, but Jimmy says they is little yellow bastards with crooked slits for eyes. They sound scary as all hell to me and I hope I never see one.

Dad's always talking about stuff that's going on overseas. Jimmy showed me once on the globe where them places are that Dad talks about. He picked up Dad's newspaper too and showed me a picture of that Hitler guy. He might be scary and mean, but I don't think he's too smart. How smart can a guy be who can't trim his mustache right? There that mustache sits, like a fishing jig, right under his nose. It don't even reach the sides of his mouth. I never see'd such a crazy-looking mustache in all my life. When Ma saw Jimmy showing me that stuff, she got real ornery. "We have enough to worry about right here at home. We don't need to be worrying about what's going on halfway around the world."

I eat the parts of my sandwich I like, then toss the crust into the empty bag. "Jimmy? That nutty guy with the chopped-off mustache, he gonna come take over Willowridge too?"

Jimmy rubs my head and says, "Don't you worry about it, Earwig. Ain't nothing ever gonna change in Willowridge. That you can count on." But I still worry.

When Delbert leaves, Dad eats the sandwich and cookies I set out for him. He's still thinking about that Europe place. I can tell, 'cause when Jimmy tries talking to him about the motor he's got torn apart in the garage, Dad don't even hear him.

That night, we sit in the living room eating warm molasses cookies as we listen to the *Bob Hope Pepsodent Show*. Dad ain't got sweat on his face no more. "That Jerry Colonna is one nutty bastard!" Dad laughs as Jerry sings some crazy version of "Blueberry Hill." We are all laughing our asses off, 'cept for Ma, who says, "I think he should leave the singing to Judy Garland."

And that's how the summer and fall of 1940 goes. Me working to pay for what I done wrong and waiting for that Mrs. Pritchard to get back on her fat feet so I can stop doing housework that Jimmy says will make me grow titties if it keeps up much longer.

When Mrs. Pritchard finally comes limping into the store, I'm hoping Ma remembers that she limped before I axed her. I hide in the kitchen, listening, as Mrs. Pritchard tells Ma all about her "recuperation" and about how she hopes Ma taught me a lesson. Ma says, "I assure you, I did." Then they talk about how that Dickens girl got healed up and how glad they are that summer's over and that polio season is gone.

'Cause Mrs. Pritchard is on her feet now, and 'cause the polio season is gone, Ma lets me run around again, but she don't take away them damn chores she added, and I can't leave 'til they're done, so there ain't much time to do anything fun anyway.

Funny how things are. You have them worst days of washing clothes and stocking shelves, and you hate them lousy days when you're in 'em. And then you have them best days too, like sucker fishing at the millpond, and later your dad saying that the sucker you speared is the best goddamn sucker he ever ate, and you figure them is the best days you're ever gonna have. Later though, when times get *real* bad, them bad days and them best days get all mixed together in your head, and you think of the whole lot of 'em as something special. Something so goddamn special that you'd give your right nut to go back to 'em.

# Chapter 4

It's Jimmy's twenty-first birthday, so Ma starts baking him a cake soon as her and me get back from church. She frosts it with seven-minute frosting, which I hate 'cause it gets this crunchy coating on top like snow that melted and then frozed up again. When I tell Ma this, she says it ain't my birthday, it's Jimmy's, and he likes seven-minute frosting just fine.

Jimmy's whole room smells like beer farts when I go to wake him up to tell him Louie and John are downstairs and wanna go over to Floyd's to do a little hunting. Since it's Sunday, John don't have to work at the Knox Lumber Factory, and Louie, who logs with his dad, he don't work on any day he don't wanna work. Floyd, he farms with his dad, and 'cept for milking so the cows' tits don't bust, they don't do nothing else on Sunday either, 'cause that's the day God says you gotta take a rest.

"You get plastered last night, Jimmy?" I ask when Jimmy rolls outta bed and clamps his hands over his head and holds it like there's a woodpecker hammering inside.

"Yeah, a little bit," he says. "Hand me my smokes and my pants there."

"Where'd you go last night?" I ask Jimmy, feeling a little bit of a lump in my throat 'cause Jimmy leaved last night while I was in my room looking at comic books and he didn't even come in first to see if I wanted to go along.

"Well, Floyd and I were heading to pick up Molly and Mary for the picture show, but we didn't exactly make it there."

Ma calls Jimmy "the birthday boy" when we get downstairs, and Louie and John snicker. Ma pats John on the arm when she's gotta scoot around him, and she gives him a smile. Ma smiles at John 'cause she says that dent he's got on his chin looks cute. Floyd says he thinks it looks like a butt crack.

"You get home in time for supper, Jimmy," Ma says as we're going out the door. "Molly will be here by six."

Floyd and his dad got 160 acres just outside of town. They don't got no ma 'cause she died when Floyd was ten years old, but they got a barn and cows, and chickens, and four goats that run up behind you and butt you in the ass with their heads if you ain't careful. They got a dog named Scout too, one of them yellow Labs, and he goes hunting with us.

"How come I can't have a dog, Jimmy?" I ask. I'm scratching Scout behind his ear, and his tongue is flip-flapping out the side of his mouth, and his tail is whacking my leg like crazy. Jimmy don't answer me. He's busy loading his shotgun with shells from his pocket, and laughing 'cause Louie is teasing John about hosing Ruby Leigh last night. John's face is some red, but it might be from the wind. "Shit, who *didn't* hose Ruby Leigh last night?" he says.

"I didn't, Pissfinger," Jimmy says.

John whistles, then says, "Well, Gunderman, that's your loss."

Jimmy laughs. "I'm missing out on a case of the clap too, but you don't see me crying about that, do you?"

Jimmy don't hose nobody no more. Not since him and Molly started talking about getting married soon as Jimmy can get together enough money for a down payment on the Williams place, which he says will be a mighty fine place once it gets fixed up. Jimmy says it's okay to hose girls like Ruby Leigh when you ain't promised yourself to another girl and if she ain't the kind of girl you wanna marry anyway. But he says that it ain't okay to hose a girl like Molly until after you marry her. He repeats then what Ma always says about men not buying milk when they can get it for free, or something like that. I never did figure what in the hell paying for milk or getting it for free has got to do with girls. Well, unless the girl you're fixing to hose is a farm girl.

Jimmy hands me a shotgun—even though Ma says I'm not allowed to carry one—and reminds me how to carry it so I don't shoot my foot off or blow somebody's goddamn head off. He makes me walk in front of him a bit where he can keep an eye on me. Floyd, he ain't walking real good, on accounta he was still guzzling Schlitz when we got to his house.

We walk along Balsam Creek, laughing and talking 'til we hear a grouse kick up from the alder brush, his wings making that loud thumping noise when he flies. Jimmy lifts his shotgun quicker than you can say "fart," then, *pow!* That grouse drops, deader than dead. Scout takes off and comes back with the bird flapping out of his mouth and brings him right to Jimmy, dropping him at his feet. Jimmy takes the bird and pokes its foot through his belt loop, then flops the bird over so it stays. He gives Scout a pat on the head. It's the damnedest thing how Scout always knows who shot the bird. Scout's one smart dog.

We hunt for a few hours, then walk through the old field, heading back toward the house. We is walking along a line, pretty close together, except for Louie, who is off to the side. Jimmy always says that Louie's got a voice loud enough to crack a guy's head open, and ain't that the truth. You go mixing his regular voice, then, with him being all excited 'cause he almost got to hose a girl last night, and we ain't having a bit a trouble hearing him even though he's a good fifty feet away.

Louie's so damn busy yammering that he don't even notice when a grouse kicks up from the brush between him and us. Floyd notices, though, and before that bird hardly rises above Louie's head, Floyd shoots.

Louie hits the ground, flopping right down on his belly. "Jesus Christ!" I yell. "You killed him, Floyd! You killed him!" And I don't mean the bird, I mean Louie!

Louie gets up before any of us can move and props himself on his elbows, shakes his head, then starts running his hands up his forehead and through his orange hair. His face goes from ghosty white to tomato red as he leaps up and grabs his shotgun. "You goddamn drunken bastard! What the fuck were you doing?"

Floyd is laughing, even though Louie's stomping through the grass, coming right at him. "You almost shot my goddamn head off!"

Floyd grabs his Lucky Strikes pack from his pocket, acting like Louie ain't even coming at him. "Oh, stop whining like a sissy. That shot was a good twenty feet above your head."

Louie reaches Floyd before Floyd even got time to light his cigarette. Louie, he drops his shotgun and butts his chest right up against Floyd's. "Twenty feet? Twenty feet, my ass! Then how come I got a fucking BB stuck in my goddamn head?" He takes his hand and pulls back his hair and, sure enough, there's a shotgun pellet stuck right in his forehead, the freckly skin around it rising up like a cinnamon bun.

"Good thing you got a hard head," Floyd says, laughing, but Louie, he ain't laughing.

"You think it's funny that you shot a guy in the head?" Louie says.

John is laughing. "Ah, relax, Olson, you ain't got nothing in that head to hurt anyway."

Louie don't pay John no mind. He's too busy screaming at Floyd. "Sure, you can laugh like a big man, Fryer. You weren't the one that got shot, you son of a bitch."

Jimmy, he lights a cigarette. "Okay, end it, girls. Let's go have a beer."

I play with Scout while Floyd, John, and Jimmy clean the birds and Louie goes to find a mirror so he can dig that BB out of his head. By the time he digs it out and has a beer, he ain't even pissed at Floyd no more.

After the birds is cleaned, we sit in Floyd's kitchen and drink his daddy's Blatz. There is food stuck to plates everywhere you look and clumped-up underwear and socks on the floor. John picks a dirty shirt off the counter and says, "You or your old man better find a wife soon, before the goddamn rats move in."

I'm leaning over, gawking at some dried mashed potatoes, seeing the way they is cracked and dark like dried-up mud. As I'm looking, I see little black turds inside the cracks. "I think them rats already moved in, John," I say.

Ain't nobody listening to me, though, 'cause Louie, he's talking about joining up with the Navy.

"What? Are you goddamn crazy?" John says.

"If I stay stuck in this shithole of a town, I'm gonna be," Louie says. "I'm going sailing. See some of the world."

* * *

That night Molly comes over for supper. I like Jimmy's girlfriend. She reminds me of a tiny piece of candy, all pink and sweet. Her hair is the color of wheat, but it don't look like wheat. Them shiny curls look soft as kitty fur. She smiles a lot too, and she's got about the prettiest teeth I ever did see, all white and shiny and lined in a neat row like buttons. Jimmy says that Molly's dad is a dentist, and that's why her teeth look so nice. Jimmy says that Dr. Franks is always staring in his mouth when Jimmy's talking, like he wants to start digging in his mouth too.

I get to sit right next to Molly, and I remember to chew with my mouth shut. Molly makes a big dent into my mashed potatoes with the back of her spoon before she pours milk gravy on real neat so it don't spill out onto my corn. "When I get old like Jimmy," I tell Molly, "I'm gonna get me a girlfriend pretty as you." Molly giggles, and her giggle feels like a tickle in my belly.

Daddy stabs a piece of grouse with his fork and stuffs it into his mouth. "Damn good," he says, forgetting to be polite and not swear around Jimmy's girl. None of them birds Ma fried up is mine. I shot once, but turns out that damn shotgun was empty. Jimmy about kicked hisself silly for forgetting to load my gun. He says that if he'd been smart enough to remember, that last bird would have been mine, so when Dad says how good that bird tastes, Jimmy tells Dad, "That one was Earwig's."

"Fine bird, Earl," Daddy says, and Ma says, "What was Earl doing with a gun?"

Ma makes us sing happy birthday to Jimmy as she brings out his cake, all wrecked with that crusty frosting. While we eat cake, she gives Jimmy his present she ordered from the Chicago Woolens' catalog. "It's one of them gangster suits, like you wanted. It's double-breasted, pin-striped, and has those nice wide lapels." She tells him this like he can't see them things for himself. "The pants have boxed pleats and suspenders too." Dad wrinkles his brow, and I know he's thinking the same thing as me—that that's about the dumbest present a guy could get for his birthday. If Jimmy thinks it's dumb when he first opens it, he changes his mind real quick when Molly starts carrying on like it's something good like a new shotgun or a fish pole.

Molly wants to help Ma clean up the kitchen, but Ma says she don't have to. We go into the living room. Dad rubs his big poochy belly and falls into his favorite chair that is the color of chocolate and has a big dent on the seat shaped like his butt. Ma calls from the kitchen to put a Glenn Miller record on, and Dad rolls his eyes 'cause he wants to listen to Edward Murrow.

Jimmy don't put Glenn Miller on. He flicks the radio on and swishes the knob until he finds some good music. When they start playing Louis Prima's "Jump, Jive an' Wail," Jimmy lets out a loud whoop as he grabs Molly and drags her into the middle of the living room. Jimmy is damn good at dancing. Molly, she don't dance all rowdy like Jimmy. She looks like a leaf fluttering from a branch when she dances, and she giggles and her cheeks turn even pinker than they already are.

Ma comes to watch at the kitchen door and she's got a dish towel draped over her shoulder, her foot tapping. When Molly sees Ma watching, she stops dancing and hurries to the sofa where I'm sitting. "Come on, Ma, let's cut a rug!" Jimmy says. Ma tosses her head back and laughs as she dances with Jimmy, their legs going like eggbeaters. I can't dance a lick, so I don't do nothing but sit on the sofa and stare at Molly's button teeth.

When the song is finished, Jimmy plops on the couch. He's breathing hard and laughing.

That night, Jimmy leaves to bring Molly home, and I sit on my bed looking at my comic books and wait 'cause I wanna ask Jimmy who he thinks is stronger, Superman or Captain Midnight. I fall asleep and I wake up in the morning 'cause Ma's shaking me good. "Earl? Earl! Where's your brother?"

"I don't know." And that's the God's honest truth.

"Earl, if you know and aren't telling, you won't leave this house until you're forty! And what are you doing, sleeping in your clothes?"

All through breakfast, Ma asks me again and again where Jimmy is. I can't hardly get my oatmeal down, 'cause every time I put a spoonful in my mouth, Ma's asking me that same question all over again and then harping at me to not talk with my mouth full when I try to answer. Then Ma, she starts yapping about how she hopes them boys didn't wrap their car around a tree on some back road or run off the road and plunge into Spring Lake. She gets my head so full of bloody pictures that I don't even bother putting no more oatmeal in my mouth. A guy could starve to death when his brother don't come home.

One thing I know for sure is that when I get twenty-one, you ain't gonna catch me running off and getting drop-dead drunk with my buddies, then going into some National Guard place with the only buddy who's still standing and signing myself up for Guard duty just 'cause the buddy with the new bigtitted girlfriend dared me to before he passed out. No sirree, I ain't gonna do that, but that's what Jimmy did.

He come home three days later, his hair matted like a collie's ass, dried puke streaked down his shirt, and Ma, who is worried sick, and Molly, who is mad as hell, they start chewing on him like he's a dead fox and they is hungry crows. Now, when you piss off a guy, you don't gotta say you're sorry even after you shoot 'em in the head with bird shot, but when you piss off a girl, saying "I'm sorry" ain't even good enough. You gotta say it about a hundred times, and you gotta yammer on and on about how dumb you are and how you don't blame 'em if they never speak to you again. Jimmy says all them things, and he looks mighty sorrowful when he says 'em, but Ma and Molly, they just stand there with their arms crossed over their titties and their lips stretched into crabby little lines.

Nobody stays mad at Jimmy long, though. Not once Jimmy gets word from them National Guard people that he's gotta show up for active duty in one week. Ma fusses at Dad when Jimmy gets the news, telling him he should go down to Janesville and get Jimmy's name scratched right off that sign-up sheet. "Tell them Jimmy is a foolish boy who did it on a dare while he was drunk. Tell them he didn't know what he was doing." Dad looks at her like she's gone nuts. Then he says, "The draft went into effect today, Eileen. Jimmy would be heading in that direction anyway."

Floyd's girl, Mary, don't stay mad at him long either. Not even with Floyd having to go off with Jimmy to the National Guard on accounta he's the other one who signed up. Mary don't stay mad at Floyd 'cause he went and asked her to marry him before he leaves.

Floyd and Mary ain't got time to put together a church wedding, which is all right by me. They get married by the justice of the peace, and me and Jimmy and Molly and the gang, along with Floyd's daddy, Mary's ma and dad, and Mary's ugly sisters, all go. The girls cry and smile at the same time as the baldy-headed justice man reads off this paper all the things Mary and Floyd gotta promise to do. I think of how I ain't never gonna get married, 'cause there ain't no way in hell I'd ever remember all that shit. When the baldy guy is done yapping, everyone shakes Floyd's hand and kisses and hugs Mary. Then we all go over to the town hall.

Ma and Mary's ma, and most of the ladies that come into the store, they put together a real nice party for Floyd and Mary. They got big banners stringed across the walls in the town hall and a big white cake with frosting flowers that look so real I gotta lick 'em a little to know they are made of frosting. The tables are all decorated in red, white, and blue. A long table is crowded with food, and another table has a big coffeepot and a punch bowl on it, the cups lined up like soldiers.

Four guys from town, old and gray as fence posts, set up their little band in the corner. They call themselves Tommy and the Toe Tappers, but their name ain't nothing but a goddamn lie. Them old buzzards don't tap their toes, and they don't play nothing you can tap your toes to either. All they do is strum their guitars while one yanks on his accordion. I look at poor Jimmy in his fancy new suit and know he ain't gonna be doing no jitterbuggin' tonight.

Mary ain't wearing one of them poofy, lacy wedding dresses. She got on a white suit, white shoes, white hat, and even white gloves. So much white she looks like she was dipped in snow. Mary ain't little and candy-cute like Molly, but she is pretty all the same. She is big, with moon titties and teeth long like a horse's teeth, only they is whiter.

It takes me a while to find Floyd in the crowd. Floyd went to Sam's Barber Shop in the morning, and Sam cut his hair short and slicked it down. All dressed up, his hair all slicked, and his fingers girly-clean, Floyd don't even look like Floyd.

Everybody is having a good time—that is, except Molly, who is being real quiet and ain't even looking at Jimmy like the other girls in the room are. As the guys are teasing Floyd and Mary about their honeymoon night, Molly and a red-haired girl go walking off. Jimmy watches her go, but he's still laughing with the guys. Then that red-haired girl, she comes back and she tells Jimmy that Molly's in the hallway crying and he'd better go talk to her. She's looking at Jimmy like he done something wrong. I start tagging after Jimmy, but he tells me to stay put, so I do. When they come back, Molly's eyes are blotchy, and she's smiling, but she don't look happy the whole rest of the night.

I'm still awake in my bed looking at my comic books when Jimmy gets back from taking Molly home. I take my comic book down to Jimmy's room and ask him the question I didn't get to ask before. "Hey, Jimmy, who you think is stronger, Captain Midnight or Superman?"

"I am," Jimmy says, and he throws a pillow at me.

"What was Molly all sad about, Jimmy?"

Jimmy takes off his gangster pants and tosses 'em on his dresser, then he unbuttons his shirt and does the same. He goes to the dresser and rummages in the pocket of the shirt he just tossed and takes out his cigarettes. He lights one, jumps into bed, and covers up to his waist. "She wants us to get married before I leave."

"You got enough to pay down on that Williams place, Jimmy?"

"Hell no," he says. He's combing his fingers through his hair. "And her daddy ain't gonna let her marry me until I have a house to move her into either. Shit, I'm only gonna be gone a year. When I get back she can have one of those church weddings like girls always want. I'll hang on to every cent I make in the Guard and see if I can save enough to make that down payment."

"Jimmy?" I ask. "You remember how you said that after you get married, I get to go live with you?"

"Yeah?"

"Okay," I say. "I just wanted to know if you still remembered."

I sit on Jimmy's bed and turn the page of my new Captain Midnight comic book. "I think Cap' could beat up Superman," I say. Jimmy, he don't say nothing. He's blowing smoke rings and thinking real hard. Downstairs, the radio is still playing. Jimmy gets up and grabs his pants. "Where you going?" I ask, and Jimmy says down to talk to Dad. I start to follow him, but Jimmy says he's gotta talk to Dad alone.

I get outta bed after Jimmy goes downstairs, and on my hands and knees I peek down through the vent next to my bed. The kitchen is under the vent, and if you poke your head so close to the vent that you can feel the strands of dust tickling your nose, then you can hear and see everything that's going on down there. Ma's alone. She's got a cup of coffee in one hand and her other hand is on her hip. She's gawking around the kitchen like she's making sure it's clean enough. Daddy's still on his chair in the living room. You can't see more than a little ways into the living room, unless you're looking down Jimmy's vent, so I just lean over and see Dad's legs that are crossed at the ankle.

Jimmy asks to talk to Dad, and Dad says, "What is it, son?"

"Can we step outside or something?"

Ma slides over to the doorway. "What's wrong?" she asks, and Jimmy says there ain't nothing wrong.

"Well, where are you guys going?"

"Just outside for a bit," Dad says.

It's a lot of hoopla for nothing, I decide, when Jimmy comes back upstairs and says Dad's gonna borrow him the money to buy Molly one of them engagement rings. "Don't say nothing to Ma, though. She'll find out soon enough."

The next morning, Jimmy wakes me up while it's still dark outside. "Hey, Earwig, you want to ride with me over to the jewelry store in Ripley?" I rub the crusty gunk outta the corners of my eyes. "Sure," I say, just 'cause Jimmy is leaving today and I'm missing him already and he ain't even gone.

We drive to Ripley 'cause we ain't got a jewelry store in Willowridge, but we gotta drive fast 'cause Jimmy and Floyd gotta be on the 2:15 bus.

"Hey, Jimmy, why do guys give their girls them dumb rings anyway?" I ask as we roar down the highway so fast the trees alongside it ain't nothing but smears.

"Well, Earwig. It's like a promise. When I give a ring to Molly, it means I promise to marry her, and if she accepts it, it means she's promising to marry me."

"Why can't you just say the promise?"

"Well, 'cause girls like promises they can show off to their girlfriends."

"Oh."

"Well," Jimmy says, "it's a promise that the girl ain't going to let anyone else feel her up too, and a promise that the guy ain't going to hose any whores."

Jimmy buys a ring that is little and sparkly like Molly, then he whistles most of the way home, and his whistle sounds all happy. I ain't feeling happy, though. Today Jimmy is leaving for one whole year, and I'm gonna miss him something fierce.

When we get back home, Molly is at our house. Jimmy goes in, and he takes Molly's hand and starts leading her up the stairs. Ma calls out, "Jimmy, what are you doing?" 'cause Jimmy ain't supposed to bring girls up to his bedroom, but Dad tells Ma it's okay.

When they come down, Molly's eyes are shining with happy tears, and Jimmy is grinning like he just caught a ten-pound walleye. "Ma, Dad . . . Molly and I are engaged." Ma's hand clamps over her mouth and her eyes look like they are gonna bug right out of her head. Molly shoves her hand out so everyone can see her new ring. Dad hurries to shake Jimmy's hand and gives Molly a hug. Ma kisses Molly's cheek, but before she does, she gives Dad a mad look like she just caught him lying. Ma's acting how she does when she wants to get the store cleaned up and some lady comes in and stays forever, flapping her gums about her aches and pains. She smiles then too, but it's a smile that don't creep up into her eyes.

When Ma and Dad stop fussing, Jimmy looks at me and says, "Well, Earwig?" and I say, "Well, what?" Dad laughs and tells me to congratulate my brother and his new fiancée. I feel sorta silly shaking Jimmy's hand, 'cause I ain't never done that before, so I'm glad when Jimmy starts jabbing little punches on my belly.

I stick out my hand to congratulate Molly too, and Molly takes it, then she gives me a big hug. I can feel her little titties right up against me, and her hair smells real good, like lemon cake. When she lets go of me, I feel downright dizzy and it feels like I got a campfire cooking under my cheeks. Jimmy grins and says I'd better not chase his girl while he's gone, and everybody laughs.

# Chapter 5

Big raindrops are plopping on our windshield as we drive Jimmy to the bus station. Ma and Dad are sitting in the front, and Jimmy and me are in the backseat, Molly smack-dab between us. Her and Jimmy got their heads tipped together, and Jimmy is rubbing Molly's hand, real soft-like. I turn and look out the back window, and there is Floyd and Mary in the car behind us and they got their heads stuck together too.

Ma, she keeps reminding Jimmy that it's just for a year, and Dad says it won't be nothing but a Boy Scout camp. Molly's eyes are dripping tears, but she don't make a peep. Jimmy lifts her hand, the one that's got that new ring on it, and he gives it little kisses, over and over again.

When we get to the bus depot, Ma starts telling Jimmy what all she packed for him, like he ain't gonna see that for hisself when he opens his suitcase. "There's stamps inside the pocket under the lid, and paper and envelopes too. You keep us posted. And I put some candy bars in the other side pocket, and don't forget to change your socks every day because you know how your feet break out if you don't." But Jimmy ain't listening. He's looking at Molly, like he wants to cry too. Dad don't say much. He just asks Jimmy if he's sure he's got enough money on him, and Jimmy nods.

"You take good care of my girl, Earwig," Jimmy says when they say the passengers gotta board the bus. I grab Jimmy's arm and tell him I want to go with him. Jimmy gives me a hug, and I bury my face right on his shoulder and cry like a titsy baby. I feel like a goddamn fool, blubbering like this, but ain't nothing I can do to make the blubbering stop.

Daddy takes me by the shoulders. "Come on, Earl. Jimmy's got to get on the bus now." I still got ahold of Jimmy's jacket, though, and I don't want to let go. Ma takes my hand away and she pinches my wrist, just like she used to do when I was little and didn't sit nice in church. She leans over to my shoulder and hisses quiet-like, "Jimmy feels bad enough about leaving without you making him feel worse." So I swallow them tears and let go.

Jimmy gets on the bus, looking like a gray ghost as he moves down the aisle. Then Floyd, he has to board the bus too. He gives Mary a big kiss good-bye. Her face is all slobbery wet with tears, but he kisses her anyway. Dad shakes Floyd's hand while he pats his shoulder, saying, "Take care, son," then Ma and Molly give him a kiss and a hug. "I'm gonna miss you, Floyd," I say, as I give him my hug. Floyd pats me on the back so hard I can hear thuds. "See ya, Earwig," he says. "Don't you go draining the millpond of suckers while we're gone, and keep an eye on Mary for me."

After Floyd gets on the bus, Mary and Molly stand together, holding each other at the waist and crying. We all wave as the bus pulls away.

We drive home with no sound in the car but for Ma's crying. Nothing feels right, and I think maybe it ain't gonna feel right for a long, long time.

# Chapter 6

It's Sunday, so I don't gotta work in the store 'cause the store ain't open on Sundays. Instead, I gotta go to church.

Ma sighs and groans as she rubs Brylcreem into my hair. That guy who sings about Brylcreem on the radio, he says that a little dab'll do, but that's a goddamn lie. Ma squeezes so much of that goo into my hair that it's making soapy sounds. She digs the comb teeth into my scalp and slaps and pushes my hair, but when she's done, it still stands up like quack grass. Ma spins me around and checks me over. She tells me to tuck my shirt into my pants better.

It ain't goddamn fair that I gotta go to church with her all the time, and I tell her so, but I don't say "goddamn" when I say it or I'm gonna be eating a bar of Lava soap and farting bubbles for a week. "You didn't make Jimmy go to church when he was old as me. And Dad, he don't gotta go on days he don't feel like going."

Dad is sitting on his chair, having his morning coffee. He looks over, but he don't say nothing.

Ma starts to say something, then she stops. She's got her lips painted cherry and her eyebrows pencil-drawed into boomerangs. She's got a blue hat on that, I shit you not, she puts on by poking a pin long as my finger right into her head. She drops her hands and looks at me, like I ain't looking so good, then she sighs and says I don't have to go.

Soon as Ma leaves, I rip them Sunday clothes off and I put on my flannel shirt and overalls. I put on a regular pair of socks, then slip one of them wool pairs over 'em, 'cause it's colder than a witch's tit now that it's December. I race down the stairs so fast I almost fall on my ass.

"I'm going over to Eddie's," I tell Dad, and he nods. By this time of year, it seems like it just gets light and it starts getting dark again. By the time Eddie gets home from school and eats his supper, and by the time Ma and me lock up the store and have our supper, it's blacker than a bear's ass and I can't go nowhere. I gotta wait 'til Sundays to have any fun in the winter.

I stand inside Eddie's front door, my boots staying on the rug so I don't slop up his ma's waxed floor. Her and Eddie are decorating the Christmas tree they got propped in the corner, even though it won't be Christmas for a lot more days. "Can Eddie come out and play?" I ask.

"Well, we *were* decorating the tree," his ma says. Her name is Pearl McCarty, and she is short and turkey-fat like Eddie. She is real nice.

I look at the tree. "Maybe you should let Eddie come out and play instead," I say, " 'cause it don't look like he knows how to decorate a tree real good anyhow. He's got all them bulbs in that one spot right there, and the rest of that tree looks butt-naked." Eddie's ma laughs a little, but she stops laughing when Eddie asks her if I can help decorate the tree too.

"The decorating can wait until later, Eddie," she says, then she comes over to me 'cause I'm standing close to where the front closet is, and she gets out Eddie's winter stuff.

"We probably ain't gonna have a tree this year," I tell her. "Ma said she don't even feel like having Christmas this year, 'cause Jimmy ain't coming home for Christmas anyway."

"Oh, your poor mother," Pearl McCarty says as she starts stuffing Eddie into his brown snowsuit. "Where is your brother now, Earl? Is he in Kentucky, or Louisiana? He's in the National Guard, right? Oh, I just can't keep track of whose son is where anymore."

"He ain't in neither place, Mrs. McCarty. First he went to a place called Fort Knox, and him and Floyd and the rest of them Janesville guys, they got sweared in to the real army and now they is Company A of the 192nd Battalion. That's a tank battalion." I can't help feeling proud when I tell her this stuff, 'cause I had to have Dad tell me them numbers lots of times before I remembered 'em good enough to tell people when they ask about Jimmy. "Then last summer, they got sent to some other camp. I can't remember where. They was learning more about how to be soldiers there. He liked it there too. They had to work hard, but Jimmy is tough, so he didn't mind. They played cards there, and guys who could play music played for 'em at night. They had a baseball team too, and Jimmy pitched and his team didn't get beat, not even once."

Eddie's ma is stuffing Eddie's hands, round and white like two snowballs, into his mittens. Eddie starts fussing 'cause his thumb ain't in the thumb part, and his ma takes the mitten off and starts over. "Well, Jimmy was always real good at baseball," she says.

"He sure always was, ma'am," I say. "But Jimmy ain't there no more. He wrote around Halloween time, and that letter come clear from San Francisco. That's way across the country, Mrs. McCarty, 'case you don't know that. Jimmy and Floyd and the rest of them guys, they were at some 'deplortment' place they called it, where they got shots so they don't get the tetanus, 'cause they was getting shipped overseas—that means they had to go across the ocean."

"I hate shots, Earlwig," Eddie says, and I tell him I know that already.

Eddie's ma is shoving Eddie's feet into his boots, and she is grunting real hard. "Straighten your toes and push, Eddie." Then she says to me, "Where overseas, Earl?"

"Well, they taked a ship over to this place called Manila. Just like *vanilla*, but with a *mmm* sound. They got there on Thanksgiving Day, Jimmy thought it was. Then from there, they taked a train to Clark Field, I think it's called, in the Philippines. You know where that is, Mrs. McCarty?"

"Well, I've heard of it, but I don't know exactly where it is," Eddie's ma says as she hangs on to the wall so she can hoist herself up, then grabs Eddie's hand and pulls him up. He's so fat with clothes he can't hardly move.

"Well, Dad showed me where it is on this map he's got in a book. You can't even see it good on there, though. Those islands look like little dots, but Dad says if you could see that place better, it would look like a thumb pointing into the water. They got palm trees there, Jimmy said in his letter. You ever see a palm tree before, Mrs. McCarty? Dad showed me in a picture. Craziest-looking trees I ever see'd. Anyway, Jimmy says it's nice there. It's hot, but it's real nice there, Jimmy says."

"You must miss your brother very much," Mrs. McCarty says.

"I sure do, ma'am, but it don't hurt like a toothache in my guts all the time no more, making me so sick I can't eat. Now it's more like when you got a bruise, how it don't hurt all the time, just when you bump it. Sometimes I still think I hear Jimmy's car, or I forget he ain't in his room and go to tell him something." Mrs. McCarty looks like she's gonna cry for a second.

"Louie is gone now too, and so is John. They're my friends. Louie signed up for the Navy right after Jimmy and Floyd left. I'd rather fly on an airplane, but Louie, he likes ships best. He's done now with that training stuff and he's on a boat in a place called Hawaii. John was gonna wait to get drafted, but then he, he"—I know I can't say that John was shit-canned at the factory, so I gotta stop a minute and think—"he didn't have a job no more, so he thought he might as well join up with the army instead of doing nothing but waiting around to get drafted. He's at Camp McCoy now. That's right here in Wisconsin."

Eddie's ma is shutting the closet door. I don't think she's listening no more, 'cause all she says is, "That's nice," when what's nice about having all your friends gone 'cept Eddie?

Eddie's ma holds the door open. I take Eddie's arm and give him a tug down the steps. She reminds us not to stay out too long and tells me to be sure and walk Eddie home when we're done playing.

Me and Eddie go to the woods off Circle Road and we find sticks long enough to be rifles. Then we start looking for swish marks in the snow, the ones that look like a feather was dragged across it, 'cause them would be rabbit tracks. When we hunt, we bring our hound with us. Eddie named our dog Spot, like in his reading book. Spot ain't no real dog, just a play dog, but just like Scout, he's one smart dog.

We don't see no real rabbits today, so we shoot at the rabbits we don't see, and Spot races to fetch 'em. He brings 'em back, and they flop, all dead, from his mouth. "Good boy, good boy!" we tell Spot, and we scratch him behind the ear.

When I get tired of hunting rabbits, I start to thinking about how maybe we should hunt Japs. I think I see one of them slant-eyed bastards behind a tree, so I yell out, "Japs!" I run real fast and dive behind a falled-over tree.

Eddie starts to screaming. "Where? Where?"

"Right there! Behind that clump of sumac! Watch it, there's some in those red pines too! Get down, Eddie! Get down!"

I prop my rifle up on that rotted tree and I shoot, "Pow! Pow! Pow!" I'm powing all over them goddamn trees, but Eddie, he's just standing there scared as shit. He drops his rifle and covers his eyes with his mittens. "Earlwig!" he screams.

I get up and run to Eddie, quick, before he pisses his pants. First I try to tell him that they ain't for-real Japs I'm shooting at, but play Japs, but Eddie, he's so busy screaming he can't hear me. I figure the only way to make those Japs be gone so Eddie stops screaming is to shoot all those bastards dead. I pick up his rifle and shove it back into his mittens. "There, Eddie. Behind the palm trees. Shoot, quick, before they kill us dead! Open your goddamn eyes, Eddie, so you can see 'em!"

Eddie opens his eyes and his eyeballs bounce all over inside them sockets. Then he grins a bit, like he finally gets it that them Japs is just play Japs, and he starts making his rifle pow too. When we is done, them dead Japs are laying all over and Spot is trying to fetch 'em. I shout to Spot to leave 'em there, 'cause what in the hell we gonna do with dead Japs anyway?

We play 'til Eddie's nose is running snot and he's whining 'cause he's cold, then I walk him home, just like I'm suppose to. "Earlwig, is Jimmy fighting Japs?"

"Dad says Jimmy ain't doing nothing but holding down the fort over there in that Pacific. But it ain't a real fort, not like Daniel Boone was in, anyway. It's what's called an army base. Him and Floyd and the rest of them Janesville ninety-nine, they is holding down that place, along with some Filipino guys, Dad says."

"Well, it's good he ain't fighting Japs, because he could get kilt if he was."

"He wouldn't get killed, Eddie," I say. "Jimmy's the best shot there is. He'd kill any Jap that even peeked at him cross-eyed from behind one of them crazy trees. He'd shoot before that Jap even had time to fart." Eddie laughs when I say "fart."

Mrs. McCarty opens the door before we even get up the steps. Her hand is wrapped around her neck and she looks all shook up. She guides Eddie by the back of his head into the house and tells me I'd better hurry on home. Something about the way she says it makes me feel scared in my stomach, so I run all the way, my breath coming in gray puffs like diesel-engine smoke.

When I get home, the whole store is filled up with ladies even though it's Sunday and the store ain't even suppose to be open. I hear men talking in the house part too. Ma is carrying a tray of coffee cups from the kitchen and Ethel Larson hurries to help her 'cause them cups are rattling on that tray. Edna Pritchard is there, and Betty Flannery, and even Eva Leigh, with that slobbery baby on her poked-out hip. Them ladies got teary-red eyes. The radio is on, but they are making so much racket, I can't tell what's on. First I think it must be that show them ladies listen to, *Backstage Wife*, and maybe they is upset 'cause that Mary Noble died or something.

When they are quiet long enough to hear anything, there ain't nothing on that radio but the Philharmonic Orchestra, and even though I don't like that program either, I know damn well that music ain't enough to make somebody cry.

I go over by Eva Leigh, figuring she'd be the most likely to tell me what's going on and 'cause she's standing the farthest away from Mrs. Pritchard. Eva Leigh is rocking side to side like she's trying to shut up her baby, but he ain't even fussing. He's just biting on his fist and making more slobber. "The

Japanese—" She don't even get her words out, when suddenly all them ladies are going "Shhh, shhh!" and waving their hands at each other.

They make so much racket saying "Shhhhh" that it takes a minute before we can hear the radio announcer say what we were suppose to shush for. "Hank!" Ma calls, and Daddy, Ben Olson, Charles Flannery, and Delbert Larson come into the store. That radio is all staticky when them news reporters are talking from faraway places, but still I make out enough words to hear 'em say that them Japs, they attacked a place called Pearl Harbor from the air, which means they flew over like Captain Midnight and dropped a shitload of bombs.

I lean down to Eva Leigh and ask her where Pearl Harbor is, 'cause I ain't never heard of that place before and I hope to hell it ain't in that Pacific where Jimmy is. Eva is busy looking across the store, where I notice that Louie's ma, Louise Olson, is sitting on the stool Ma keeps in the store for when her legs get tired. Louise Olson is crying, and Ma is rubbing her back a bit with one hand and dabbing at her worried eyes with the other.

"I didn't know either, until your ma told me. It's in Hawaii," Eva finally answers.

"Where Louie is?"

Eva is rocking so hard she's bumping against me, but she don't notice. "Yes," she says, and her voice ain't hardly more than a whisper.

That reporter, he says that the bombing in Pearl Harbor, it's been going on pert' near two hours. Louise Olson lets out a little cry. Then that news guy says he's got to get off the air so that goddamn orchestra can play some more, but he don't say "goddamn."

Dad slams his fist down on the counter. "We're getting attacked, for crissakes. You'd think those goddamn advertisers could give up enough airtime to let us find out what in the hell's going on."

My legs don't feel like they are there anymore, and my insides are so jumpity that I'm scared I'm gonna start slapping my head. I don't even see Dad come up to me. He don't say nothing, he just puts his arm across my shoulder, and his arm holds that fear down a little bit.

The radio starts playing music again, and everybody is talking. Daddy leaves me and joins the guys. They are cussing about the Japs, who they say was talking out of their asses when they was talking peace to Washington.

Ma takes Louise Olson's arm and says to her, "Why don't we go in the living room, Louise." Mrs. Olson, she gets up like she's got so many heavy rocks in her pockets she can't hardly move herself. Ma leads Mrs. Olson to the doorway, them other ladies following like ducks.

All afternoon this goes on, people coming in and out of the store, everybody waiting for them news guys to break in to the shows and tell us what's going on.

Later, a news guy comes on again. The radio is so goddamn staticky that I don't think Dad can hear, even though he's bent over with his ear practically stuck on the speaker. Dad hears enough to know that the news guy is talking about the Philippines now. He don't get to hear much, though, 'cause some lady from the telephone office, she cuts in and says the reporter's gotta get off 'cause the line is needed. Dad slams his fist on the radio and cusses. "Hank?" Ma calls. Her and them ladies are back in the store again. "What did they say about the Philippines?" Ma sounds real scared and I hope she don't forget to hang on to Louise Olson, 'cause she's looking real tippy.

"Sounds like the Japs have hit there too," Dad says. "He didn't get to finish the report. The operator cut him off."

"She cut him off?"

"Well, it's wartime controls, Eileen. They don't want the

enemy knowing what's going on, plus, the military needs those phone lines now." Dad rubs his belly, then strings his thick thumbs though his belt loops.

And that's how it goes all day. Ladies and men coming and going, dirtying up so many coffee cups that I gotta keep washing 'em. Everybody talking about how we is at war now, then shutting up when a news reporter comes back on.

I don't know where to go, 'cause I don't wanna see the ladies cry no more, and I don't wanna listen to the men talk about war. So I go up to my room and I sit on my bed, and I think of how I shoulda gone to church so God wouldn't be pissed off, 'cause now He sure as hell ain't gonna listen to me if I ask Him to do me a favor. I scooch up against the headboard, even if I still got my boots on, and I wrap my arms around my legs. I feel all cold, inside and out, so I pull them covers up over me and I think about how I don't want Jimmy and Floyd and Louie to be bloody-dead.

When Ma says she's going to church to pray for them boys 'cause Preacher Michaels is holding a special prayer service, me and Dad say we'll go too. And we do, even if that means getting on our Sunday clothes and slapping down our hair. I pray real hard, telling God how sorry I am I went hunting rabbits and Japs instead of going to church, but even if I did, could He please still make sure Jimmy and Floyd and Louie ain't dead?

The next day, Dad goes to the station and Ma opens the store, and people come in to both places, but nobody buys any food or asks to get their car fixed. Instead, they crowd by the radio waiting for somebody to say what's going on in Pearl Harbor. Most of 'em don't ask nothing about the Philippines, like they don't even know it was bombed too, but when Ma or Dad says Jimmy and Floyd are there, they start to worrying about what's going on there too.

I mop the kitchen floor, even though Ma don't tell me to, and I keep myself busy 'cause I don't know what else to do.

That night, President Roosevelt comes on to give one of his Fireside Chats. Dad sits in his butt-dented chair, and Ma sits on the edge of hers, and she's got a dish towel in her hands that she's tugging and twisting so hard that, if it was made of paper, it would be all shredded up on the floor.

I don't understand all of what the President says, but best I can tell, he's saying that we tried hard to be friends with them Japs, but nothing much worked. He starts talking about them places in Europe and how the Nazis are attacking countries all over and without warning them first. This don't surprise me none. You'd have to be pretty goddamn dumb to tell somebody that you was gonna wail on 'em before you did it, and I ain't sure even a Jap or that Nazi bastard is *that* stupid.

Roosevelt, he talks about us being at war now, and how we all gotta be in it together. I hope to hell he don't mean me. Then he starts talking about that bombing in Pearl Harbor. Even he, the President of the United States, don't know how bad they got bombed there, imagine that, but he says that it's gonna be bad, he thinks. And he's talking about how it's gonna be a long, hard war, and how we gotta make more weapons for it. "It is not a sacrifice for any man, old or young, to be in the Army or the Navy of the United States. Rather it is a privilege," the President says, and Ma grunts and says, "Privilege!" and she sounds real pissed off at Roosevelt. Dad tells her to hush and he turns the radio up louder.

I don't listen to all of what the President is saying, 'cause I get busy wondering if he's sitting in his wheelchair as he's talking or if they got him propped up by that fireplace. And I get to thinking about how maybe, if people let a cripple man be

President, three whole times, then maybe they'd let a dumb person be President at least once. I ask Dad about this, soon as Roosevelt says we is gonna win this war and stops talking. Dad says, "Well, Wilson was no genius, but I guess you wouldn't exactly call him simpleminded. Course, the way this world is going to shit, I don't doubt that one of these years, we'll have a downright idiot for a President." Ma gets pissed at me and Dad for talking about this. "Our Jimmy is in trouble and this is all you two can think about?" she says, and then I feel kinda bad.

Days go by, and still we don't hear if Jimmy's alive or dead. We listen to Gabriel Heater's war reports every night. He's got the best voice I ever did hear on the radio. He tells where the army is, and which buncha guys is getting shipped where, but he don't say no guys' names, so we don't know nothing about Jimmy, or Floyd, or Louie.

It takes a long time, but one day, while me and Ma is pricing bottles of Epsom salts and I'm putting them on the shelf, label side out, the mailman stops in to hand Ma the mail. He's got his fist full of letters and he's sorting through 'em looking for ours as he's talking to Ma about how cold it is. Ma sees a Western Union letter poked out from the heap in his hand, and she sees them two stars in the corner that lets the mailman know that he's bringing bad news to somebody. Ma makes a godawful noise and she grabs on to the counter. "No, no, Mrs. Gunderman. This telegram isn't for you. Look, see, just the usual mail for you." Ma gulps hard and my stomach floats back down to where it should be. "I'm sorry, Mrs. Gunderman. I shouldn't have let you see that telegram." Then Ma asks him if that telegram is gonna go to Louie's folks or Floyd's Dad, and he says he can't say.

Mrs. Pritchard don't waste no time waddling into the

store, big snowflakes dropping off the back of her ass onto the scrubbed-clean floor. "I just come by Louise Olson's place," she tells Ma, and she shakes her head real sad-like, so we know that telegram was about Louie. I hear everything she says, at least my ears do, but my heart, it don't hear a goddamn thing.

Ma gets so upset as the day passes that she starts screaming at Dad, right at the supper table, where we ain't suppose to yell. "I told you we should have gotten Jimmy out of the National Guard. He was drunk, for godssakes. He didn't know what he was doing. My God!"

"It's water under the bridge now that war's been declared. It won't be long and *all* our boys will be called up to fight."

"You're right about that, Hank! One by one, they'll take them, just like before. And you know as well as I do just how many of them will die, buried where they fall, no mother to cry over their grave."

Ma don't ever cuss, but she cusses now. "You goddamn men and your war! You're all the same. Just itching to go fight. To fight for what? To save the goddamn world like last time? Do any of you even give a damn that you take away our sons, our husbands, our brothers? Damn you all!" Ma runs into the bedroom and slams the door. Dad stops eating, his fork and knife just hanging there in the air. "They are *our* sons and brothers too," he says, but Ma don't hear him, 'cause her bedroom door is shut, and he ain't said it with more than a whisper anyway.

I think about what Ma says when I'm laying in bed. I don't think nobody gets to be the boss of a country unless he's a man, and I know that men like to kick ass. I get to wondering then about how things might be if ladies was the boss of countrics, instead of men. I think maybe there wouldn't be no wars then. I think if any guys even got the notion to shoot somebody's head off or toss a grenade in somebody else's yard, a lady president would yell her fool head off and make them work twice as hard until they learned their lesson.

# Chapter 7

Louie's body ain't coming home, on account of it's stuck inside that ship that is sunk to the bottom of the ocean, all blowed to shit. So there ain't no casket at Louie's funeral, just a picture of Louie in his Navy uniform, propped up at the front of the church, right alongside of a flag folded up like a napkin, and the letter saying Louie is dead, signed by the President himself. I think of how it's a damn shame you gotta get killed by the Japs before the President writes you a letter, 'cause Dad sure would like a letter signed by President Roosevelt. All around that picture and letter and flag, there is flowers. So many flowers that the whole church stinks like perfume.

I feel real sad when I see Louie's ma and dad sitting up at the front of the church, her shoulders moving like they is panting, and his all drooped down like they was hit by a bomb too.

Preacher Michaels, he starts talking about God's love and something called mercy, but I don't pay much mind to that 'cause I can't make heads or tails outta what he's saying anyway. I just look around and think about how it ain't right that Jimmy and Floyd and John ain't here, and I think of how the kid next to me should stop picking his nose in church.

I feel sad to start with, but when this girl stands up and starts singing "Amazing Grace" in a voice as pretty as an angel's, then that sad grows so big and runs so deep in my guts that I start to crying. I think of how Louie won't be going sucker fishing with us no more, and how I ain't never gonna get to open him another Schlitz. I think about how scared Louie was when Floyd shot him in the head, and I think about how much more scared he musta been when it was big-ass bombs aiming at his head, not just a little spray of bird shot.

Before I know it, I'm slapping the sides of my head just like there is blood right in front of my eyes. I am making so much racket that Dad takes me outside. Dad don't get all frazzly and harpy at me like Ma does when I do this. He just takes my hands away from my stinging face and holds 'em and says, "It'll be okay, Earl. It'll be okay." Then it's like I'm a popped tire and I'm done hitting my head and I'm leaning on Dad and crying and I don't even care if I look like a titsy baby.

Dad leads me down to the church basement for sandwiches and pickles and cake when I'm done with my fit. Mrs. Pritchard's fat ass is the first thing I see when we get down there. That chair don't look no bigger than a teacup under that ass.

It's noisy with so many people talking and little kids playing tag around the tables, even though their mas are yanking their arms and telling 'em to settle down. The men are talking about when Spring Lake is gonna freeze over enough to ice fish, and the ladies are talking about if there is enough coffee, or if they should make some more. None of 'em are talking about Louie, and I wonder if they forgot that that's why we come here, to talk about Louie and say good-bye to him. Ain't nobody, it seems, who remembers why we is here except maybe Molly and Mary, who is sitting together holding hands and sniffling into their hankies. I know I forget things sometimes, so I get to thinking maybe even smart people forget things sometimes too, so I decide to help 'em remember. I stand up, and I shout real loud, "Louie's dead!"

Everything in the room gets dead quiet. I can see they ain't remembering nothing, 'cause they look all dazed, like they got clobbered over the head or something, so I say, "He got shot up by the Japs, and now he's stuck in the ocean, so we come here to say good-bye to him." Nobody moves. Everybody just sits there all frozed up like their bodies and even their eyelids got the polio. Everybody 'cept Ma, that is. She comes running across the room so fast her skirt is flapping, and she tugs me down to my chair and says, "Earl, what on earth has come over you?" Then she calls to Dad and I gotta go outside again, even though I ain't slapping my head.

That night Dad comes into my room. He looks as tired and old as a grandpa. "You all right, Earl?" he asks. I shrug 'cause I know I'm suppose to say yes, but I don't wanna say yes 'cause that would be a lie, and I'm thinking I got God pissed off at me enough already.

Dad sits on my bed and he pats my leg that's lumped up under the covers.

"Dad, is Louie in heaven?"

"Well, Earl, I'm not much of a religious man, but I guess at times like this we all get a bit more religious, don't we?"

"Is Louie in heaven?" I ask again, 'cause he ain't answered me the first time.

"Well, son, the Bible says if we love Jesus and live a good life, then yes, we go to heaven after we die."

"Are you living a good life if you drink Schlitz and go chasing girls with big titties in Janesville, and if you cuss a little bit?" Dad drops his head and smiles some and the chubby red skin under his chin poofs out.

"Louie was a good boy, Earl," he says, and I sure am glad to hear Dad say that.

"Dad, you worried about Jimmy?" I ask.

"Course I am," he says.

"I'm worried too. Jimmy's the best brother I ever had."

Dad smiles again, and it might just be he got something in his eye, since Dad don't cry, but he blinks hard like his eyes are stinging him some. He gives my leg a quick squeeze and tells me to try to get some sleep.

After Dad leaves, I lay there and listen to the quiet. Jimmy's room is right next to mine, and when he was home, I never heard nothing coming from that room at night 'cause Jimmy don't snore and his bed don't creak. Still, there was something that come from that room that let me know he was there, even if it wasn't a noise. For months now, though, that room stays empty-quiet inside at night, and that makes me feel all empty-quiet inside too.

Dad told me to get some sleep, but I can't 'cause my head's wondering about some things. I'm a-wondering if there's anybody in that heaven place at all besides that Jesus guy. Seems to me there can't be, 'cause even when we try to be good, we do bad things sometimes. Things like axing fat ladies' legs, or drinking Schlitz, or shooting our friend in the head. Preacher Michaels says we is all sinners, so if we're all a bunch of sinners, how's a damn one of us gonna get let in to heaven?

Betty Flannery, who teaches our Sunday school, calls God our "Heavenly Father" and says He loves us more than any dad in the whole world. I'm trying to sleep like I'm suppose to, but I just keep on thinking. Ma says Dad cusses like a sailor, and even though I don't know how much a sailor cusses, I know Dad cusses a lot. He don't pick up after hisself either, and sometimes, when somebody pays him cash for fixing their car, he don't jot it down in that book so he knows how much he's gotta pay the government. He just slips that money into his pocket, even though that's being a cheater. Dad ain't perfect. That's what Ma says, and I guess she's right. Still, sinner, cusser, and cheater of the government that he is sometimes, I know one thing for sure—I know that Dad would never get so pissed off at me or Jimmy that he'd lock us out of his house. And he'd never, ever, let some mean red guy poke us in the ass with a pitchfork and drag us into the basement and stuff us into the woodstove to burn for that eternity, which is a long, long time. If Dad can be that good of a dad, and he ain't perfect, then I wonder how in the hell God, who is suppose to be perfect and the best dad in the whole world, can do those things. So before I go to bed, I ask God to please be as good of a dad to Louie as my dad is to Jimmy and me.

# Chapter 8

This Christmas is like any other Christmas, yet it ain't.

Dad says maybe we should go to church with Ma on Christmas Eve, so we go. Afterward, Ma straps an apron around her waist and starts making pies for Christmas dinner. I ask her if I can help and she tells me I can. Ma don't let me roll the pie crust, 'cause she says if it's fussed with too much it gets tough, and she don't let me cut up apples, 'cause I scare her when I wave knives around, so I just sit at the table and wait for her to tell me what I can do. She lets me open the cans of pumpkin, then she spoons the squished pumpkin into a bowl. She adds them spices that smell real good, and then she cracks the eggs and dumps 'em and the brown sugar into the bowl. After she pours the canned milk in, she tells me to stir it up real good. I stab at the eggs 'til the yolks bust, then circle my spoon around, going faster and faster like the propeller on an airplane. I'm Captain Midnight's plane, taking him off across the ocean to fight evil. "Nrrrrrrrrrr."

I don't mean for pumpkin to slop up on my shirt and on the table, but it happens. "Good grief, Earl." Ma takes the spoon away from me and tells me to go sit with Dad.

Dad's in the living room and it's empty on Christmas Eve without Christmas songs, but Ma said she don't want any this year. I ask Dad if we can put music on anyway. I remind him that Ma didn't want a Christmas tree either, but he brought one home all the same, so why can't we play Christmas music anyway? Dad says no.

Dad is drinking coffee and munching on a cookie shaped like a bell and I go off into the kitchen to get me one. When I come back, Dad is watching me eat my cookie. Even when my cookie's gone, he is still watching me. He stares at me for a time, then he gets up and yells to Ma that he's goin' out for a bit. Ma pokes her head out of the kitchen. "Where on earth do you need to go on Christmas Eve?" Dad don't tell her, he just says he's got something to do.

By the time Dad comes back, the kitchen is filled with the smell of pies, but Ma says we can't have any 'til tomorrow. Dad is grinning when he gets back. He jokes with me about Santa coming and I gotta remind him that I'm big enough now to know that Santa ain't nobody but somebody's fat uncle wearing a cotton beard.

In the morning, we open presents. Ma gets a new Toastmaster toaster and holds it up and smiles into the shiny chrome. Me and Dad get new winter boots and Dad says that's a good thing, 'cause with the war on now, soon we won't be getting anything new.

Ma starts picking up the ripped wrapping paper, but she stops when Dad says he thinks he forgot to bring over another present for me that he stashed at the garage in case I went snooping around the house. "Hank, what are you talking about?" Dad don't answer, he just tells me to get on my coat and new boots while he goes to start the car, and I can go with him to fetch the present.

It's cold and snowy and I shiver as I stand outside the garage waiting for Dad to unlock the door. "Well, let's just see what else Santa brought you," he says as he shoves the door open. The floor of the garage where the cars get fixed is concrete, and so is the floor in the paying part where the counter and cash register are. That painted concrete is scuffed and muddy already, so we don't ever have to stomp the snow off our shoes when we go inside.

Dad ain't even shut the door behind us yet when I hear something whining and scratching. Dad points to a box tucked under his messy desk, and I see a little black nose peeking over the top of the box. I look at Dad, 'cause I can't figure out why in the hell there's a puppy stuck in a box in his garage.

"Merry Christmas, Earl," Dad says, and he's smiling.

I run to the box and there that puppy is, shuffling around inside. A work shirt with squished puppy turds stuck to it is bunched up in the corner. The puppy ain't a kind I ever see'd before. He's got white and gray fur that looks like the bristles on Ma's scrub brush, and he's got one pokey-up ear and one droopy-down ear. He's got a puny tail and legs that look like someone chopped 'em off at the knees, and there is some gunk stuck in the corners of his eyes. I pick him up. He's about the damn cutest thing I ever did see. Even cuter than Scout or Spot. He squirms in my arms, making puppy grunts, and he licks my face and my hands and just about anything else he can stick his tongue to.

"He's the best dog in the world, Dad!" I say as I go dancing around the garage, not exactly doing the jitterbug, but something kinda like it.

"I'm glad you like him, Earl. He was the last pup Mrs. Lark had left."

On the way home, that puppy stays right on my lap. When I start scratching him good, he rolls over on his back and I can see he's got a little pecker, so I know he's a boy for sure. "I'm gonna name him Lucky," I tell Dad, hoping he don't know that I'm naming him after somebody he thinks is a Nazi bastard. I pick Lucky up and hold him to my nose. He smells good, even his paws. I poke him up by Dad's nose and tell him to take a sniff.

"Oh, Hank, how could you?" Ma says when I walk in with Lucky. She starts harping about how we're gonna be stepping in puddles now, and how we don't need a dog to feed. Dad lets her yammer on a bit, then he says real slow, "Crissakes, Eileen. The boy needs something to hold on to right now, don't he?" and she shuts up.

That night when I go to bed, I don't leave Lucky in his box like I'm suppose to, 'cause when I try, he starts to crying. So I tuck him under the covers, and he curls up against my armpit, making me all toasty warm, and he goes right off to sleep. I think of the box Ma shipped off to the Red Cross, even though she don't know if Jimmy will get it. In that box she put razors and socks, candy bars, a fruitcake, and cigarettes. I sure do wish that box coulda had something extra good in it, like a puppy.

# Chapter 9

I pedal my bike to the garage and Lucky follows. He's growed a lot, but his legs ain't, so I don't pedal too fast or else the rope I got him tied to is gonna drag him, scuffing his belly on the sidewalk. I got Dad's ham sandwich and a piece of pie in my basket.

The front door of the Skelly is open even though it ain't even sucker-fishing time yet, 'cause on the first warm-enough day of the season, Dad opens the doors to let the gas and oil stink get out. Lucky and I go inside and I put Dad's lunch on the counter. I hear Dad in the garage part. I'm gonna go in there soon as I get my shoe tied, which ain't gonna be real quick 'cause Lucky's biting my hair.

"Ed, our boys are getting crushed over there. But what do you expect, outdated rifles, goddamn lightweight M-3 Stuart tanks from World War One . . . Crissakes, Ed, those tanks are riveted. Can you believe it? Riveted. You know what's got to be happening to them when they're hit? Those goddamn panels have got to be buckling and dropping like playing cards." Ed is Floyd's dad. Ed Fryer.

"Shit, Hank. Least they could have done is welded them. Lightweight or not, they'd have a chance of holding together if they were welded." Floyd's dad talks soft, probably 'cause he ain't got much wind on accounta he's skinny as a piece of straw. Hearing that Jimmy and Floyd are in trouble is enough to make my guts feel sick.

"Shit, I don't even know if it would make a difference at this point. Those boys weren't trained for this kind of combat, and crissakes, the Japs got control of the water and the air now. We can't even get supplies in. What in the hell was MacArthur thinking, running those boys down into the peninsula without supplies enough to last until reinforcements could get in? Our planes are all blown to shit, and our boys are starving and sick. That son of a bitch sent our boys to fight to the death, while he holed himself up in some tunnel in Corregidor. Coward bastard."

"They'll be better off now with Wainwright, Hank," Floyd's dad says.

"You're goddamn right about that."

Dad and Mr. Fryer get quiet.

"I'm even scared to go to the mailbox these days," Floyd's dad says, and them words sound like metal scraping on metal when they come out. "That boy is all I have left."

"It's rough, Ed. I lost a brother in World War One, and now I got my boy in war too. Course, I don't like to show how worried I am. Not around Eileen and Earl anyway, but I'm worried, Ed. I'm plenty worried. My guts have been giving me trouble ever since their base was hit, so I know how you feel."

Lucky's teeth, sharp as sewing needles, bite into my ankle and I let out a yelp. I hear Dad cuss, then him and Mr. Fryer come into the paying part. "Lunchtime already?" he says, and his smile looks like a belt strapped tight across his face.

"Well, I'd better get home," Floyd's dad says. He pats my arm when he walks by. "I got that Anderson kid coming over after school to help with chores, but I've got work to do before he gets there." Mr. Fryer reaches down and pats Lucky, who is jumping up on his leg. "Nice dog you got here, Earl," he says.

Dad opens his lunch bag and starts eating his sandwich. He pulls a string of ham fat out from between his teeth and tosses it to Lucky. Dad grabs two Coca-Colas out of the cooler and hands me one. "Here you go," he says. I take the bottle, but I don't take a drink, 'cause ever since I heared Dad and Mr. Fryer talking, I got about a million scary thoughts jumping into my head, screaming "Boo!"

Dad is watching me. "Son, did you overhear Ed and me talking?" I nod. "Don't you worry, Earl. Jimmy's going to be all right. Jimmy and Floyd will look out for each other."

I hand my Coca-Cola back to Dad and tell him I gotta go, and I don't wait around to explain why. I scoop Lucky up, run him outside to where my bike is propped, and plop him into the basket. When Lucky tries to jump out before I can even get my leg swinged into place, I yell at him to stay put, then I get on and I pedal my bike like my ass is on fire.

In our store window, we got a paper flag hanging there (just like the flags other folks who got a boy or two fighting in the war gots hanging in their windows) and on that flag, there's a big star. If our soldier is alive, that star is blue. If our soldier gets killed dead, that star turns to gold.

When I reach the store, I jam my brakes on so hard that the

ass end of my bike kicks sideways, and the whole thing tips right over, dumping me and Lucky out onto the grass. Halfway up the store steps I run, Lucky crashing into the back of my legs when I stop, lickety-split. There that flag is, and the star is still blue. Whew! Jimmy ain't dead.

I swear that when Lucky was a little pup, he musta got that same damn fever I had, 'cause this dog can't learn nothing new, it seems. I'm in the yard with him, throwing a stick and telling him to fetch it, but he don't do nothing but hop around my feet. I pat him on his head, where his hair stands straight up like mine, and tell him it's okay if he's dumb as a stump. He's my dog, and even if he ain't a smart dog like Scout or Spot, he's still one good dog.

I don't go inside 'til my hands get cold, 'cause Ma and Dad are in the living room, and if Ma and Lucky are in the same room together longer than two minutes, she starts fussing over what he's licking or sniffing, and if he even starts to walk behind a chair or the sofa to take a nap, she starts bellering 'cause she thinks he's going off to take a piss or a shit, and she makes me take him outside again.

Ma and Dad got the radio on and Dad holds up his hand for me to be quiet. I can tell the man who's talking is a reporter giving the war news. The first thing I think is how I hope if it's bad news he's saying, it's about that European Theater, not the Pacific Theater. That's what words they use, depending on if they're talking about the war in that Europe place or about the war in that Philippines place. I don't know why they call them two wars theaters—unless maybe it's 'cause if you go down to the theater to watch a picture show, they always show a little movie about one of them wars first. I remember then that John is in the European Theater, so I whack myself in the head for hoping the bad news is about that Europe place.

The reporter is talking. "Bataan has fallen. The Philippine–American troops on this war-ravaged and bloodstained peninsula have laid down their arms. With heads bloody but unbowed, they have yielded to the superior force and numbers of the enemy."

Ma turns her head fast as a chickadee and says, "They surrendered?"

"Wait, Eileen," Dad says. Dad finishes listening to the report, then he lets his back fall against his chair.

"They've all surrendered? What does this mean, Hank?" Ma's picking at her skirt, just like I pick at my pants when I get scared. "What will happen to Jimmy now?"

"They are prisoners of war, Eileen."

"Oh, my God! What will they do to him, Hank?"

"There's international laws about how countries have to treat war prisoners, Eileen. Jimmy will be fine." Dad don't look at Ma when he says this. He gets up and stuffs his hands in his pockets. He walks in half a circle, stops, and walks back to where he was.

"Dad?" I ask. "What did that reporter guy mean when he said that Bataan falled?" I don't want to, but in my head, I can see that little thumb of a place snapping off and falling right into the ocean, just like Louie's ship did.

"It means, son, that our boys had to give up because the Japs were winning."

That don't sound right to me. Jimmy, he always says you never give up. Never. That no matter how many times you fall down when you're learning something new, you gotta keep getting up and trying again, even if your goddamn knees and elbows are all scraped to shit. That's what Jimmy telled me when he helped learn me to ride a bike.

Ma don't even notice when Lucky starts chewing on the leg of the sofa. I notice, though, and I give him a scoot with my foot. I'm feeling skittery 'cause I got pictures of Jimmy and Floyd's bloody heads sinking down into that ocean. It don't seem right to me, our army losing that battle like that. Jimmy never gives up, and no team Jimmy's ever played on loses.

Ma's eyes go buggy, and her hands start to shaking. Those shakes creep right up her arms and then crawl right down the rest of her, not stopping 'til they reach her feet.

Dad looks scared when this happens. Lucky, he sees Ma's shoes hopping and he thinks she's play-teasing him, so he crouches and hops and barks at her feet. Dad picks him up and gives him to me. "Take Lucky and go upstairs, Earl."

I run up them stairs, planning to take Lucky and head under the covers of my bed, but then I hear Ma crying hard, and I don't go to my bed. I go to Jimmy's room that is whistle-clean and quiet. I set Lucky down and I get on my hands and knees and look down the vent that shows into the living room.

Dad is bent over, his butt poked out. He's got Ma's shoulders in his hands. "Eileen, look at me. Jimmy's going to be fine. You hear me? Jimmy's going to be just fine."

"I can't do this, Hank," Ma says. "I can't do this."

"Yes, you can, Eileen. You have to. Earl needs you and so do I."

Ma, she leaps out of her chair and she starts pacing. Her hands are rubbing the top part of her arms like they's freezing and she's trying to thaw 'em. "I don't care who needs *me*. Right now, *I* need my son!"

"I know, Eileen. I know. But we have to be brave. For Earl, and for Jimmy when he comes home."

Ma, she starts picking at her head then, like she's got lice crawling around in them spit curls. "Comes home? We don't even know if he's coming home, Hank. He could be dead already. How would we even know? We haven't heard from him in weeks. Neither has Molly. Oh, my God, he could be dead already!"

I ain't suppose to bug Ma and Dad after Dad tells me to get lost, but seeing Ma with her worst case of the nerves ever, and Dad not knowing what in the hell to say or do to make her nerves stop, I run down them stairs and I take Ma's hand. "Come on, Ma," I say. "I gotta show you something that'll help."

"Earl, I don't think your mother wants to look at anything right now," Dad says, but Ma, she lets me take her hand and lead her out the back door and around the house.

The way the streetlight is hitting the store window, I can't see nothing but shiny black glass. I drop Ma's hand, and I hurry halfway up them stairs and lean over the bent pipe. I look real hard, and there that flag is. "Come on, Ma," I say, reaching out my hand. "Come up here and have a look."

Ma, she moves like she is sleepwalking. When she gets to me, I lean my head down to touch hers so I can see where she's looking. I point at Jimmy's blue star. "Ma, when you get them scared thoughts banging around in your head, you come out here and take a look, same as I do. Long as that star there is blue, Jimmy ain't dead." Ma, she looks at Jimmy's star, then she buries her face against my chest, and she bawls hard.

# Chapter 10

The Army lost Jimmy! That's what the letter we got in the mail from them says. Mary, she got a letter saying they lost Floyd too, and Dad says every other family of them ninety-nine boys got the same letter, saying their soldier is lost too.

After Ma gets that letter and reads it out loud to me and Dad, she lets Dad put his arms around her, and she flops against him like a bug splattering on a windshield. "We always pay for our mistakes," she cries. Her head is laying sideways on Dad's shoulder. "We always pay." Dad pulls her off him and gives her a little shake. "You aren't paying for anything, Eileen. You hear me?"

I don't know what the hell Ma and Dad are talking about,

but I know I don't like the way it makes my guts feel. I don't stick around to hear what else Dad says to Ma. I call Lucky and we go upstairs. I help him get up on our bed and pull the quilt over us. I hold Lucky real tight, and he licks the tears offa my face. "Lucky," I say, "I wish me and you were over in that place. We'd find Jimmy and Floyd and the rest of them guys, for sure." Lucky barks a little, and that means, "You damn bet we would, Earwig."

Pert' near every day Ma writes a letter to Washington asking 'em if they found Jimmy yet, and I pedal it down to the post office. They don't answer, but Ma, she keeps writing anyway.

Ma ain't the same no more. She wears the same dresses, and she wears the same pin-curled hair, but she don't look the same. Her face looks all hard, like it's made of Bakelite, and Dad says she's getting too skinny. She don't act the same no more either. She don't fuss at me about washing behind my ears, or changing my socks, and she don't tell me to finish my vegetables so I can stay healthy and not get the polio, which is all over Willowridge again, dropping kids like flies.

Dad says we gotta get up each morning and do the same things we always do. He says we have to do this so we don't get all buggy and fall off our rockers. So that's what we do. We get up every goddamn morning, even if we don't want to, and I let Lucky out to take a piss and a crap while Ma makes breakfast and Dad shaves. After we eat, Dad goes off to the garage, I tie Lucky up by his doghouse, and then me and Ma get busy in the store.

We gotta keep busy, so it's probably a good thing when we have to start messing with those ration books that the government comes up with so we don't hog up all the food, leaving the soldiers shit out of luck. They call off school for a couple days so the teachers can start figuring out who-all needs sugar and how much each of us needs. That means Eddie don't got to go to school.

Ma is busy pricing Karo syrup (that she says she knows is gonna sell like hotcakes when people can't buy as much sugar) when Eddie comes in. Eddie is eight years old now, and in the third grade.

Eddie don't talk to me first. He goes right up to Ma, and says, "Good morning, Mrs. Gunderman. Would you like to buy some Victory Seeds?" Eddie says it just like he's one of them salesmen that come around now and then, selling Bibles or them encyclopedia books.

Mrs. Lark is in the store, and so is Mrs. Flannery, and they both go over to Eddie so they can get a good look at them green packages with a big red V on 'em. "Our school's selling them," Eddie says. "The seeds are to plant in Victory Gardens. Whatever room sells the most gets to carry the flag on Fridays when we march around the school."

Mrs. Lark, she don't know nothing about Victory Gardens 'cause she don't keep a radio. Like she says, she can't sit around listening to a radio all day when she's got cows to milk and fields to plant. So Eddie tells her about the Victory Gardens Roosevelt is asking everybody to plant. Eddie talks real good. He don't get all balled up with his words like I know I would if I had to sell them seeds.

"Well, I'll be," Mrs. Lark says. She rubs her hand on the leg of her trousers, and she takes a package of string-bean seeds. "Where are people planting these gardens? Most people in town don't have yards big enough for much of a garden."

"Well, Mrs. Lark," Eddie says, "in some towns, folks with more land than they are using are divvying it up, borrowing a little plot to families so they can grow some food for themselves. They have to plant and weed their plot themselves and pick the stuff when it's ripe. Lots of times, they have to give the landowner some of the stuff too, just as a way of saying thank you, I guess."

"I'll be," Mrs. Lark says. Then she says that she has a lot of land, and that people can use her land for a big-ass Victory Garden. Mrs. Lark don't say big-ass, but that's what she means, 'cause she's talking about donating a lot of acres.

Ma and Mrs. Flannery say that's right nice of her for offering her land, and Mrs. Flannery says she'll place an announcement in the paper so people know about the Victory Garden, since she's going to the paper anyway to place an ad to sell their old Ford.

After Eddie sells them ladies some seeds, he asks Ma if I can go along with him while he sells more 'cause he wants his room to carry the flag. Ma says she guesses I can, since it's for a good cause.

We go door to door, selling them seeds, and we put the dimes and nickels in our pockets. We sell so many packages that by the time Eddie's legs are tired, our pockets are lumpy as an old man's knuckles.

"Hey, Earlwig," Eddie says as we walk back toward home. "Know what?"

"What?"

"At school now, sometimes a teacher goes into the hall and blows a horn, real loud. Then we gotta hurry up and crawl under our desks."

"How come?"

"'Cause. Teacher says it's an air-raid drill. I guess we got to do it so we're practiced up in case them Jap or German planes get over here and start bombing us. If we get under our desks, then we ain't going to get killed, I guess."

This makes me all skittery inside. "Well, what if you ain't got no desk? I ain't got no goddamn desk."

"Well, I don't think it's gotta be a desk, because if we're in the lunchroom, then we gotta dive under the lunchroom tables."

"That's good," I say, " 'cause I ain't got no desk."

I walk Eddie home, even if his ma don't say I gotta anymore. I walk him home 'cause Eddie wants to show me something in his new Captain Midnight Flight Control Newspaper. Eddie's real lucky to get Cap's newspaper in the mail. I want to get it too, but Ma says it don't pay 'cause it's mostly words, and I can't read worth a damn. She don't say damn, though.

"Wait until you see what we can get, Earlwig," Eddie says, as he's looking for the right page.

"Hey, Eddie," I say. "You think now that you ain't such a little kid no more, you could call me by my real name, instead of 'Earlwig'?"

"Sure, Earl," Eddie says.

"Not 'Earl.' 'Earwig.' It don't seem right, no one calling me Earwig no more."

"Sure, Earlwig," Eddie says, then he whacks himself between the eyes. "I forgot already. But I'll start remembering."

Eddie finds the right page and jabs his fat finger down on a picture. "See this thing that looks like a spyglass? It's a MJC-ten plane spotter. You look in this end, and you can see planes in it."

"Now, that'd be good to have," I say to Eddie. "Then if the Jap or the German planes come to bomb us, we'd see 'em and know when to dive under a table or a desk even if there weren't no teacher around to blow a horn."

Me and Eddie like Captain Midnight best of all the heroes 'cause he flies a plane, just like Charles A. Lindbergh. Captain Midnight don't just fly to get across the ocean, though. He flies places to fight evil. He even fights dirty Nazis and Japs. Me and Eddie are lucky 'cause we are members of the Secret Squadron. We even got certificates to prove it.

"Know how we are saving up for decoder rings?" Eddie says. "Well, I was thinking maybe we shouldn't send our premiums in for those decoder rings after all. Maybe we should save them to get ourselves two swell plane spotters instead."

"Yeah, Eddie, let's do that."

"If we get enough premiums, we could each get a plane spotter *and* a code-o-graph. How swell would that be, Earwig?"

I grin 'cause Eddie remembered to call me by my real name. "That would be real swell, Eddie. You think we could get enough premiums for both?"

"If we drink up enough Ovaltine, we could. Too bad you still can't get premium points at Skelly gas stations like in the old days. Then your dad could have given us a whole mess of them and we wouldn't have to drink so much, huh, Earwig?"

"Yep," I say. "Man, Eddie, if we get code-o-graphs, then we can call up Washington if them bombers come, just like Chuck does when him and the Cap is in trouble. Washington'll send help then, sure as shit."

Eddie's ma calls up the stairs, "Eddie, your soup is getting cold. Earl, you want to stay for lunch?"

"No thank you, ma'am," I shout, real polite-like. "I gotta go bring Dad his lunch." When I'm going out the door, I hear Eddie tell his ma he don't want no plain old milk for lunch. He wants Ovaltine.

A couple days later, Ma tells me I gotta watch the store for a little bit 'cause she's got to get down to the high school and sign up for the sugar ration. She scoops up the papers she's got on the counter that she says are forms so the government knows how many people we got in our house, and how big and old we are, so they know how much sugar we gotta have.

"Ma, what if I gotta make change?"

Ma is busy tying her scarf under her chin. She rolls her eyes.

"Earl, I've showed you a thousand times. Just do your best, and ask the customer to help double-check your figures if you aren't sure."

No one comes into the store while Ma's gone, except for Eva Leigh. Little LJ's got a big head now, with hair that only grows on the top. If you run your hand over that hair, it stands straight up and follows your hand around like a puppy. LJ walks now too, but if Eva Leigh lets him loose, he rips crap off the shelves, so even though he's a walking baby, Eva Leigh still pokes out her hip and props him on it, 'cept now he's heavy enough that she's gotta lean herself way over in the other direction so he don't tip her over. LJ kicks his legs and screams to get down unless she gives him a cracker or something from her purse to shut him up. Once I even see'd him bite her shoulder when he wanted down, and it made me hope that he ain't getting the orneries like his dad.

Even with LJ fussing at her hip, Eva Leigh don't look so skittery no more. Not since that nasty Luke got drafted and sent off to Germany. She don't droop so much when she walks either. I heared her tell Ma after Luke left that, awful as it is, and as much as she misses him, it sure is nice not being scared that she's gonna do something wrong and get hit.

"Morning, Mrs. Leigh. You look real pretty today, with your hair all curled up like that."

"Thank you, Earl." Eva Leigh smiles, with her new lips that are painted the color of a rose. "Where's your mother?" Eva Leigh is roaming around the store. She puts a couple cans of evaporated milk and a box of Tide on the counter. I know I'm gonna have to make change if Ma don't get back before she's done shopping, but I know too that if I have trouble, Eva Leigh will help me and be nice about it.

"She went to the school to sign up for them sugar books."

"Oh," she says. "I did that this morning."

"I can check you out, though, Mrs. Leigh. If you help me make the change, I can do that."

"I've got to have it written down, Earl. But I'll help." Oh, boy, I think. I never even thought of having to get the book out of the drawer. That would be the charge book. When folks are broke 'cause the weather's been bad and wrecked their crops or mudded up the woods so they can't get wood hauled, they ask Ma to put what they owe down in that book. When times was hard, that book just sat on the counter and never got put away. Ma was right proud after those hard times passed and people who got their stuff wrote up in that book told her that they wouldn't forget how she kept 'em eating through that bad Depression. Now when Ma rings 'em up, they sometimes hand her a little extra and tell her to put it on their old bill. Ma says people know when they've been done a good turn, and then they do a good turn back. Even if a Piggly Wiggly goes up in Ripley, those people say that they is still gonna shop at Gunderman's Grocery.

"I won't have to charge for much longer, though," Eva Leigh says to me. Then she comes right up to the counter and says, "I got a job, Earl!" Her eyes got a sparkle in 'em that I ain't never see'd there before. "My sister-in-law, Luke's sister Ruby, she got me a job at the Ten Pin Bowling Alley where she works. I'm going to take the bowlers' money and rent out shoes and balls. Things like that."

"Ruby Leigh, she's a relation of yours?" I try not to sound all shocked 'cause the town whore is her relation, but it comes out sounding that way anyway.

"Yes, she's Luke's sister. Earl, I know what people say about Ruby, and, well, I guess most of the stuff they say about her is true, but Ruby's got a heart of gold. She's always been good to me. It was real nice of her to get me that job."

"It sure was."

"I start tonight. I'm so nervous!" Eva Leigh giggles some. "I've never had a job before, Earl."

"You'll do real good at that job, Mrs. Leigh. You can count change, so you'll do real good."

Ma says that good girls like Molly and Mary shouldn't be seen with girls like Ruby Leigh. Ruby don't come into the store much, 'cause she lives with her ma, Elsie Leigh, and her ma does most of the grocery shopping. One time, though, I see'd Eva Leigh and Ruby Leigh in the store at the same time, but I didn't figure they was relation. Lots of times people who ain't relation shop in the store at the same time. After they left, Ma said that Eva Leigh shouldn't lower herself by even walking next to Ruby Leigh. I was too busy thinking about Ruby Leigh's big titties and rocking hips to pay much mind to what Ma was saying.

"I know it's silly, me being a married woman and a mama, but still, just knowing I got this job now, well, it makes me feel different. More grown-up, or something." I force myself to stop thinking about Ruby Leigh's big titties, 'cause Eva Leigh is looking straight at me and it gives me the nerves to think she might figure out what I'm thinking.

"Luke won't like it," Eva Leigh adds as she swats at LJ's hand 'cause he's leaning over and reaching for stuff. "But what am I supposed to do? Luke's only making nineteen dollars a month in the army. I can't make it on that. I figure if the President himself signed papers opening up jobs to women and coloreds, then I'm just doing my duty by getting a job. I just won't write Luke about me working, and I hope my mother-in-law won't either. He'll be fit to be tied when he comes home and finds out, but I can't worry about that now. I've got to think of LJ."

Eva Leigh ain't ever talked so much to me in her whole life. She's just chattering away like a squirrel on a branch, but I like it. She's got a real pretty voice.

"Maybe ol' Luke will get shot dead by one of them Nazis and won't come home anyway," I say. "Then you don't ever have to tell him and get cuffed for lying." The minute I say it, I'm goddamn sorry, 'cause Eva Leigh is looking at me like I'm one of them monsters up there on the picture-show screen. And worse yet, Ma comes out of the kitchen, her scarf still tied under her chin, her cheeks still pink from the cold, and she's looking at me like she wants to swat me with her purse.

"Earl Hedwig Gunderman!" she shouts. "That was a rude, insensitive comment. Apologize to Mrs. Leigh this minute!"

"I'm sorry, Mrs. Leigh." I turn to Ma. "Ain't like I want Luke to get killed. I don't, even if he's rotten-apple mean. I was just telling Eva Leigh the God's honest truth. If Luke gets killed, then he ain't coming home, and she ain't never gotta tell him." Ma tells me to shut up and then she apologizes to Eva Leigh. She tells me to go finish pricing the bags of split peas.

Eva Leigh don't stay rattled long. She starts telling Ma all about her new job and how she's gonna exchange baby-sitting with some other lady so she don't have to pay a sitter, since the other lady works days at the Knox Lumber Factory now, and she'll be working nights. "Well, if you have to work, then a sitter is the way to go. Those day-care centers they're putting up now are nothing more than orphanages."

While Eva Leigh's telling Ma this stuff, I see her take a jar of Ovaltine off the shelf and bring it to the counter. "Mrs. Leigh?" I call out. "You think after that Ovaltine there is drunked up, you could save me the label and the foil under the cap, please? There's premium points there, and me and Eddie are—"

"Earl!" Mom snaps. "Will you *please* mind your manners!"

"I said please, Ma. I'm sure I did!"

Eva Leigh smiles and tells Ma it's okay, then she tells me she'll be glad to save me the premium points.

"Eva, about this job. I realize you have to do something, but couldn't you find another place to work? I hate to see you working in an establishment that sells liquor. It's just not good for a girl's reputation."

Eva Leigh turns away and starts looking on the shelves. She don't say nothing.

Outside, Lucky is barking, like he always is when he's tied. Ma is pulling the charge book out from under the counter. She slams it on the counter. "Earl, can't you teach that miserable dog not to bark like that when he's tied?"

"No, ma'am," I say, "I sure can't. That dog can't learn nothing."

Ma sighs, hard. "Earl, go run the carpet sweeper in the living room." As I leave, Ma is telling Eva Leigh that if the worry over Jimmy don't kill her, her frayed nerves from dealing with me will.

While sweeping the big rag rug in the living room, I get the notion that maybe I'd better have myself one of them air-raid drills since I don't get those drills at school. So I just whistle as I sweep, like I don't even know it's coming. Then I make a loud honking noise like a horn. Real quick-like, I drop the handle of that carpet sweeper and make a beeline dive for the kitchen table. I don't duck quick enough, though, and I catch my forehead right on the goddamn edge of the table. I get whacked so hard, I yell like I'm getting killed and kick my legs out, knocking a chair with my foot. *Kapow!* Down goes the chair.

Ma comes running into the kitchen, yelling, "What on earth are you doing in here, Earl?" I start telling her I was having a air-raid drill since I don't get 'em at school, but she just snaps at me to shut up. "Get your jacket on and help Mrs. Leigh out with her groceries." As I fetch my jacket, I decide I better practice them air drills more often, 'cause if them bombers come over Willowridge, I'm gonna kill myself whacking my head before that big-ass bomb even reaches the goddamn ground. Before I even get my jacket zipped up, Ma, she starts bawling. "Earl, when are you going to grow up? I can't take much more of this!" And I don't know how to answer that one, 'cause I don't know when I'm gonna grow up.

# Chapter 11

At first, sugar is the only thing we can't hog up, but before long, it's a whole buncha things. We have to close the store down for pert' near a whole week, and we gotta count every goddamn thing we got in there so we can tell the rationing board. We got to do that in our kitchen too, and so does everybody else. Them ladies sure get in a uproar about that. Mrs. Pritchard says it ain't fair 'cause you lose eight points if you canned a jar of snap beans, but beans that week might only take three or four ration points, so look how many points you lose. Ma agrees that it ain't fair, but says we gotta do what we can for the war effort.

Ma don't seem to give a shit about doing what we can for the war effort when them ration stamps come out, though. There is red stamps for meat and butter and cheese and margarine and canned fish, and there is red and green stamps for vegetables and fruits. Fruit costs so goddamn many stamps that two bites of canned peaches could practically hog up your whole book.

Everything we sell in the store now is got a price on it for money and a price on it for ration points, and like Ma says, you can't memorize the price of nothing 'cause them ration points change on a dime. If a lady buys a can of sugar peas for six ration points, she ain't got no coupons to use but for them ten-point ones. She don't get no change 'cause there ain't no ration change, so that customer, she gets miffed enough to dig through the whole store looking for something worth three points. Them ladies make a goddamn mess of them shelves, and I'm the poor sucker who's got to straighten 'em up.

It's a goddamn pain in the neck, this rationing, and Dad thinks so too, 'cause he's got his own rationing mess down at the Skelly.

First they ration the tires, and people gotta count how many tires they got on every one of their cars. Then they gotta count the tires they got laying around and turn in the ones they don't need.

Then comes the gas rationing, which Dad says is happening 'cause people ain't doing so good on the tire rationing. When that starts, Dad goes into a whizzy-tizz. "Crissakes, just look at this mess," he says as he's staring down at the papers he's got spread out on the counter. "Everyone's gotta fill out these forms now, telling how many miles they drive back and forth to work. The ones who drive farthest will get a C sticker to put on their windshields, and those who don't drive far will get an A stamp, and I've gotta keep track of it all. Crissakes, how are people with the A stamp going to even get by on this little bit of gas, and how in the hell am I supposed to keep my business afloat?

"It's a goddamn pain in the ass," Dad tells Delbert Larson one day while we is standing in the Skelly parking lot. "Ben Olson was in here yesterday. His tire had a big ol' slice in it. He had to go all the way down to the goddamn ration board, pick up a paper that me and the guy at Texaco across town had to sign saying his tire couldn't be fixed, then he had to bring our signatures back to the board to get a ration coupon to buy a new one. Now he's got to look all over kingdom come for somebody with a tire to sell him. I sure as hell didn't have one the size he needed. Shit, I don't hardly have any tires left, period. Soon folks won't be fixing their cars either, if they can't drive them anyway. Things keep up like this too long, and I'm gonna go belly-up."

"Did the Texaco have it?" Delbert asks.

"Hell no. And now what's he suppose to do? He can't drive over to Ripley if he don't have enough gas coupons to even get himself there and back."

Dad gets so crabby, he don't even sit still and listen when *Fibber McGee and Molly* comes on. Before things went to shit at the station, Dad sat in his chair and laughed his ass off whenever Fibber came up with some harebrained fib to get hisself outta work or a hitch. And Dad used to about piss his pants when Fibber got to talking to that little girl, Teeny, the two of them getting their words so balled up that neither of 'em knew what the other one was talking about. But Dad, he don't hardly even crack a smile no more. Then one night at suppertime, while Ma is dishing up raisin pie for dessert, he tells us some news that about makes Ma's jaw drop off its hinges.

"The Oldsmobile plant in Janesville, they rolled their last car off the line last week and turned their whole production over to making shells. With most of the young men gone now, and women taking over the assembly lines, they're looking for a few men to fill the foreman positions. I contacted them last week, Eileen. I start on Monday."

"Without even discussing it with me first?"

"I'm sorry, Eileen, I knew you'd be upset, but I don't have a choice, honey. The garage is barely making overhead costs. I'm hiring Delbert Larson to run the station, at least so people can get their piddling-ass drops of gas to get to work and back. He'll work for forty-three cents an hour."

"But the drive, how can you make that drive now with—"

"I won't be driving it every day. That wouldn't work. I'll put myself up in a boardinghouse during the week and come home Friday nights."

Ma drops her fork onto her plate. "You're leaving me here by myself, Hank? At a time like this?"

"You won't be alone," Dad says. He wags his fork toward me. "You have Earl here. He's almost eighteen now. He's good company, and he's a good helper. You'll take care of your ma, won't you, Earl?" I nod.

I'm busy staring at my pie. I don't like raisin pie, and seems it's the only dessert we get anymore since the sugar rationing. Don't that just figure, I think every time Ma cuts me a slice of that pie that looks like it's made with rabbit turds and snot, that goddamn raisin pie is the only kind of pie that don't need sugar. I scrape the innards out and eat the crust. When I'm done, Dad tells me to take the supper scraps outside to Lucky.

Ma scrapes the leftovers onto my plate, her fork moving all jerkity-jerk, then she hands the plate to me. Lucky gulps them scraps up like a pig, raisin filling and all. I scratch him behind his pokey-up ear as he eats, and when he's done, he starts to licking me.

It's almost dark now, so I untie Lucky to bring him inside. Ma and Dad are in the living room arguing, so I scoop up Lucky and take him quick up the stairs.

Used to be back when Jimmy was home, Ma and Dad, they hardly ever had one of them arguments. Now it seems that's about all they do.

I don't like hearing Ma and Dad fight, yet I can't make my ears not listen. It's like them times when somebody comes into the store and starts telling Ma about so-and-so who got hurt bad or killed bad on the farm or in the woods while they was working. You want your ears to close up, 'cause you don't wanna hear how somebody got their hand caught in their corn chopper and how that machine chewed their arm clear up to the shoulder, or how they got clobbered over the head by a falled tree and their head cracked open like a egg. You don't wanna hear it, yet you just can't get your ears to stop listening. Worse yet, you even find yourself moving closer to the counter so you can hear every goddamn bloody word they say. It's like that when Ma and Dad fight. I don't wanna hear what they're saying, yet I go straight to that vent and lean over so I can hear every goddamn word.

"You can't stand the sight of me anymore, Hank. That's the real reason you're leaving," Ma says.

"What on earth are you talking about, Eileen? I've got to work, for crissakes."

Ma starts crying. Seems that's about all she does since Jimmy left. Cry and yell and work. Cry and yell and work. "You're leaving home to punish me," she says.

Dad scratches his head, right on that bald spot that is shiny and a bit bumpity. "For crissakes, Eileen, what is with you, anyway? I've been as good of a husband to you as I can possibly be for twenty years, but it's never enough. No matter what I do, the second things get tough, you accuse me of holding the past against you."

"Oh, Hank," Ma says, shaking her head in quick, skittery jerks. "Don't tell me that every time you look at Jimmy you aren't reminded."

Dad sounds like he's all tuckered out when he answers. "Maybe *you're* the one who can't let the past go, Eileen. Maybe *you're* the one who remembers every time you look at Jimmy."

That room down there gets cold then. So cold it feels like Old Man Winter is sending ice farts up the vent. I don't know what they are talking about, but I know it ain't something good, 'cause I feel it in my guts.

I hear the back door open and close, and it don't open again until pert' near two o'clock in the morning.

Three days later, Dad leaves for Janesville. Ma has his suitcase packed, and she's bagged him a couple sandwiches to take along, but she ain't hardly talking to him at all. Dad pretends like nothing's wrong. He sneaks breakfast scraps from the table to Lucky and he asks to look at my MJC-10 plane spotter. "Well, look at that," he says. "It's just like the aircraft recognition silhouettes the Civilian Defense plane spotters use." I run upstairs and get my code-o-graph to show him, and Dad thinks that's real swell too.

An hour later, Dad is putting his suitcase in the trunk and tapping his pocket to make sure his wallet is there. Ma waits on the back porch, her hands holded together. She don't even harp at him to be sure and change his socks every day so he don't get itchy feet.

My stomach feels sick over Dad leaving. "Now I can't bring you lunch no more." Dad reaches up and rubs the top of my head, just like Jimmy used to do. "I'm gonna miss that too, son," he says. Then he tells me this won't be forever, 'cause the war can't last forever, even though it seems it already has.

Dad puts his arm up around my shoulder and gives the top of my arm a squeeze. Then he looks like he's gonna go to the porch to give Ma a kiss like he does every morning when he leaves to go to the Skelly, but he don't. Instead, he lifts his hand, just a little, and that's suppose to be a wave. Ma does the same. "I'll see you two Friday night," he says, then he drives away.

When I can't see Dad's car no more, I turn and look at Ma. Jimmy's gone. Dad's gone. Louie's gone. Floyd's gone. John's gone. Now there ain't no one left but me and Ma and Lucky. And that don't make me feel so lucky.

# Chapter 12

My birthday is on a Thursday, but I gotta wait to have cake 'til Friday night when Dad comes home. Ma makes me a chocolate cake from the sugar she saved up, and she puts a bit of real frosting on it, not that crappy seven-minute frosting that I hate.

Ma says Eddie can come over for cake, so he does. He wears a nice school shirt, and he brings a present wrapped in blue paper. Ma tells him he can set it down right beside the little present she got for me. Molly surprises me and comes over too. I ain't see'd Molly for a long time, so I get all happy when she comes through the door. She got her hair cut into one of them new hairdos she says is called a pageboy. I can tell Molly likes it by the way she keeps swooshing her hair around so it bobbles on her head. She got on new shoes too, and I can see some of her little toes peeking out of the hole up front, and her toenails are painted pink.

We eat spaghetti, 'cause I like that best, and after we eat, Ma sponges Eddie and my shirts off before we have cake and I open my presents. Ma and Dad give me a war bond, and I wonder what in the hell kind of present that is. Dad tells me they bought it to help the war effort, and Ma says it will be worth twenty-five dollars in twenty years.

Eddie wrinkles up his nose, probably 'cause he thinks it's a dumb present too. "Open the present I gave you next, Earwig. Mine's good." Molly laughs when Eddie says that, and she says then maybe I should open her present next and save Eddie's for last. Molly gives me a little box that is filled with these candies they call M&Ms. They are little chocolate pieces and they got colored candy over 'em that makes little crunchity noises when you chew 'em. "They made this candy for the soldiers," Molly says. "They coat the chocolate with hard candy so they won't melt when the soldiers take them into the fields. You're eating the same candy Jimmy eats," Molly says. Dad tells Molly she must have good connections to get ahold of those candies, and Ma tells me to share with Eddie, so I do.

Inside the blue wrapped box from Eddie is a toy airplane. And not just any old airplane either. It's Captain Midnight's airplane, I shit you not. "Thanks, Eddie!" I say, and I pick up that plane and I fly it around the room, right over the heads of those damn Japs and Nazis, and I drop a few bombs.

While I'm zooming my plane around, Eddie tells me his ma let him order one just like it, so he runs home to fetch it so we can both play. I can't go with him, 'cause I got company, so I fly my plane around and wait for Eddie to come back. Dad and Ma and Molly talk while I "Nrrrrrr" around the room, fighting evil.

They talk about Washington not answering Ma's letters, and Dad says how we just gotta go on believing Jimmy's still okay. "How can twelve hundred American GIs be lost? They've got to be somewhere. A prison camp is the most likely place." My plane flies lower when Dad talks, but not so low that Lucky can bite it or the Japs or Krauts can shoot it down.

Ma sighs, like she's been doing lots these days. "I wish Jimmy had never signed up for the Guard. It was the most foolish thing he could have done."

"Jimmy would have had to go anyway, Eileen," Dad says, "but I wish he had waited until he got drafted. At least he would have gotten decent equipment to work with and had better training. It's like those poor Guard boys were nothing but throwaway soldiers. The army used them to distract the enemy, bide themselves some time to put together an effective army, and now that those things have been done, they don't care what happened to the first batch they sent in."

"They were sacrificial lambs," Ma says.

"I pray for him every night," Molly says, and Ma smiles.

Ma's smile don't last long, though. Not when Molly tells us she's gonna go live with her aunt in Chicago. "My uncle, he's a doctor, and he's been drafted. My aunt's health is poor and she has six little ones to tend to." Ma's smile sorta freezes. Then, when Molly adds, "I'm going to watch my cousins during the day, then at night I'll be working as a hatcheck girl at the Starlight Ballroom," that would be the part that knocks that smile right off Ma's face.

"A hatcheck girl at the Starlight Ballroom? I'm not sure Jimmy would approve of that, Molly."

Molly dabs at the corner of her lip, like maybe she thinks that her lipstick is smeared, then she clears her throat. "Well, Mrs. Gunderman, I'll make good money. Who knows, maybe I can make enough for that down payment on the Williams place. I think Jimmy would appreciate that, don't you?"

I set my Captain Midnight plane back in its box to wait 'til Eddie gets back, and I say, "Sometimes, I almost forget what Jimmy looks like. I ain't never gonna forget him in my heart, but sometimes I think my eyes are starting to forget him." I think maybe I ain't said the right thing, 'cause Molly starts fussing with her skirt, even though it ain't got a speck of dog hair on it.

"How about some coffee?" Dad asks, and Molly says that sounds good, 'cause their house is fresh out of coffee 'til the new books come out tomorrow. "Eileen," Dad adds, "maybe you need to take Jimmy's Guard picture out of our room and put it out here where Earl can see it."

When Eddie gets back, Molly leaves, and me and Eddie, we run missions with our planes up and down the stairs 'til Ma says that's enough and sends Eddie home. Dad, he don't listen to Ma harp about Molly being a hatcheck girl. He listens to the nine o'clock news and he gets happy when they say that our Navy won the battle at Midway, wherever to hell that is.

With Molly and Eddie gone and the radio shut off now, there ain't too much talking going on. Dad sits in his chair, squirming his butt around like the cushion don't fit him right no more. I hold my airplane and look at the way it's put together. Ma is sewing a patch over a tear in the knee of my trousers. When she finishes, she pats her work and says, "Use it up, wear it out, make it do, or do without." Then she asks Dad if he wants coffee, 'cause there's some left from earlier. Dad says no.

Both nights, Dad sleeps on the couch 'cause his back is hurting him, then on Sunday, he leaves.

Them Schlitz bottle caps I saved up when Jimmy and the guys was here, I got 'em in my closet. One night I take that box out and I put it on my bed. Then I sit on my bed like a Indian and run my hands through 'em, listening and liking that tinky-chinky noise they make when they slip through my fingers. I ain't got a clue why I saved 'em. Just 'cause I like bottle caps, I guess. I like the smell of 'em and the sound of 'em, and I like to stick my fingernail in that soft cork part underneath.

I pick up a handful and pick through 'em, turning one in my hand, trying to remember exactly which good time it come from and whose bottle it came off of, but I can't remember that. Downstairs, Ma's playing Glenn Miller, and 'cept for the music, and the tinky-chinking of my bottle caps, I don't hear nothing but Lucky's snores.

I drop the whole handful of bottle caps into the box, real slow-like, watching 'em plink on the others. Then I pick up more handfuls and watch those fall. I get to thinking about how these bottle caps are like the days since Jimmy left. First there was only a few of 'em, but before I knowed it, there got to be so goddamn many I couldn't count 'em no more. Ma says Jimmy's been gone over two years now. Don't seem right to me, but if Ma says it's true, then it's true, 'cause she's real good at counting.

When I'm done hearing my bottle caps, I pick up the box and haul it back to my closet. Ain't a damn thing to do at night no more with Dad still working at that plant in Janesville and Ma not wanting to listen to the radio at night in case they say something bad about the war. She don't even wanna play checkers.

Before I shut my closet, I see a little piece of black poking out from under the box where all my winter clothes are kept, and I pull it out. It's the felt hat Ma made me one Halloween so I could be a pirate. I put it on, but it don't fit real good no more. I scrinch it down the best I can and hope my quack-grass hair will keep it in place. I dig more and find the wood sword Dad made me to go with it, and I stick it through my belt loop. I wake up Lucky so he can be my parrot, even if he's too big to sit on my shoulder, and I tell him we is going treasure hunting. "We gotta have our treasure hunt up here, though," I tell Lucky, " 'cause Ma has got the nerves tonight and she'll yell if we go digging around downstairs."

I look down at my treasure map, which ain't a real treasure map but a page that come loose from my Superman comic book, and then I head out on my adventure. I look for a treasure under beds and in closets, and my parrot follows me. There ain't nothing good anywhere. Even in the closets. Just clothes lined neat on hangers, boxes of Christmas ornaments and old knickknacks or outgrowed clothes. Nothing good at all. That's when I get the notion to head up to the attic, where there might be something good. I got a flashlight in my drawer in case I gotta pee in the night, so I take that flashlight with me 'cause there ain't any lights in the attic.

I pull the attic stairs down real careful-like, hoping Ma don't hear 'em groan, and I pick up my parrot and up we go. It's hot in the attic. So hot it could fry a ghost.

That attic is spooky in the dark, all shadowy and smelling like dust and mothballs. I whack my knee hard against a old sewing machine, and I cuss like a good sailor. Lucky is sniffing all over the place.

I dig through piles of junk, old books, old lamps with no shades, a bag of baby toys, and them chairs Ma might have recaned someday. Then I see it. A treasure chest. A real pirate's treasure chest! "Lucky, look!" I say, pointing to the wooden chest that has a rounded top and everything. I take the bag off the top of it and get down on my knees. "We're rich! We're rich!" I tell my parrot, who don't give a damn about being rich, just about sniffing.

When I open that lid, I can see right off there ain't nothing in there but ladies' stuff. So I tell Lucky this is a queen's treasure chest that Blackbeard stole off her ship when she was sailing on one of them trips queens take. "Bet the queen will give us lots of money if we steal it from Blackbeard's hiding place and give it back to her."

That queen, she sure does like lace, 'cause she's got all kinds of lacy things in there. A tablecloth, folded pin-neat, and doilies, and even a white nightgown that's all frilly with lace.

She's got squares of material, like for sewing them quilts, and they is all tied together with a ribbon like they is gonna be a present or something. She's got a tea set in there too, and I bet it's worth a pretty penny, 'cause when I peek under the newspaper the pot's wrapped in, it looks pretty damn fancy to me with that gold stuck all over it.

Toward the bottom of the treasure chest is a album filled with pictures of people from the old days. I tell Lucky that them sourpusses are the queen's dead family. There is little ribbons and hair pretties under that photo album, along with a mirror and brush that have backs all shiny and rainbowy like seashells. Then there is another box. A small box made of wood, and it's got a picture of an old-timey lady on the lid. The box is the last thing in there, 'cept for a few dried-up dead bugs and some mouse turds.

Inside that box, there is a little bunch of squashed flowers with a ribbon still on it. When I lift it out, some of them petals, they fall right off even though I'm trying to be real careful so the queen don't say I wrecked her things. There is a necklace in there, and a book of matches, of all the crazy things.

When I tip my head over to get a peek at the photographs at the bottom of that box, my pirate's hat falls off, bounces off the box, and rolls onto the floor. I just leave it there, 'cause I ain't a pirate no more when I pick up the flashlight and get a good look at them pictures. Ma is in the first one. Just how she looks in that wedding picture that sits on her dresser. And she is standing next to a man who's got his arm around her. That man, he is wearing a uniform with wings on it, and I ain't kiddin', he looks just like Jimmy. He's got the same wavy hair that's bright like the sun, and he's got Jimmy's same mouth, 'cept it stretches farther across his cheeks.

I look through the other photographs, and sure enough, there that man is in every one of 'em, and if he don't look like Jimmy, then my name ain't Earl Hedwig Gunderman.

In one of them pictures, that Jimmy-looking guy and Ma are standing in front of a porch, and Dad is there too, looking all young and skinny. It ain't Dad's arm around Ma, though, it's this Jimmy-man's arm, and him and Ma are standing so close the sunlight can't even sneak between 'em. On the last picture, there is Ma, giving this guy a big kiss, her arms wrapped around his neck, his arms wrapped around her waist.

Lucky comes sniffing around, and I shove him away with my arm. My head is all mixed up now, wondering why Ma is kissing this guy that looks just like Jimmy.

There are some letters too, and they is tied together with a ribbon braid, one strand red, one white, and one blue. Them letters are all yellowed like old things get, and I'm kicking my own ass for getting kicked out of third grade, 'cause now I can't read a word they say.

The braid is tied with a knot and I ain't good at getting tiny knots out, so I work the braid until I can slide one end off. Then I pull out a couple of them letters. It ain't easy to do that when you got a flashlight in your hand either.

I got 'em in my hand when I hear Ma. She sounds right at the bottom of the stairs when she yells, "Earl, what are you doing up there?"

I look down and I got a heap of junk laying out. When I hear her coming up them stairs calling my name, I know I ain't gonna be able to get it all throwed back in time. I don't know what to do, 'cause I ain't suppose to dig around and I ain't suppose to touch nobody's mail. So I stick them two letters I got out into my pocket, 'cause there ain't a whore's chance in heaven that I'm gonna get 'em back in the bundle quick, and I toss them pictures back into that old-timey box and start dumping the rest of the junk back in the treasure chest any which way. I ain't even got the lacy stuff back in when Ma's head and shoulders peek up out of the floor.

"What on earth are you doing up here?" She is leaning this way and that, trying to get a good look at what I'm up to, which ain't easy 'cause it's dark as shit up here but for the log of light shining from my flashlight on her old sewing machine.

I stand up, 'cause I don't know what else to do. "I was just looking around."

Ma is all the way up now. She puts her fingers on a box of old junk so she don't trip. Like the idiot I am, I let my arm fall down and that light spills out right over the lacy junk that's still heaped on the floor.

Ma hurries to me and she yanks the flashlight outta my hand. She wobbles the light over the mess I made and I know I'm in big trouble. "What are you doing, digging around up here?"

"Just playing, Ma," I say.

She leans over and picks up the stack of lacy stuff and she brushes it off, then hugs it to her like it's a baby that's falled and needs some holding before it can stop crying.

She's already got the nerves tonight, and now she's pissed too, so I know I should just shut my mouth and take Lucky downstairs real fast, but I don't. Instead, I reach down and dig in that old-timey box until I feel them pictures, and I pull a couple of 'em out. "There's a man in these pictures that looks just like Jimmy," I say, holding them out. "You're kissing on him in one of 'em." Ma snatches 'em right out of my hand and clunks me right on the side of my head and tells me I ain't got no business snooping in other people's things. She tells me to get downstairs, right now.

I scoop up Lucky and carry him down the stairs, 'cause he

don't know how to climb stairs that are more like ladders than steps. I hurry back to my room. My hat is in the attic, but I'm still wearing my wood sword, so I take that off and shove it back in the closet. Then I sit on my bed and wait for Ma and the good harping I know I'm gonna get when she comes down.

I wait a long time. A good long time. Finally I hear the creak and the thud that means she's putting the stairs back up. I hear her footsteps coming, but they don't stop at my door. They go right past, and down the stairs.

I stay upstairs until me and Lucky gotta piss so bad we can taste it, then I go down quiet-like. I don't go to the bathroom, 'cause that's too close to Ma's room, where she is with the door closed, so I slip outside with Lucky and we both take a leak by the tree.

Ma don't say nothing to me the next morning. She puts my bowl of oatmeal on the table, then starts telling me all the things we gotta get done in the store today. I mind my Ps and Qs all day, and I wait 'til after supper before I go to Eddie's, them two letters in my jacket pocket.

Mrs. McCarty lets me in and she tells me Eddie's up in his room. She asks me how my dad's job is coming.

"His job's coming real good. He says them ladies work as good as any man. He says they do everything from heavy machining operations to forging. I don't know what that exactly means, but that's what Dad says they do. He says they is all Rosie the Riveters, but that ain't what he calls 'em. He calls 'em 'Wings,' 'cause they got wings on their uniforms even if they ain't pilots."

"It's a shame he couldn't get a foreman's job right here in town, but I suppose they had their help already. I'm sure your mom would rather he was home, her worrying so much about your brother. And I'm sure your dad would rather be sleeping in his own bed at night too. People never seem to rest as well when they have to sleep in strange beds. I know I don't," Mrs. McCarty says.

"Well, Dad can't sleep in a bed no more," I tell her. "His back's been bothering him for a long time now, so he sleeps on the couch."

"Oh?" Mrs. McCarty is looking at me funny as I start up the stairs, so I stop and lift up my feet to check the bottom of my shoes, thinking maybe I brought a gob of dog crap in on 'em, but I didn't.

"Hey, Earwig," Eddie says.

"Hey, Eddie."

I pick up a piece of paper that's on his bed and sit down. Eddie's got words printed in neat rows down that paper. "You write real good, Eddie," I tell him. He tells me he's making a list of things he wants for his birthday, which ain't coming up anytime soon.

"You want to go fishing tomorrow, Earwig? Dad says the crappies are biting real good at Spring Lake."

"Nah, I can't fish tomorrow," I tell Eddie. "I gotta work in the store in the morning, then I gotta go weed our garden over at Mrs. Lark's when I'm done."

"That stinks," Eddie says, and I remind him that it was him that talked Ma into buying them damn seeds in the first place.

"I can't do nothing fun right now 'cause I ain't mopped the floor in the store yet either. I just come by real quick so you could read something for me." Then I take them two letters out of my pocket and I show him.

Eddie takes one and looks at the writing on the envelope. "Where'd you get these?"

"I found 'em."

"They're addressed to a Miss E. J. Lasky. Who's that, Earwig?"

"I don't know. Just hurry up and read 'em, Eddie. I got

Lucky tied to your fence and, 'case you ain't noticed, he's barking like his nuts are caught in a bear trap."

"It's from a guy in the Army Air Corps. Hey, Earwig, look, that's your name—Gunderman. William Gunderman, it says, and this here, this is his rank and stuff."

"Get to the goddamn letter, Eddie," I tell him.

Eddie unfolds the page and it is thin like onion skins. *"My dearest,"* Eddie reads, then he stops and giggles. "Hey, this is a love letter!" he says, and I gotta tell him again to just read the goddamn letter.

*"Not much time to write. Just got back from the front, north of . . ."* Eddie pauses and scrinches up his eyes 'til they ain't nothing but two skinny black lines. "Must be like our letters now, how they cut out names and stuff in case the enemy gets ahold of them." Then he starts reading again. *"We saw little action, so don't fret. We were there mainly for pilot practice."* Eddie stops again. "Man, oh, man, he was a pilot, Earwig! A real flying ace like Cap!"

"Just read the goddamn letter, Eddie."

Eddie rolls his eyes. "Jeez, Earwig. What crawled up your hind end to make you so crabby?"

"Just read the letter, Eddie. I ain't got all day." Eddie sighs, then he starts reading again.

*"Rumor has it we'll be reassigned tomorrow. My plane is running smooth as a shooting star as it is and will run even smoother as soon as it gets overhauled with a Liberty engine. Sorry, I'm doing it again, aren't I? Writing about things a girl finds dull. Know, though, my darling, that as much as I love flying, that love doesn't compare to my love for you. Memory of your sweet kisses sends me higher than any plane could."* Eddie stops reading so he can giggle, but I ain't giggling 'cause I know who them words was writ by and I know who they was writ for.

*"I await each of your letters, and read them over and over. I can't wait until this bloody war is over and I can come home to you. We'll be*

*married then, honey. The same day, if possible. That is my only regret. That we didn't have time to marry before I left. I hope that is your only regret too. Give my regards to my family and yours, my dearest. If you have any word on my brother, please let me know, as I have not heard from him after his training and Ma didn't mention him in her last letter. With endless love, Your Number One Ace, Willie.*"

I snatch the letter out of Eddie's hands and fold it up real quick. "Wow, Earwig, a real flying ace from World War One. Can you believe it?"

Eddie goes to grab the other letter, but I lift my hand up high so he can't reach it. I don't wanna know what it says no more. "I gotta go, Eddie, before Lucky pukes from barking so hard."

"You want to go down to the crick one of these days or something, Earwig? See if that beaver's got his dam finished?"

"Maybe."

"What you going to do with them letters?" he asks.

"Put 'em back where I found 'em," I tell him. Eddie asks where that is and I say, "In the queen's treasure box," and then I go home.

# Chapter 13

When you figure out something that nobody told you, that means you put two and two together. I ain't good at numbers, but I still can put two and two together, I guess, 'cause that's what I do after I see the photographs and Eddie reads that letter. I put two and two together, and now I know that my ma and my uncle Willie was sweethearts once upon a time. I know something else too. I figure it out when I see them dogs at Mrs. Lark's, when I go to weed our plot over in the Victory Garden.

There them dogs is, and I know which one is Lucky's ma 'cause figuring out which dog is the ma is easy. She's the one that got them pink titties hanging down, and them would be for feeding her pups. The other two dogs, they got peckers plain as day, so they is the boys.

Mrs. Lark shows me the new pups that is curled up on hay in the barn. Them new pups are still scrawny and their eyes ain't even open yet. Their fur still looks more like stains on their skin than fur. Still, you can see what color that fur is gonna be. The ma dog, she is yellow, and one of them pups is yellow just like her. Three more got white and gray patches like Lucky, and two more is all blotched up with black and brown and white spots. Them two boy dogs sniff around as we look at the pups, and I ask Mrs. Lark which one of them dogs is the daddy. She points to the one that looks like Lucky, 'cept he's got two pointy-up ears, not one. "Well, that mutt there is the father of these two pups at least. That other dog there, the beagle, he's the daddy of these two spotted ones. I don't know who fathered the yellow one; could be either, I suppose."

"You mean to say, ma'am, that pups can have two different daddies?"

"Yep, they sure can, Earl. Just like two kids in one family can have two different daddies."

Her words about make my teeth fall out. "Well, how can that be, Mrs. Lark, if that ma and dad is married?"

Mrs. Lark laughs a bit. "Earl, I think somebody should talk to you about the birds and the bees."

"I know about the birds and the bees, Mrs. Lark. What I'm asking about is people."

Mrs. Lark scratches her chin, and there is dirt rimmed around her fingernails. "Earl, you know about mating, don't you? The kind of mating that animals do? Well, people do that sort of mating too. It doesn't matter if they're married or not. If they do the mating, they can have a baby, and if they mate with more than one, the babies they end up with can have different daddies." She gets up then and brushes off her dirty knees.

My head, it's swirling like there's a tornado inside it, and I ain't liking none of them thoughts that's swirling in there. I don't get to say nothing else to Mrs. Lark then, 'cause she is leaving the barn, but the next time I go weed the garden, I ask her to come by the pups with me. I point with one hand at the white and gray pups and with the other hand at the blotched pups, and I ask her, "These pups, is they still brothers if they got different daddies?" and Mrs. Lark, she says, "Well, they are half brothers, not whole brothers." It feels like my heart falls right down into my work boots when she says that, 'cause now I think I know. Me and Jimmy might got the same ma, but we probably ain't got the same daddy. I look like Dad in some ways, but Jimmy, he don't look nothing like Dad. He looks just like that uncle in them pictures. I think now we ain't whole brothers, only half brothers, and even an idiot knows that half a something ain't as much as a whole of something.

It's a knowing that won't leave me, even after I sneak back into the attic while Ma's at the rationing board turning in coupons and I put them letters back. For days and days, I think about what I know, and I can't get it outta my head. I wonder if this ain't one of them things that everybody knows except me. Back when I still thought there was a fat guy with a beard who brought presents on Christmas, Ma, Dad, and Jimmy, they all knowed there wasn't, but they didn't tell me. Just like I don't tell Eddie. I wonder if this ain't like a Santa thing too, and maybe they all know about Uncle Willie being Jimmy's real dad, but nobody told me.

Funny how knowing something that's big and sad makes a person feel different. It takes the happy right out of you, and that makes you feel old. Old as a grandpa.

When Eddie comes over to play, I tell him I don't want to,

and I don't. When Ma sees that I ain't playing, not with Eddie, not with Lucky, not with my Captain Midnight plane, she says I am finally growing up. Her saying that makes me wonder if that's what growing up is—feeling too sad to play anymore. I decide if it is, then I hope to hell Eddie never grows up.

Weekends, when Dad's home, we listen to the radio, and on the news they talk about what's going on in the war. I don't know what to hell's going on with the war no more. Not when I listen to the radio, or when I listen to Dad and Mr. Larson talk when Dad and me go to the garage to check up on things. There's so many goddamn battles, in so many goddamn places, how's a guy suppose to keep it straight? I don't care anyway. Unless they got something to say about MacArthur going back to that Pacific place to look for Jimmy and Floyd and the rest of them guys, I don't wanna hear nothing they got to say.

I watch Dad on weekends, and I watch Ma too. Dad's back is better and he's sleeping in his own bed by Ma now, but something still ain't right, 'cause even when they is sitting in the same room, their chairs almost touching, they look like they is sitting miles apart.

I wait 'til Dad and me is walking to the Skelly again and I ask Dad a couple a questions about Uncle Willie. Dad, his legs suddenly get stiff 'til he looks kinda like he's a marching soldier. "What do you want to know, son?"

"Anything," I say. " 'Cause I don't know nothing about him, 'cept that he was your brother."

"I guess we don't talk about Willie much, do we? He was a wonderful man, Earl. Everybody loved him. That guy could fix anything."

"Like Jimmy," I say, and Dad clears his throat, even though it don't sound like there is any snot in there.

"I ever meet Uncle Willie?" I say.

"No. He died in the war, long before you were born. He was a pilot. One of the first in the Army Air Corps. The Germans shot his plane down over the Marne."

"Did Ma know Uncle Willie?" I ask. I'm stiff as a soldier too while I'm walking, 'cause just asking these questions is making me feel like I'm gonna get the shits.

"Yes. She knew him. She knew him before she knew me."

"That Uncle Willie. He ever get married?" I think I must be half crazy asking these questions, but I can't stop myself.

"No. He never married. He was just a young guy when he died," Dad says.

"He ever have any kids?"

Maybe it's a good thing that Lucky takes off after a squirrel before Dad can answer, running between Sam's Barber Shop and the dime store and not coming when I call him, so I gotta chase after him. Maybe it's a good thing, 'cause when I get ahold of Lucky and get back to the sidewalk where Dad's waiting, Dad looks all saggy and I'm sorry I even brought up Uncle Willie. After that, I try to push them thoughts I'm having right outta my head. I try not to think about Ma being one of them bad girls that give their milk away for free and what a goddamn pity it is that Dad's only brother got killed in the war. I try not to think that my best brother in the whole world ain't my whole brother, but how does a guy stop thinking about something like that?

When New Year's Eve comes, Ma and Dad invite people to stop over, and the men drink beers and the ladies drink punch and all of 'em munch the itty-bitty treats Ma's got on fancy plates stuck all over the place. All night long, they talk about the war, and about who beared sorrows this year. Ma, she even put up a sign she made, and it's got the names of the soldiers in town whose blue stars turned to gold. Everyone thinks it's real nice of Ma to do this. "Maybe '43 will bring an end to this god-forsaken war, and our boys will come home," Ma says. Everyone nods and says things like "We can only hope." Dad, he don't hope right along with 'em. He says to Delbert Larson, real quiet-like, "Wish in one hand and shit in the other and see which fills up the quickest."

Me, I just sit on the sofa trying not to look at Mrs. Pritchard's legs, which ain't looking so good in that brown makeup the ladies paint on their legs now 'cause they ain't got real stockings no more. Them lines running down Edna Pritchard's legs are all ziggity-zaggity over her lumpy skin. They look like a drunk man drawed 'em on. That brown makeup, it don't take too well to axed parts, I can see, 'cause that scar is shiny and silvery as a smelt.

"This seat taken?"

I look up and it's Eva Leigh standing there. She's fixed up all pretty for New Year's Eve. "No, there ain't no one sitting here but me," I tell her.

Eva Leigh sits down and holds her cup on the lap of her papery dress. "I was hoping to get a chance to talk to you, Earl."

"What for?"

"Well, today we lost another pinsetter at the Ten Pin. Slim, that's the guy who owns the place, he's having a real hard time trying to keep pinsetters. About the time he breaks one in, that boy quits to join up or to run off to the city to work. Anyway, I told him I have someone in mind for the job. Someone who's honest and a real hard worker."

"Who's that?" I ask. I don't feel much like talking, but I'm trying to be polite.

Eva Leigh laughs and her teeth are almost as pretty as Molly's. "You, silly!"

"Me?"

"Sure. Why not? The job is nights, Thursday through Sunday, so you'd still be able to help in the store. You'd get your own uniform shirt, and a check every two weeks." Eva Leigh sighs, one of them happy kind of sighs like the one you get after you eat a really good supper and you're so full you could puke. "Earl, I feel so grown up now that I got a job. A real job. Not just helping Luke's ma stitch quilts, even though she paid me a little after she sold them. It keeps my mind off of things, you know? It keeps me busy and gives me something to feel good about. I think working there would be good for you too."

"I could use something to keep my mind offa things," I tell her. Eva Leigh grabs my hand then, and hers is small and Lux soft. She gives mine a little squeeze. "Good. Let's go ask your folks."

Eva Leigh, she rounds up Ma and Dad, and she tells 'em about the job. Ma starts putting up a fuss, saying she don't know how I'd do without being prodded and Slim won't have time to prod me, but Dad, he just asks, "Earl, you want this job?" I tell him I sure do and he says, "Then it's settled. You're a man now, and men make their own decisions. If Slim is willing to hire you, you can take the job." I get so happy, I give Dad a hug.

The next day, I go to Eva Leigh's house, like she said I should do, and me and her and LJ walk down to the bowling alley. The wind is whipping, so Eva Leigh asks me to pick LJ up so we can walk faster. I pick up LJ and he looks kinda scared, so I fly him in Charles A. Lindbergh's plane. Soon he's laughing and making the sound of the engine too.

Slim is in the bowling alley, even if it ain't open. Slim is a little skinny man with gouges on his face 'cause he had infections in his pimples when he was young. He got a Lucky Strike hanging out of his lips, and his lips are fat and purple like somebody punched 'em. Eva Leigh introduces us (even though I see'd Slim lots of times when I came here with Jimmy and the guys, so he knows who I am), and Slim and me shake hands, just like two people who ain't never met before. Eva

Leigh tells Slim I want to set pins and Slim says we'll give it a try.

I follow Slim down a little walking path alongside the shiny lanes to a door that would be the door to the little back room where the pinsetters work. It ain't really a room, though. It ain't nothing but a skinny hallway back there.

"Each pinsetter is responsible for two lanes," Slim says. "You'd be responsible for lanes one and two here." I'm glad that they is the first two lanes you come to, 'cause I know that will make remembering easier if I get the job.

Slim shows me how you peek through the little triangle window so you know when the ball is coming. He yells out to Eva Leigh and tells her to throw a ball down. Eva Leigh laughs something silly when she's gotta throw three balls before she gets one to knock down any pins. I like the sound the ball makes when it rolls down the alley. It sounds like thunder. Then *crash*!

Some of them pins stay on the alley, and some, they drop down into the pit. Slim shows me how to rake away the falled-over pins to get 'em out of the way, and then after the second throw, he shows me how to put all the pins into them holder spaces, one for each pin. Then he pulls a lever, and up that holder thing comes, and that triangle of pins is all standing up, ready for another crack. He shows me, too, how to grab that bowling ball and fling it along this gouged place that looks like a long gutter. He shoots it along and it rolls right back to Eva Leigh.

Slim shows me first, then he tells me it's my turn. Slim taps his foot a bit, then he says he'll go make a few throws or we might be here all day waiting on Eva Leigh to give me a strike. I wait, peeking out that little window, hoping I don't mess up so I get myself fired before I even get hired.

Slim is a real good bowler. He picks up that ball and cranks it back as he runs a few steps, then *whoosh*, it flies from his hand, spinning and rumbling down that lane like nobody's business. I grab ahold of the bars on both sides of me, just like he showed me, and I hoist myself up, holding my legs up so my feet are out of the way. *Wham!* Them pins, every one of 'em, they get whacked, about scaring the shit outta me as they crash against each other and the back wall. I jump down quick as I can, and I start grabbing them pins that is shaped like fat beer bottles, and I drop 'em into the round spaces, lickety-split. Then I toss that ball back and peek out the window.

Slim puffs smoke out of his nostrils, his eyes squinting, and I wonder if he can see me too. He's got the ball back, but he ain't throwing it. He don't even take his cigarette out of his mouth when he shouts down the lane, "You gotta pull the lever there, kid," he says. I whack myself in the head for forgetting, then I pull the lever and them pins drop down all neat again.

Slim practices me over and over again, throwing that ball first down lane number one, then down lane number two. Back and forth until I've worked up a sweat hopping from lane to lane, raking pins that go down, resetting the rack, and sending that ball back. Then Slim stops and tells me to come out.

I shut the door and walk back down that little path next to the wall. I'm nervous as a whore in church. When I get to Slim, he sticks out his hand and says, "Welcome aboard, Earl." Eva gets all hippity-hop happy and she gives me a little hug, so I guess that means I'm hired. Slim tells Eva Leigh to give me Ralph's old shirt and says he'll order a patch with my name on it, then his old lady will stitch it on for me when it comes.

"Can I have my real name on it, Mr. Slim?" I ask. And he says I can have any name on that shirt I want, so I tell him how to spell *Earwig*.

That night, I lay in bed scratching Lucky and wishing that Jimmy could get mail, and that I could write. Then I'd go down to the post office and write to him on one of them special papers that makes a envelope when you fold it, them V-mailers. I'd write that I hope he is fine and not dead under one of them goofy trees, and I'd sign it, *Your brother, Earwig. Pinsetter. First Lane, Second Lane. Ten Pin Bowling Alley*.

# Chapter 14

By the time I get my first payday, my shirt patch comes and I don't have to be *Ralph* no more. I rub my hand over them stitched letters and I walk right past Ruby Leigh at the bar, six times, 'til she notices that I got my name patch and says, "Hey there, Earwig. Pretty fancy! Pretty fancy!"

Ruby Leigh, she is about the prettiest thing I ever see'd. Well, not pretty, I guess you'd say, but she sure is something. A guy can't look at Ruby and not stare at them titties that is poking out so far that they almost bump you when you ain't even standing that close. And she's got them hips that rock like boats when she walks, and, boy, is that something. She's got about the prettiest legs I ever see'd too. Even prettier than that

Rita Hayworth's legs in that picture hanging up on the inside of the door in the men's shitter.

Ruby Leigh serves drinks to the bowlers. She laughs real loud and springy, and she smokes cigarettes and licks her red lips when she talks. Ruby Leigh ain't never gonna get married, I don't think, 'cause she gives her milk away for free. I ain't an employee at the Ten Pin longer than three nights when I put two and two together and figure out what men not buying milk when they can get it free means. I figure it out when I walk into the men's bathroom one night after Slim closes up the lanes.

I open up that shitter door and there they are, Ruby Leigh and Skeeter Banks, who ain't more than seventeen. Ruby Leigh, her blouse is unbuttoned clear down to her waist and her brassiere is all twisted up around her armpits. Ruby Leigh's got Skeeter's head pressed up against them titties and he's sucking at them titties like he's starving to death or something. Ruby Leigh, she's got one leg slung around Skeeter's skinny hips, and I shit you not, he's got his hand creeped right up her dress, right between her legs.

I know I ain't suppose to gawk at guys that is sneaking a feel, but I can't get myself to turn around and walk out. Not when I gotta piss so bad I can taste it. And not when I'm looking at the two of 'em banging up against the wall, moaning and groaning like they is in pain or something.

I don't hear myself make any noise, but maybe I do, 'cause suddenly they stop and Skeeter turns his head. Ruby Leigh, she opens her eyes. I can see her whole tittie now, that nipple part Easter egg pink and all shiny from Skeeter's spit. They is both gulping for air like they is drowning.

"Get outta here, Earwig!" Skeeter snaps, so I turn and go, even if I still gotta piss. Later, they both come out of the bathroom. Skeeter, he's tucking his uniform shirt in and he's grinning like he just bowled a 300 game. Ruby Leigh don't look at me when she comes out. She don't look at Skeeter either. She goes straight to the bar and starts wiping it clean. "Skeeter?" I say real quiet-like as we start tipping chairs upside down on the tables. "Did you get Ruby's milk for free?"

"Huh?" he asks.

"Did you have to pay Ruby Leigh for sucking on her titties?"

Skeeter laughs. "Hell no, Earwig. Ruby don't charge nobody. She's a whore, not a hooker, you dummy."

After work, Thursday through Sunday, I walk Eva Leigh and Ruby Leigh home—that is, if Ruby Leigh ain't walking home with some guy. Ruby Leigh and Eva Leigh and LJ all live together now, right in town. Used to be, back before the war and before Luke got drafted, all of 'em lived out on the farm with Mrs. Leigh, who would be Elsie. But with no tires for their car and gas being all rationed, them ladies, they moved above Sam's Barber Shop so they can walk back and forth to work.

One night in February, when it's a-snowing and blowing so hard and so goddamn cold that the boogers freeze in your nose, Eva Leigh says I should come up to her apartment and warm myself before I finish walking home.

LJ ain't there 'cause he sleeps at the sitter's and who would want to tote a sleepy kid who gets cranky if he gets waked up from one apartment to another if they don't have to. Ruby Leigh puts a Frank Sinatra record on her phonograph, and she starts singing along to "Stardust." Ruby Leigh's got the kind of voice that makes you get all tingly warm where you ain't suppose to get tingly warm if you're minding your Ps and Qs. I mind my Ps and Qs, though, when I hear them words she's singing, about how sometimes she wonders why she spends her lonely nights dreaming of a song. Them words sound like tears when they come outta her mouth.

When Eva Leigh goes into the kitchen to make hot cocoa, Ruby Leigh, she grabs my hand and says, "Dance with me, Earwig."

I can't jitterbug, but that slow kind of dancing, it don't seem there's much to it, so I tell her yes, ma'am, I sure will dance with you. Ruby Leigh, she helps me out. She takes my arm and she wraps it around her waist and, I shit you not, it's like I'm touching an electric fence when my arm goes around her back. Then she puts her hand in mine and she starts moving, all dreamy-like.

Ruby Leigh sings as we dance, tossing her head back now so I can see her neck real good, and it's white and long like a goose neck. Then, like she's tired or something, she drops her head right down on my chest and I can feel her titties squished right up against me and I feel something else. Ruby must feel it too, 'cause she pulls away a bit and looks up at me and laughs that laugh that sounds like teasing, but not mean teasing.

Eva Leigh brings in our cups and pulls Ruby Leigh away. "Your cocoa's getting cold," she says. She gives Ruby Leigh the same look she gives LJ when he's touching things in the store that he ain't got no business touching.

Ruby Leigh sits down, lights a cigarette, and grabs an ashtray. She takes her cup and scoots sideways in the chair, her head on one armrest, her legs draped over the other. When her dress creeps halfway up her legs, she don't bother to tug it down. Eva Leigh turns the phonograph down, then comes over to the sofa where I'm sitting and sits down.

"So you like working at the Ten Pin, huh, Earl?"

"I sure do. I appreciate you getting me this job. That was right nice of you."

I drink my hot chocolate and wipe my mouth on my sleeve, so I know I ain't wearing no chocolatey mustache. Ruby has got her head tipped back and she's looking at the picture of Eva Leigh and Luke that's hanging on the wall. A cloud of smoke circles above her. I look at the same picture Ruby Leigh is looking at. Luke, who is big and handsome, he's got one arm around Eva Leigh and one hand holding a beer. Eva Leigh is standing under Luke's arm, and she has got her shoulders scrinched up like she's afraid something's gonna fall on her head.

"Tell me something, Eva," Ruby Leigh says. "What in the hell did you marry that no-good son of a bitch for, anyway?"

"Ruby! That's your brother you're talking about."

"He's still a son of a bitch," Ruby Leigh says. "Just like our old man was. All my brothers are like him. Not one of them is worth a damn."

"Luke can be very sweet," Eva Leigh says, but it don't sound like she means it, not really.

"Yeah, when he ain't using you for a punching bag." Ruby Leigh takes another puff from her cigarette and it curly-swirls out from her lips. "I guess that's the way it was bound to go, though. Luke learned how to put his arms up around his head to protect himself before he was old enough to even lift a fucking spoon to his mouth."

"Your daddy sure was mean, from what Luke told me," Eva Leigh says.

"That ain't all he was," Ruby Leigh says. She sits up and sets her cup down on the rickety end table. She stands up then, and I shit you not, she lifts her sweater over her head and I can see her slip. Eva Leigh says, "Ruby!" and Ruby just laughs as she unzips her skirt and steps out of it. When she bends over, I can see almost all of her titties, and ain't that something. Eva Leigh runs to get Ruby Leigh a robe and throws it at her. "You have no shame, Ruby," she says, and Ruby Leigh says, "Quite the contrary, sweet Eva. I got all the shame in the world."

Eva Leigh starts talking to me about what a good job I'm doing setting pins and how Slim is pleased as punch with my work. She don't say nothing about the times I get whacked in the legs 'cause I don't get outta the way fast enough, and I don't say nothing about them purple and yellow blotches I got running up my shins.

I tell Eva Leigh how much I like it at the Ten Pin. How I like the jukebox music and the sound of them balls rumbling and pins cracking. I tell her how much I like them new shirts that Sam's Barber Shop's team is wearing now, all shiny gold with green sleeves.

I can't think of any more things I like at the Ten Pin—well, 'cept for looking at Ruby Leigh's titties, but I can't say that, so I just shut up.

"Hey, we should start a women's league," Ruby Leigh says all of a sudden. "It would keep the place busier until this goddamn war is over and the boys come home. Hell, if women can work, they can play too. Shit, Eva, you and me could be captains of our own teams."

"I can't bowl, Ruby!" Eva Leigh says, and she's laughing.

"Sure you can," Ruby says, and I say, "No, ma'am, she sure can't bowl." Ruby Leigh says she ain't going to let it drop.

Eva Leigh asks me if we heard any news about Jimmy. I tell her no. "Ma writes the army all the time, asking about him. They ain't wrote her back, though, only that one time when they telled her they lost Jimmy. He ain't dead, though," I say, " 'cause his star is still blue."

Ruby Leigh asks me if Molly is being true to Jimmy, and I tell her that I think she is. Then Ruby asks about Floyd and John, and I tell her their stars are still blue too. "That John," Ruby Leigh says. "He thinks he's God's gift to women. What an arrogant bastard." Then she laughs and says, "But all men are bastards, so where's the surprise?"

Ruby Leigh picks up her empty cup to take it to the corner that would be the kitchen. She stops by the end of the sofa and she takes her hand and bunches up my mouth, and she says, "Well, except you, Earwig. If all men were sweet as you, even

Eva Leigh here would be cheating." Then she leans down, I shit you not, and she pops me a kiss right on my bunched-up lips.

Eva Leigh says I'd better run along home now before my ma starts worrying, so that's what I do.

Ma is still awake, sitting on the sofa with an open book on her lap, 'cause when she can't sleep, she opens a book but she don't read. "You're late," she says, and I say that I sure am.

Ma's eyes are red and the skin ringed around them is pink, like it was rubbed hard. "Ma? Is something wrong?"

"I'm just feeling a little blue, that's all," she says.

Ma, she looks up at me and smiles, but her smile don't look too happy. Then she cocks her head sideways and stops smiling. "Earl, what's that on the top of your lip? Is that lipstick?" And I say, "Yes, ma'am, it sure is," and I feel real proud saying that.

"Who on earth would do such a thing?" She says this like she's talking about somebody spitting on me or something. I don't tell her, though, 'cause Jimmy telled me once that even if a girl is the biggest two-bit whore in town, a decent guy don't kiss and tell.

Next day, I'm in the backyard splitting up some firewood when Eddie comes along. He's dragging his rickety sled. "Hey, Earwig," he says.

"Hey, Eddie," I say.

"You want to go sledding over on Lark's hill?"

"I ain't got time for playing, Eddie. I am a working man now. I got one job at the store, and one job at the Ten Pin, and I gotta help Ma out. I ain't got time for playing."

Eddie, he just stands there for a bit, watching me. He swipes his mitten across his nose, then he says, "You ain't never got time for playing no more."

I stand up real tall and I tell him that's exactly right. "Yep, things is different now. I got two jobs, I got sorrows, and I got a sweetheart too. I ain't a little kid like you, Eddie." Eddie picks up the rope that's tied to his old sled, 'cause he didn't get no new sled for Christmas on accounta all the wood and metal are going to the war now, and he says, "You're being a jerk, Earwig."

Eddie turns his sled, the blades making scuffing sounds in the packed snow. He's halfway down the block before I run to the sidewalk and yell out, "I ain't trying to be a jerk, Eddie. I'm just trying to be a man!"

I ain't really got a sweetheart, like I told Eddie. Ruby Leigh, she's got a sweetheart, all right, but it ain't me. His name is Elliot Birmingham, and ain't that a fine name for a gentleman, which is what Ruby Leigh says he is. He wears fancy suits and a long coat that looks Montgomery Ward-new, and he always tips his Stetson when he greets a lady. Ruby Leigh thinks he looks like Cary Grant.

Mr. Birmingham, he ain't in the war 'cause the army wouldn't take him on accounta he's got one of them ruptures, but the government lets him work for 'em, rupture or not. He travels all over, making sure the factories are making enough stuff for the war. He come to Willowridge 'cause he says that the Knox Lumber Factory's gotta stop making lumber for houses and gotta start making stuff for the war. It's his job to convert the mill over. That's what he tells Ruby Leigh.

Mr. Birmingham stays in town for pert' near two weeks the first time, and every night he comes to the Ten Pin for drinks and a little of Ruby Leigh's free milk.

"I don't know what's wrong with me," Ruby Leigh says one night in spring when we're walking home, leaping over the sidewalk puddles. "I can't sleep, I can't think of anything but him. Crissakes, I never thought I'd go ga-ga over some guy like this. I must be nuts."

"You must be in love," Eva Leigh says.

After Mr. Birmingham comes along, Ruby Leigh stops leaving the Ten Pin with other guys at night, and she starts wearing dresses that don't show as much of her titties. It's a sorry day for Skeeter and me for sure when that happens.

I'm happy for Ruby Leigh, but most guys coming in to the Ten Pin ain't. When Ruby Leigh don't rub up against 'em no more, and when she won't leave with 'em at closing time, some of the guys start getting all pissy-mouthed. One night Bottoms Conner, who's got a fat beer belly and is sweaty even in winter, he gets downright nasty with Ruby Leigh. "What the fuck you acting all uppity for, Ruby?" Ruby Leigh tries to ignore him. She is washing beer glasses real fast and pretending she don't hear nothing he's saying. Eva Leigh and me are tipping chairs upside down on the tables, 'cause it's closing time. Eva Leigh stops, and she gets real still when she hears that meanness coming out of Bottoms's mouth.

"You think you're too good for me now, just because you got that city boy sniffing around you? That it? Shit, you aren't nothing but a two-bit whore, and don't think City Boy ain't figured that one out. You listening to me, bitch?"

"Go home, Bottoms. We're closing," Ruby Leigh says without looking up.

Then that fat bastard, he gets up from his stool, real fast for a fat man, and he stomps right around to the back of the bar. He jerks Ruby Leigh by the arm, hard, and spins her around. "You listen to me when I'm talking to you, whore."

I drop the chair I'm holding. I go right behind the bar where I ain't suppose to go, and I pop Bottoms Conner so hard that his back slams against the back bar. A few of them drippy-wet glasses, they crash to the floor, slices of glass shooting like little missiles. I pin that sucker right to the bar. "Listen here, mister, I think you better start minding your Ps and Qs."

"Get off me, you fucking idiot," Bottoms says, and he shoves at my chest, then uses his fat hand to catch the blood that's coming outta his nose. I let him go then, not 'cause he tells me to, but 'cause I can tell he's done being nasty to Ruby Leigh and 'cause there ain't no way I'm gonna stare at that blood. I give him a little shove. "You go on home now. Your wife's gonna be wondering where you are."

Eva Leigh runs to Ruby the minute Bottoms is gone. "Are you all right?" Eva Leigh is all skittery, but Ruby Leigh, she is just plain pissed. "Fat, ugly prick!" she says. "Who to hell does he think he is? Limp-dick bastard!" She spews them cuss words 'til every one of 'em is outta her, then she starts to crying.

I go fetch the broom to clean up the broken glass, and Eva Leigh steers Ruby to a stool. I'm real glad that Slim went home early or I'd be shit-canned for going behind the bar and punching a paying customer.

When I come back with the broom and dustpan, Ruby Leigh gets off her stool and comes to me. "Thank you, Earwig," she says, and her eyes get all glittery with tears. "In my whole goddamn life, no guy has ever stood up for me. Not once. Thank you." It's enough to break a pinsetter's heart, the way she says that. She gets on her tiptoes and she presses her lips right against my cheek.

When I get home, I go up a couple steps out front of the store and lean over the pipe rail, and, yep, Jimmy's star is still blue. I think of Jimmy, and Floyd, and Louie and John, and wish they was here so I could tell 'em I kicked somebody's ass tonight. I know damn well if they were here, I'd get the first beer.

# Chapter 15

I'm in the store working the morning Edna Pritchard comes in. She is showing Ma a picture of Irene Rich, from the *Irene Rich Drama*, and oh, my, don't Irene look trim and slim after being on the Welch's Reducing Plan all these years. "You drink one glass of Welch's before each sensible meal," Mrs. Pritchard says, and I'm thinking she better drink maybe five or six glasses if she wants to get rid of that fat ass.

Edna Pritchard plops a can of Welch's on the counter, and she says she don't care if it takes every blue stamp she's got, she's buying it. Ma tells her that she don't know when we're gonna get any more Welch's in, on accounta fruit and fruit juice is getting mighty hard to come by now. Mrs. Pritchard says she'll have it shipped in from Ripley if we run out, or have her sister hunt some up in Chicago if she has to.

Ma and Mrs. Pritchard are still talking about her reducing plan when Mrs. Banks comes in. Mrs. Pritchard starts to tell Mrs. Banks about her reducing plan, when Ma says, "Just a minute, Edna. What's wrong, Selma?"

Selma Banks, she shakes her head, real pitiful-like. "I just heard that the little Leigh girl, Eva, she got her telegram this morning. Luke Leigh is dead."

Ma's hand goes over her mouth and she shakes her head, her eyes welling up. It don't matter what GI dies, even if they was as mean as a rabid skunk, or even if she don't know the dead guy from Adam. Ma still starts to crying and gets the nerves every time she hears bad news about a soldier.

"Oh, my, poor Elsie," Edna Pritchard says about Luke's mom. "As if she's not had a heavy enough cross to bear, married all those years to that horrible man, then raising a pack of kids just like him."

"Poor Eva," Ma says. "So young to be left alone with a child."

I don't ask Ma if I can leave. I just do. I go to Eva Leigh's apartment, right above Sam's Barber Shop, and I give Eva Leigh a hug, 'cause even if that Luke was a no-account son of a bitch, Eva didn't want him dead. She is sitting on the wored-out sofa, still holding that paper that says that Luke did a good thing dying for his country, the paper that is signed by the President hisself. "I can't believe it. I just can't believe it," she says.

"I'm real sorry, Eva. Luke was mean, but it's still a shame he got killed."

LJ, he wants to play airplane, so I play with him a bit. "LJ is just a little boy. He doesn't know what dead means," Eva Leigh says. "He don't even remember his daddy."

I ain't there but fifteen minutes or so when Ruby Leigh

comes home. She's crying too. She hugs Eva Leigh and they sit on the couch together. "How's Ma?" Eva Leigh asks, and Ruby tells her that Elsie is like you'd expect. I know I can't stay, 'cause I got to clean the storage room and I got things to price, but I tell Eva Leigh that I'll come by later. When she hugs me good-bye, she feels all small and sad in my arms. "You're a good friend, Earl," she says. As I'm going down them stairs, ladies is coming up. I can smell baked beans and something like stew coming from the pots they is carrying. I know that soon enough, Eva Leigh's table is gonna be full of things to eat, 'cause that is what them women do when they get the nerves. They bake. And they give them baked things to people with sorrows.

Luke Leigh ain't even had his memorial service yet when Elliot Birmingham comes around again. He drinks his beers and talks to the guys at the bar like always, but he don't hardly give Ruby Leigh the time of day. She waits 'til the place is almost empty, then she goes up and leans over the bar to talk to him.

Even though I'm watching from my triangle window and can't hear a thing they is saying, I know that Mr. Birmingham is saying something that makes Ruby Leigh sad. I know it 'cause Ruby Leigh, she looks like she's shrinking.

When Mr. Birmingham gets up to leave, Ruby Leigh yells, "Elliot!" so loud I can hear it above the jukebox. She comes right out from the bar and she runs to catch up to him. The way Ruby Leigh starts pawing at his jacket reminds me of Lucky when he's begging for something from my plate.

Elliot Birmingham, he grins and shakes his head like he can't believe she's grabbing his jacket like that. He jiggles his arm until her hand drops away, then he leaves.

Elliot Birmingham, he's got a wife and three boys it turns

out, and that's all there is to it. "He thanked me for the good time," Ruby Leigh says. "The bastard thanked me for the good time." Ruby, she's as broke up as Eva Leigh now.

Ma and me go to Luke's memorial service together. Dad don't go, 'cause he's in Janesville on accounta it's a weekday, but Ma told him about Luke when he called. They didn't talk long, 'cause the war rules say you can't hog up the long-distance lines longer than five minutes, but they talked long enough for Dad to tell Ma to tell Eva Leigh that he's really sorry about what happened to Luke.

Ma, she hugs Eva Leigh real nice, and she cries when she says how sorry she is. I can see Ma out the side of my eye as Preacher Michaels talks on and on about how wonderful it is that Luke gave his life for his country. Ma is crying into her hankie, and I start to wonder if she's crying for Luke or if she's crying for a different dead soldier, 'cause Ma never cared a lick for Luke Leigh.

Up front, Eva Leigh and Ruby Leigh sit by Luke's ma, who is small and bent and looks like she got beat up lots of times. LJ is on Ruby Leigh's lap 'cause his mama's crying too hard to hold him. Used to be Eva Leigh and Ma and Ruby Leigh, they seemed so different that I wouldn't have even had them in my head at the same time. But now I think maybe all three of 'em are pretty much the same. They is all ladies who loved the wrong man and got their hearts crushed when their man got gone.

First night Eva Leigh comes back to work, I walk her and Ruby Leigh home. We sit in the living room and Ruby Leigh makes coffee. We get to talking about all the sorrows we got. Ruby Leigh talks about Elliot Birmingham and how he's the first guy she ever loved and how he's gonna be her last. Eva Leigh talks about Luke. She says he sure was ornery, yet he gave her a wonderful little boy, and things were good for a time. Ruby says Luke was a son of a bitch, but he was still her brother, and she cries some after she says it. I talk about my brother too, and about how he's probably a "P.O.W." now, which is what Dad says is short for "prisoner of war." I tell 'em I get scared that one day I'm gonna go out front of the store and look and his star is gonna be gold. Them girls, they listen real good, and they pat my hand and rub my shoulder when I talk my turn. Before you know it, we is all crying.

We get quiet for a time, except for our sniffling, then Ruby Leigh, she says the damnedest thing. She says, "What a sorry-assed bunch we are. A widow, a whore, and a simpleton, bawling and carrying on like there ain't no tomorrow. I've never seen anything more pathetic in my whole goddamn life. A widow, a whore, and a simpleton. Now, don't that beat all." And even though we is all filled up with sorrows, we start to laughing then. We laugh until we can't hold ourselves up no more and topple over like dominoes.

# Chapter 16

Ma scoops up change out of one of the cubbyholes in the till and starts counting while I turn off the outside store lights like she told me to. That change is clinky-plinking as I take the sign from the window and spin it around so customers can see that we ain't open no more. I just get the sign propped back in the window when I see Mrs. Pritchard's Ford pull up. "Mrs. Pritchard is here, Ma!"

Ma plunks the rest of the change she's holding back into the till and grumbles. Pritchard's car is rocking like a boat as she hoists herself outta it. "Here she comes!" I say.

"Sorry, Eileen. I know it's past hours," she tells Ma as she thumps her purse on the counter. "But I felt I just had to come and tell you this because I'd rather you hear it from a friend. I didn't want to come in while the store was busy, when there are extra pairs of ears around." She waves her fat hand toward the stool that sits behind the counter. "My legs have been giving me trouble," Mrs. Pritchard says, and she shoots a look my way as Ma brings her the stool. She sits down, her breath making a big whoosh.

"What's wrong, Edna?" Ma asks. I pick up the broom and go back behind the meat counter and start sweeping the floor like I'm suppose to after the store closes.

"Eileen," Mrs. Pritchard says, "you know I don't like gossip, but there's a difference between passing along stories just for the sake of gossiping, and telling the plain truth for the sake of being a good friend." Edna Pritchard pauses while she catches her breath. "Well, Eileen, you know my sister, the one who moved down to Chicago so her husband could take a better job?"

Ma nods. "Yes, of course. Ruth."

"Well," Mrs. Pritchard says, "I just got off the phone with her. She was telling me how last Sunday, her and Owen took in a movie, then stopped for coffee and dessert afterward. Well, Eileen, she ran into Molly in the restaurant.

"She doesn't really know Molly, of course. When Ruth left here, Molly was still in that awkward stage, but Ruth said she'd know Judith's grown daughter anywhere. Molly is the spitting image of Judith, and Ruth and Judith were close friends, as you know. Anyway, Ruth doesn't have a shy bone in her body, so she went right up to Molly and asked her if she was from Willowridge."

"Yes, Molly does look just like her mother," Ma says. I can't figure out for nothing why Pritchard's gotta come by after hours to tell Ma that Molly looks like her ma.

"Eileen, do you think I could have a nice cold glass of water? I'm a bit weak, or winded, or something. I don't know what's wrong with me these days. Maybe it's this reducing plan." Ma tells me to bring Mrs. Pritchard a glass of water.

When I'm coming back with the water, I hear Mrs. Pritchard say, "No, Eileen, there was no mistaking the situation." Mrs. Pritchard takes the glass of water from me and she don't say thank you. She peers down, then holds the glass up to the light and looks through it like she's expecting a booger or a tadpole to be swimming in it.

"Molly was cozied right up to this young man—that is, until Ruth went up to her and asked her if she was from Willowridge. Ruth said this young gentleman was very well dressed, and the way he carried himself it was plain to see that he comes from money.

"Well, Eileen, I just thought you should know. I hate to be the one to tell you, but it's better if it comes from a close friend." Mrs. Pritchard don't look sorry she has to be the one to tell Ma at all.

Ma waits 'til Mrs. Pritchard leaves, then she explodes like a stick of dynamite. "I knew that girl was trouble from the start! I told Hank, Molly would end up thinking she was too good for Jimmy, but he told me to keep my nose out of it. I knew it, though, I knew it! Little two-timing hussy! 'I hate to be the one to tell you . . .' " Ma says, just like Pritchard. "Oh, you bet she hated to tell me. She was gloating the whole while!" Then Ma's anger gets all used up. She rubs her forehead first, then rests her hand on the side of her face. "Poor Jimmy. He's going to be so hurt."

I don't say nothing. I just finish sweeping and think about Molly, all tiny and pink like candy. I think of Jimmy, and the way he was kissing on her hand before he left. They made a promise. A promise she could show her girlfriends. They was gonna get married and I was gonna move with 'em into that Williams place, which will be a right nice place when it's fixed up. Now when Jimmy comes home, he ain't gonna have no girlfriend, and I ain't moving nowhere with him and Molly. It pisses me off enough that I decide that after Jimmy comes home, I'm gonna ask Ruby Leigh if she'll give Jimmy a little milk for free since he don't have a girl no more. I bet Ruby Leigh would do that, on accounta she's gone back to her old ways now that Mr. Birmingham is gone.

Me and Ruby Leigh walk home alone after work 'cause Eva Leigh, she caught the pukes from LJ, so she didn't work tonight. While we's walking, Ruby Leigh, she reaches up and taps my head with her fist, but she don't do it hard. "Hello? Anybody in there?" she says.

"I am," I say.

Ruby Leigh, she puts her hand on my arm. "What's wrong, Earl?"

Ma says there's things you should tell other people, and there's things you shouldn't. I have a feeling the things stuffing up my head are things I shouldn't tell her, but the way I see it, who would know more about this loving stuff than Ruby Leigh, who's always loving on somebody? "Ruby Leigh? If I was to ask you some things about loving, would that be something I should ask?"

Ruby Leigh smiles. "Sure, Earl."

"Well," I say, "how come some people stop loving each other, and some people don't?"

Ruby Leigh, she is swinging her purse a little as we walk. She looks up at me, like she's studying on something, then she says, "Earl, you talking about somebody in particular?"

"Well, I guess I am. I'm talking about Jimmy and Molly, and I guess I'm talking about my ma and dad too." My voice kinda cracks when I say that.

Ruby Leigh, she puts her hand on my sleeve. "Oh, Earl, what's going on, honey?"

"Well, Molly, she's two-timing Jimmy. And my ma and dad, well, there's trouble there too."

Ruby Leigh stops walking, and she leads me to the bench in front of the barber shop. It's so late, there ain't even a drunk on the street. "Oh, Earwig, I'm so sorry. Come on, honey, sit down and we'll talk."

My throat gets all tight, like I'm gonna strangle on my own spit, when I tell her how Molly is gonna up and marry somebody, but it ain't gonna be Jimmy. "Ah, poor Jimmy." Ruby Leigh sighs. "It's happening a lot, though, Earl. The soldiers have been gone a long time, and long separations have a way of cooling a girl's heart down."

"Not my ma's heart," I say.

"What do you mean?"

So I tell Ruby Leigh about how I was playing pirate and how I found that old treasure chest with pictures of Ma kissing that guy that looks like Jimmy. "Turns out that guy in them pictures is my uncle Willie—well, he ain't really my uncle no more, 'cause he's dead. He got killed in that other war.

"And that ain't all, Ruby Leigh. I put two and two together, and now I'm thinking that me and Jimmy ain't whole brothers at all, just half brothers."

She asks me lots of questions. She asks me how old Jimmy is now, and I tell her I ain't exactly sure but that he was twenty-one years old when he joined up with the Guard. Ruby Leigh says that was in 1940, so she figures it out and says he's twenty-four now. Then she asks how long Ma and Dad been married, and I gotta think hard, 'cause I ain't sure on that one, on account of I heard Dad say to Ma that they been married twenty-one years, but I knowed I heard her tell Mrs. Pritchard not that long ago that they been married for twenty-five years. When I tell Ruby Leigh this, she looks down at her hands. "Earl, it sounds to me like your ma and your uncle were lovers first. It sounds like she got in the family way and probably didn't realize it until after your uncle left for the war. I suppose your daddy married her after your uncle died so Jimmy would have a daddy, and probably because he loved her."

"Ruby Leigh, this means my ma was giving her milk away for free, don't it? I never did think of my ma as one of them bad kind of girls, but now I'm thinking it." The minute I say it, I'm sorry, 'cause I remember that Ruby Leigh is the town whore. "I'm sorry, Ruby Leigh. I, I—"

"It's okay, Earl."

We sit for a minute without talking. Ruby Leigh, she takes my hand and holds it real soft.

"My uncle Willie's been dead for a long time, but seems to me Ma is feeling as sad as if it just happened yesterday."

Ruby Leigh bites on her lip that looks near black in the dark. She says, "I think your ma had all those memories come back to her when Jimmy went off to war, like his blood daddy. She probably didn't feel those sorrows over him being killed back then, with all the worrying she had to do about being in the family way and not having a husband. Bad girls like me, we don't worry about our reputations because most of us never had one to begin with. But girls like your ma, they worry about their reputations a lot.

"Feeling our sorrows is just something a person's got to do, though, Earwig. We have to feel our sorrows, or else they stay locked up inside forever, making our hearts close up like fists and making us do crazy things."

"You think my ma loves my dad?" I ask Ruby Leigh.

"I can't really say, because I don't know your mom and dad well. What do you think?"

"I don't know, but I hope so. I don't think Molly loves Jimmy no more, though." I give a sigh so big that my belly sucks in, skinny as Floyd's. "It just don't make no sense. Ma loving a dead guy after all these years, even though she ain't suppose to, and Molly not loving Jimmy after only a couple, even though she's suppose to."

"Well, Earwig, there's not much about love that does makes sense."

I get home late from the Ten Pin, and I'm hanging my uniform shirt up real nice in my closet when I hear Ma and Dad's bedroom door open. Then I hear Ma say, "What are you doing up, Hank? Can't you sleep?"

Dad don't say nothing, so I peek down the vent. He is taking a loaf of bread outta the breadbox and getting out a knife. "You want a sandwich, Hank? I'll get that. Here, let me." Ma takes the knife from Dad and tells him to sit down. "I'll reheat the coffee. There's a little left."

"I'll just have bread and butter."

"You want some apple butter on it? I found a jar stuck back in the pantry."

"No, butter's fine."

"You sure you don't want me to make you up a sandwich with the leftover chicken?" Ma is fluttering around the kitchen like a moth.

"Eileen," Dad says, "you don't have to do this."

Ma stops in her tracks. "Do what?"

"Try so hard."

For a little bit, they just look at each other and there ain't a peep of sound but for the hum of the Frigidaire. "Yes, I do, Hank. Yes, I do." Ma starts bawling then and Dad sits for a minute, then he gets up from the chair and goes to her. He wraps his arms around her.

"I'm so sorry." It's hard to hear what else Ma is saying, 'cause she's got her face mashed up against Dad's shoulder.

Dad pulls Ma back and he holds on to the sides of her face.

"Eileen, I know you loved him. That's never been a secret between us. I never expected it to be. I just need to know that you learned to love me somewhere along the line too."

Ma starts shaking her head. "Oh, Hank, I spent so many of our early years together mourning Willie, building him up in my head until no one could compare. I was just as blind with my young, starry eyes as Jimmy is with Molly. All these years. All these years no one could hold a candle to the boy in my memory. But, Hank, I'm not a girl anymore, and with having you gone so much now . . . Oh, I've been such a fool."

Dad tells Ma she ain't no fool, and Ma tells Dad how much she loves him, then they start to kissing.

I get up from the floor. I'm real glad they're kissing, but I don't wanna watch, in case he starts grabbing at her titties or something.

The next morning, Ma turns on the radio as she scrambles eggs, and Dad, he whistles in the bathroom as he shaves. Everything feels right again. At least as right as it can feel with Jimmy still gone.

# Chapter 17

Things get right again with Eddie and me too, after a long, long time. One Sunday, when the leaves are all orange and yellow, there is a knock at the back door and I open it up. Eddie's standing there. He don't ask me to come out and play (which is a good thing since I'm still growed up); instead, he asks me if I wanna work with him.

Eddie's got papers with him that come from the War Production Board that his dad brought home from the Knox Factory. Eddie points to the picture on the bottom of the page. "See this here picture of the sailors on their raft? It says here, *Life belts saved these sailors who had struggled seventeen hours in storm-tossed seas.* You see, Earwig, life jackets, they used to be made out of this stuff called kapok fiber filler. That kapok stuff, it came all the way from a plantation in the East Indies. A plantation is a big farm."

"Where's the East Indies, Eddie?"

"I don't know, Earwig, but that ain't the point. The point is, the Japs, they captured the East Indies and now we can't get any more of that kapok stuff to make life jackets with. If the soldiers ain't got any life jackets, they could drown. This guy, I can't remember his name, he figured out that we could use milkweed floss instead of that other stuff. You know the round fat part that we used to pick off milkweed plants and use for hand grenades back before you got too old to play? You know that white stringy stuff like hair inside those milkweed pods? That's the stuff they're gonna stick inside life jackets now. Anyway, we can pick them pods and make money for turning them in at the factory." Eddie ain't as fat as he used to be, and he ain't as dumb either.

"I know you got two jobs and a girl and sorrows, Earwig, but if you got time and want to pick milkweed pods with me, then you could do that."

So that's what me and Eddie do. We wake up early every morning before I gotta be in the store and Eddie's gotta be at school, and me and Eddie and Lucky go picking milkweed pods. Mr. McCarty, he lets us take his old pocket watch along, and we take turns carrying it. Eddie one day, me the next. And when I carry it I gotta keep an eye for when the big hand gets on the twelve and the little hand gets on the eight, 'cause then we have to head back, so we ain't gonna be late.

We head down on Honey Road, 'cause there is lots of milkweed growing up along that road. Ma gives us bushel-sized onion sacks she got saved up from the store, 'cause that's what we gotta put 'em in. We find milk pods that has got nice brown seeds inside, like the paper says those seeds gotta be, and we fill them sacks. Eddie says each bag's gotta have about eight hundred pods in it. I tell Eddie I can't count that goddamn high, and Eddie says we don't have to actually count 'em.

Them bags are bulky when they is full, so after Eddie ties 'em tight, I carry 'em back to Eddie's house. We hang 'em over the fence in the backyard, 'cause if we toss 'em on the ground and leave 'em there, they're gonna rot and mold and the mill ain't gonna pay us one red cent for 'em. We wait 'til we got that fence filled with a whole shitload of sacks, then Eddie's dad takes 'em in the back of his truck to the mill. We get twenty cents a bag for them milkweed pods and split the money right down the middle, fair and square.

When we get done working in the mornings, Mrs. McCarty, she feeds us pancakes or Malt-O-Meal, and then I gotta get to work and Eddie's gotta get to school. Before I leave, I always say, "See ya tomorrow, Eddie," and Eddie, he always says, "See you tomorrow, Earwig." It sure is nice hanging around with Eddie again and laughing about farts and stuff. I am too growed up to play now, but I ain't too old to laugh about farts and stuff, 'cause even Dad still does that.

Dad, he says if I keep working and putting my money away like I am, I'm gonna turn into another Rockerfeller. I tell Dad that I ain't working hard so I can get Rockerfeller-rich. I'm working hard so I keep busy and don't get all buggy and fall off my rocker.

# Chapter 18

Like I said before, the busier you get, the faster them days pile up like bottle caps. I work hard and a whole season goes by, and then another, and they keep piling up 'til it's the summer of 1944 and I'm saying, "How in the hell did that happen?"

Funny how things go. One day, time is whooshing along so fast you can't count them days, then, *wham!* that time slams into something so big and awful that it can't even budge.

I head for Eddie's house on a Sunday morning. I go early, when the birds is just waking up and making a racket in the trees. Me and Eddie is going to look for arrowheads, and the day before, Eddie said, "Come early, Earwig." I think Eddie wants to go early 'cause he don't like running around a lot on summer days that get so hot by the time the sun gets right over your head that you got sweat running down your ass crack.

If you go digging around in the dirt in the right place, and you find something that is a rock but is shaped kinda like a triangle, that would be one of them arrowheads. Indians used to make 'em out of rocks and tie 'em to the tops of their sticks so they could poke animals and each other. After me and Eddie find some arrowheads, he is gonna tie 'em on sticks and go play-hunting with Spot. I'm all growed up now so I ain't gonna play with Eddie, but me and Lucky might go along anyway to help him scout animals and keep Spot in line, 'cause Spot sure does mind me better than Eddie.

When I get to Eddie's, his ma says Eddie can't come out, 'cause he's sick. "He's got the flu, Earl," Mrs. McCarty says. "Maybe in a day or two."

I go home and try to find something fun to do. I wait 'til the next day, and after work I go back to Eddie's to see if he wants to go look for arrowheads now, 'cause there's plenty of time left before dark, but Mrs. McCarty, she says he's still sick. She says now he's got the pukes and a fever.

After a couple more days, Eddie's feeling better, but I don't get to see him anyway 'cause Ma's making me work like a dog again, and I didn't even do nothing bad. Next day after that, Eddie wakes up in the morning, only he can't walk on accounta his legs are freezed up with the polio. I heared all about it from Mrs. Pritchard, who said poor little Eddie went to swing his legs out of his bed and they wouldn't budge. Not even a smidgen. So Eddie, he got real scared and started hollering for his ma. Mrs. McCarty got all skittery then, and called Dr. McCormick, who come over right away and said, yep, Eddie's got the polio.

Ma, she gasps when Mrs. Pritchard tells her. She calls me to the counter and she asks me over and over again when I see'd Eddie last, and did I go inside his house, and am I feeling punky at all, and do my legs ache. I gotta say no about a hundred times.

Eddie, he has to go to the hospital in Ripley, and Ma says he's probably gonna have to be there a long time, 'cause that polio ain't nothing to mess around with. I get real scared, thinking about how Eddie maybe is gonna die.

It just figures that whenever something bad happens, I ain't been to church for a long time. Now Eddie's got the polio and God is pissed and I can't ask for nothing, so I use my head and ask Ma to pray for Eddie instead.

Ma musta prayed good enough, 'cause Eddie don't die, and that polio, it don't creep up to his lungs so that he's gotta go in one of them big metal things, but maybe she didn't pray enough days, 'cause Eddie, he don't get all the way better either. Mrs. Pritchard, she says that Eddie is hurting bad in his muscles and that he's laying in that hospital bed wearing braces on his legs. Mrs. Pritchard knows this 'cause she talked to Pearl McCarty. "Of course, I didn't go inside. I didn't even go into the yard. Pearl was hanging laundry so I just talked to her over the fence. Poor dear, she's worried sick and missing that little boy so much."

One thing I know for sure from listening to Edna Pritchard is that when Eddie comes home, he's gonna either be in a wheelchair or he's gonna be walking using them short sticks that are sorta like a extra pair of legs. I want to tell Eddie that if he has to walk with them sticks, I'll walk real slow so he can keep up, or if he can't even do that and has to be in one of them wheelchairs, I'll push him where he needs to go. I want to tell him these things, but I can't. Eddie's in the hospital and nobody can go see him. Not even his ma and dad.

With having Jimmy and Floyd and John to worry about, and now Eddie too, I get whacked by them bowling pins a lot. "What's the matter, Earl?" Eva Leigh asks me after days go by and I'm still getting whacked. "You still upset about your little friend?" I nod. "Earl, I hear that Eddie is getting better and will be home soon. He'll be in braces, but at least he's alive and will be able to get around."

"I know that," I tell Eva Leigh. "I'm just wishing I didn't get mean at Eddie like I did when I growed up and didn't want to play no more."

Eva Leigh, she pats my arm and says, "Earl, we all think like that when something happens to somebody we care about. We start adding up the times we weren't the best to them and we feel bad about those times. If we think about it too long, we can even start thinking we caused that person to get sick or to die because we didn't love them enough. That's not true, though. Even the nicest person in the world has some parts of him that aren't so nice now and then. You don't need to blame yourself or feel bad, Earl. It wasn't your fault Eddie came down with polio."

Eva Leigh, she tells me that maybe I'd feel better if I drawed a picture for Eddie. She says if I do, she'll address it off to Eddie at Saint Mary's Hospital in Ripley for me. So that's what I do. Only I draw Eddie a few pictures (on accounta I think I wasn't so nice to Eddie way more than once). I draw him a picture of Lucky Lindy's airplane and three pictures of Captain Midnight. I ain't real good at drawing, so I ask Eva Leigh to write on them pages what those pictures are. On Cap's picture I draw a bubble coming outta his mouth like in the comic books, and I ask Eva Leigh to write in the bubble, *Don't be scared, Eddie. I'll beat up that polio for you.*

I draw Eddie a picture of me and Lucky too, but I don't ask Eva Leigh to write on that one, 'cause I drawed turds coming out of Lucky's butt so Eddie can have hisself a laugh. I think Eddie will figure them things out for hisself even if Eva Leigh doesn't put on the page, *This is Earwig. This is Lucky. This is Lucky's turds.*

Nobody goes to visit Eddie in Ripley, and nobody goes to

visit Mrs. McCarty while Eddie's in the hospital either. They are too scared of getting the polio from Eddie's house. Mrs. Pritchard, she says that Pearl McCarty says that people even cross the street so they don't have to walk too close to her house. I feel real bad when I hear this, 'cause Mrs. McCarty is a real nice lady. I ask Ma if I can go see her, but Ma says I can't. She says what I can do, though, is bring Mrs. McCarty a box of groceries. Mrs. McCarty, she ain't coming into the store now 'cause she don't want to make the ladies get the nerves, so she calls Ma with a list of things she needs, and Ma and me, we shop for her and Ma writes the stuff in the charge book. Then I carry the box to the McCartys', but I can't go inside. I knock on her door so she knows the groceries come, then I leave her box on the steps and go back on the sidewalk like Ma says. I wait for Mrs. McCarty to open the door, then I yell to her and ask her how Eddie is doing. Every day, she says he's about the same and, nope, he can't come home yet. One day on my way to the McCartys' with groceries, I see some violets growing up alongside a tree and I pick some and put 'em in her box. When she sees them flowers she puts her hand up against her cheek and starts bawling. I didn't know she was gonna cry when I gived her those flowers. I feel bad 'cause I didn't mean to make her cry, so I don't pick her no more violets after that.

On days Mrs. McCarty don't need groceries, I still walk to their house, knock on the door, then run back to the sidewalk and wait for her to come out. When she gets out on the front steps I ask her how Eddie is and when he's coming home, and she tells me. "You don't need to come ask every day, Earl," she says one day. "I could call you on the telephone and keep you updated." But I tell her it ain't no bother coming by every day.

It takes weeks before Eddie comes home. When he does, Ma calls Dr. McCormick and asks if Eddie is still catchy, and Dr. McCormick says no, he's not, so I can go see Eddie.

Eddie's laying in his bed, his legs strapped in them metal braces that run down the sides of his legs and curl around under his shoes. Eddie don't look turkey-fat no more. He looks little and he's white as a snowflake.

Eddie don't look at me when I walk into his room. He's busy looking out the window. I go over to the window to see what he's looking at. It must be something good, since he don't stop looking out there even long enough to say "Hey, Earwig." I look this way and that, but there ain't nothing in that sky. Not even a cloud.

"Hey, Eddie," I say, about a hundred times, but he still don't say "Hey, Earwig" back.

Mrs. McCarty brings up two glasses of Ovaltine and two thick slices of homemade bread gobbed with peanut butter. She sees that Eddie ain't talking to me, and she sets down the tray and curls her finger at me a couple times, so I know to follow her into the hallway.

"Eddie's just feeling embarrassed right now, Earl. He doesn't want anybody to see him in his braces. He's afraid people will make fun of him."

"I wouldn't make fun of Eddie, Mrs. McCarty. I sure wouldn't."

"I know that, Earl," she says, "but that's what Eddie's afraid of."

I go back in and sit down by his bed, and after a time I say to him, "Eddie, you ain't gotta be worrying about me seeing you in them braces. I don't care if your legs are crippled up by the polio. Well, I mean, I do care, 'cause I'm real sorry they is, but what I mean is that I ain't gonna poke fun at you or nothing. Hell, Eddie, you see me being a dumbhead every day and you still like me just fine anyway. Even if I see you being crippled up every day, I'll still like you just fine too."

Eddie, he turns to me then and he says, "Yeah, guess so." Big fat tears start dripping down his face. "I just don't want to be a cripple, Earwig."

"I don't want you to be a cripple either, Eddie, but it's better than being dead, ain't it?"

"Yeah, I guess so," Eddie says, and I pat him on the head the way Dad does to me sometimes.

As we drink our Ovaltine and have our peanut butter bread, I make Eddie laugh by talking about boogers and farts.

After a few days, Eddie can go outside. He's not doing good on them sawed-off sticks, so his ma says he better go out in his wheelchair so he don't tip over on the sidewalk and get hurt. At least until he gets stronger. His ma dresses him up like it's winter, so by the time I get Eddie to the sidewalk, he's sweating like Bottoms Conner.

I get Eddie's old bike rim—the one that come from his outgrowed bike—that is propped up against the wall inside the garage, and I bring it to Eddie. "Here, this can be your steering wheel and that chair can be your car."

There is a girl with skinny legs walking down the sidewalk. She sees Eddie in his wheelchair, and she gets all skittery, like she's scared of him. She starts walking faster and faster. It kinda pisses me off, the way she's looking over her shoulder at us, like she's afraid we is gonna come too close to her and give her the polio. Eddie sees this too, and he wants to go home, but I don't want to. "Hang on, Eddie," I say. I push real fast, *rhmmm, rhmmm,* down the sidewalk, until we is close up behind that girl, then I yell, "You better watch it there, missy. Eddie here's got the polio and he's gonna give it to you, sure as shit." Eddie starts to laughing so hard he almost falls out of his chair.

We chase that girl pert' near four blocks before she ditches inside a house and slams the door. "Uh-oh, Earwig. She's gonna tell her ma." I think Eddie's right, so I spin his chair around, lickety-split, and race him back to his yard. "If she comes over here with her ma, we'll just say it weren't us, Eddie," and Eddie says it's a deal. He's still laughing.

* * *

"What's this, Edna?" Ma says as she picks up the book Mrs. Pritchard plopped down on the counter. Ma reads the cover out loud. "*And They Shall Walk*, by Sister Kenny."

"It's a book my sister sent me after I wrote her, telling her how many of our precious little angels here in Willowridge are coming down with polio. I took a look at it, and I think it's something Pearl needs to read. I don't have time to run it over there today, so I thought maybe your Earl could."

Ma pages through that book as Edna Pritchard yammers. "It's an autobiography of this Australian woman who is now working at the University Hospital in Minneapolis. This woman is a miracle worker for children crippled from polio, Eileen. An absolute miracle worker!"

Ma's still got her nose stuck in that book.

"She says that doctors have it all wrong, putting polio victims in braces and immobilizing them like they do. They do it to stop deformity from occurring, but she says that is the very thing that causes the deformity. This Sister Kenny—who, incidentally, is not a real nun at all, but that's what nurses are called in England, where she was working before she came here—well, she believes that a patient's muscles need to be reeducated."

Edna Pritchard, she keeps flapping her gums until she's told Ma about everything there is in that book. Ma sets the book down. "Well, thank you for bringing it by, Edna. I'm sure Pearl will appreciate it. I only hope it doesn't give her false hope if there is no real hope to be had."

"Well," Mrs. Pritchard says, as she lifts her head up high, her chins wobbling, "it seems to me that she could not make these claims in a book if they weren't true."

"Yes, I'm sure," Ma says. "I'll have Earl run it over to Pearl right away." Ma, she gets out a little piece of paper to jot Mrs. McCarty a note explaining where the book come from, then she tucks that note into the book and gives it to me and tells me to run it over to her. "But no staying, Earl, it's a workday, remember."

When I get back to the store, that Edna Pritchard, who said she didn't have time to run the book over to Mrs. McCarty herself, she's still there, propped on Ma's stool, gossiping her fool head off. I go back to work and think about how I hope that book ain't no goddamn lie.

Mrs. McCarty gets all happy after she reads that book and she calls the hospital where that sister, who ain't a real sister, works. She sets up an appointment for Eddie and tells Ma on the phone that she don't care if they have to use every cent of their savings and a whole month's supply of gas coupons, Eddie's gonna get into that hospital and get the best help he can get.

I go see Eddie before he leaves. Eddie, he don't want to go back to no hospital and he's crying. Mrs. McCarty, she is crying too 'cause she don't want Eddie to go away either, but she tells Eddie that if this lady can make his legs work again, then he's got to go. "You want to be able to walk again without braces, don't you, honey?" she says, and Eddie nods.

I bring Eddie some of my comic books to take along, and he sniffles and says, "Thanks, Earwig."

"How long does Eddie got to be gone, Mrs. McCarty?"

"I don't know, but it will be awhile."

"How long is 'awhile'?"

"It's some time, Earl. I don't know for sure."

Eddie wipes the snot off his lip. When his ma tries to kiss his face, he pushes her away, probably on accounta a guy don't like his ma getting all mushy on him, at least not when his growed-up buddy is watching.

"You'll have a good time there, Eddie," she says—like he is

going on a fishing trip or something. "They told me when I called that there are hundreds of children there."

"Oh, great," Eddie says. "Just what I want, a couple hundred creepy, crippled kids gawking at me."

"Hey, Eddie," I say, "them kids got the polio too. If they laugh at you for having crippled-up legs, you can laugh at them for having crippled-up legs too."

Eddie is gone for a long, long time. I go to his house every day after work, on days that I don't have to work at the Ten Pin, and every time Mrs. McCarty says no, he ain't comed back home yet, then she asks me if there's any word on Jimmy, and I tell her no, we ain't heard nothing yet. Then one day Mrs. McCarty says to me—just like she said when Eddie was in the hospital in Ripley—"Earl, how about I call you on the telephone when Eddie comes home? And if it takes a long time, I'll call you every few days to give you any news I get." I tell her she ain't gotta do that, 'cause I gotta give Lucky some more exercise anyway, 'cause, like Dad says, Lucky is getting fatter than a pig and needs more running.

So I keep walking Lucky around the same blocks, and I keep stopping at the McCartys' every day. Then one day, after the summer is almost gone, Mrs. McCarty says that her and Mr. McCarty is going to Minneapolis to pick up Eddie on Friday! They says Eddie had one of them miracles and now he can walk real good! So good he don't even have to wear them braces no more! I get so happy when Mrs. McCarty says that that I give her a big hug that lifts her right off the ground. She is giggling when I set her down. "Oh, Earl, isn't this a blessing?"

The day Eddie comes home, I wait on their steps with Lucky. It takes a long time, but finally I see their car coming down the street, and there is Eddie, bouncing on the backseat, waving so fast that his hand ain't nothing but a blur. I wave back just as fast as he does.

I can't hardly believe my eyes when Eddie jumps right outta the car and runs over to me and Lucky. He ain't even got no braces on his legs. Lucky jumps all over him and licks his face, and I pat Eddie on the back, while Mrs. McCarty smiles and cries, and Mr. McCarty just smiles.

A few days later, Eddie walks home with me to show Ma and Dad his fixed legs. Ma slaps her hands over her cheeks when she sees Eddie walking so good. "My legs got reeducated, Mrs. Gunderman," Eddie says. Then he tells Ma and Dad what he telled me. How that Sister Kenny sure was a nice lady and that his ma says she's an angel. "She felt around my legs when I first got there," Eddie explains. "She was looking for some twitching that told her my legs weren't all the way dead, I guess. She took my braces off and left them off. Lots of times, I had to have hot wool rags wrapped over my legs. That felt good, though, because polio makes your legs hurt bad and those rags sure made them feel better. Then she had me work real hard, doing that physical therapy stuff. It was a lot of work but, little by little, my legs started moving again. Ma says Sister Kenny is a miracle worker."

"Well, I'd say she is!" Ma says.

Dad says, "Well, the way Edna Pritchard is carrying on, you'd think that *she* was the miracle worker. She's making sure that everybody in town knows it was her idea for you to go see Sister Kenny."

"You can say that again," Eddie says, while he rolls his eyes. "She brings over ladies from her clubs, and she tells them all about the book about Sister Kenny that she sent over. She makes me walk in circles and jump up and down to show them how I'm all better. Then she tells me to show them how bad I was before she sent over that book. When I won't, she shows them herself. She gets out of her chair and walks all stiff-legged and wobbly and groans like she's dying or something." Eddie rolls his eyes again. "I told Earwig that if I looked like that when I had polio, I would have had him come over with a twelve-gauge and shoot me."

Dad laughs and shakes his head, and Ma, she says, "Well, thank goodness Edna found that book." Then she gets up and says she's gonna make some hot chocolate so we can celebrate Eddie's reeducated legs.

While we is drinking our hot chocolate, I realize that, for a whole buncha days, my head was so stuffed up with worry about Eddie that I plum forgot to worry about Jimmy. I get real scared when I realize this, and I jump up and run out the back door. "Where you going, Earwig?" Eddie calls, but I ain't got time to answer. Down them porch steps I go and circle round the house so fast Lucky can't hardly keep up. I let out the breath I been holding ever since I left the table.

Yep, Jimmy's star is still blue.

# Chapter 19

One morning, Lucky is barking like crazy out by his doghouse. Ma is counting them paper coins that the ration board gived out a long time ago so customers can get change. Ma is counting away, then she stops and slaps her hands down on the counter. "That barking dog messed me up. I was almost done too. Shoot! Go see what he's barking at." I don't have to go outside to find out, though, 'cause I can see the mailman heading up the steps, and I know it was him that got Lucky all skittery. Lucky ain't a puppy no more and he don't bark for just any old reason. It takes a mailman, a squirrel, a car, a bird, a blowing leaf, or a tumbling scrap a paper to get him stirred up now.

"Morning, Mrs. Gunderman," Mr. Peale says, then, slow-like, he hands Ma a letter that any fool can see is from the army.

"Oh, good Lord, what's this?" Ma says. I hurry to the counter.

"I don't know, ma'am," Mr. Peale says. Ma turns that letter over in her hands, like she's looking for them two red stars, but there ain't none.

I get scared clear down to my toes, waiting for Ma to finish ripping open that letter. Mr. Peale, he stands right there, like he's thinking maybe he's gonna have to catch her if she gets the shock.

Ma's hands shake as she reads. "Ma, is it bad news?"

Ma shakes her head then and she starts crying and laughing at the same time. "It's a letter confirming that Jimmy is in a prison camp! In the Pacific. Earl, he's alive! He's still alive!" Ma reaches over the counter then, and she gives me a hug, and she hugs Mr. Peale too. "Over three years now, and all we had was hope. Now this letter!"

"That's real good news, Mrs. Gunderman," the mailman says. "I'm glad when I can deliver some good news."

Ma hops all over the store after Mr. Peale leaves. "Oh, thank you, God, thank you!" she says, right up to the ceiling, like God is in them boards. "Oh, Earl, this is wonderful news. All these months. These horrible months. He could have been dead the whole time. . . ." Then Ma, she does the damnedest thing. She sits down on her stool and she cries like there ain't no tomorrow. I think maybe she is just getting rid of some of them sorrows she's been carrying around all this time.

Ma don't wait 'til Dad is off work and back at the boarding-house that he says always smells like sauerkraut. She calls him right at work and asks whoever answers the phone to please get Hank Gunderman. When Dad comes on the phone she is about shouting as she reads him the letter. "Yes, Hank! That's what it says!" And Ma, she starts laughing up a storm. Ma, she hands me the phone, and then me and Dad, we laugh together for a bit.

Friday night when Dad gets home, he tells me Jimmy might be coming home soon, 'cause it looks like we is winning the war. We winned some islands called the Marianas Islands and that's good news, he says, but the Germans didn't win at clipping off that Hitler guy last month, which is a damn shame, 'cause that crazy Nazi is killing a whole bunch of people just 'cause they is Jews. He's killing 'em all, putting 'em in ovens. Gobs of 'em. That's what Dad says while we is eating our breakfast. He says Hitler don't like any people 'cept people with blond hair and blue eyes on accounta he thinks they're the best, smartest kind. It don't make no sense to me. That Nazi bastard ain't got blond hair, and he ain't smart either, so what's he got to brag about?

"Hank! Don't go telling Earl that awful stuff."

Dad's eyebrows scrinch down. "Well, it's the truth."

"No one knows that for sure," Ma says.

"Jesus, Eileen, we've known about this for two years now. What do you mean, no one knows for sure? *The New York Times* reported it back in '42. It's no goddamn secret."

"What does 'Jews' mean?" I ask Dad.

"Well," Dad says, "a Jew is just a person. They go to a different kind of church, and Hitler doesn't like that, I guess you could say."

"Why's he killing them just 'cause he don't like their church?"

Dad thinks a minute, then he says, "Who to hell knows what's going through his mind, Earl. He's a goddamn lunatic who's trying to play God."

"I think he's trying to play devil," I say.

Ma drips syrup on the tablecloth and hurries to the sink to get a dishrag. She comes back all crabby and says, "Let's change the subject now."

I know I should shut up, but I can't. Not just yet. "Dad? Do we go to a church that lunatic likes?"

"Yes, Earl."

I think a minute and I ask Dad what kinda church that Hitler guy goes to, 'cause seems to me it can't be worth a damn, if what he's learning there is that it's okay to go around killing people just 'cause you don't think they're the right kind. Ma tells me to never mind and to finish my pancakes.

Ma says we can't talk about the war at the table no more, so we don't. That is, until a couple months later, when Dad says we got troops back in the Pacific now, and that soon we'll take back that thumb of an island from them Japs.

For a long time, I didn't listen to the nightly news, but I listen now on nights I ain't working at the Ten Pin. And even on nights when Dad ain't around to explain some of what I'm hearing, I understand enough of it to know that we are kicking some ass now.

It about knocks the wind out of me when I hear the news that President Roosevelt is dead. Dropped dead, just like that, from a vein popping in his head, blood exploding all over in there. I'm on the back steps pluckin' wood ticks off of Lucky when Ma opens the porch door and tells me the news. I don't even bother picking off that gray, swelled-up one next to his eye after she tells me the news, 'cause I feel too heartsick to do anything but follow Ma back inside.

Everybody is heartsick, just like me, when they hear the news. Eddie's school and all the stores, even Gunderman's Grocery, close up tighter than a drum.

When Dad comes home that night, he says he can hardly believe it. He is walking real slow, like his best friend up and died. He says that Harry Truman will make a good President, but that there ain't never gonna be another President like Franklin D. Roosevelt. Ma says she hopes the war won't drag on longer now that we lost our President. Dad says he don't think it will.

Couple weeks or so later, that scary Nazi with the chopped-off mustache, he kills hisself. Dad says he did it 'cause he knew the war was over and he knew we was coming to get him. I think he knew that when we found him where he was hunkered down in that bunker we woulda strung him up by his balls. Least that's what the guys are saying down at the Skelly.

A few days later, them Germans surrender. Me and Eddie whoop and holler when Sam steps out of the barber shop and stops us on the street to tell us. "I hate them goddamn Krauts!" I tell Eddie after Sam goes back inside and we get to walking again.

"You shouldn't say that, Earwig," Eddie says. "You're a Kraut too."

"You're a goddamn liar, Eddie!"

"You *are*," Eddie says, and he don't even flinch, even though I'm so mad I'm wanting to pop him right on the head. "Your name is *Gunderman*, and that's a German name. Lots of folks around here are Germans."

Soon as we get to the station, I give Dad his lunch and I ask him if we is Germans.

"Well," Dad says, "my daddy was born in Germany and immigrated here with his family when he was still a boy."

I scratch my ear a bit while I'm thinking, then I turn to Eddie. I stand up real tall so he knows I mean business. "Well, there, Eddie. We used to be Germans, 'til Dad's daddy come over here, then we started being Americans. Ain't that right, Dad? We is Americans now—no matter what we used to be—

and that means we ain't bad no more. You wouldn't see us Americans go around killing a whole buncha people like them Germans is doing, just 'cause we don't like the church they go to, or just 'cause we think they ain't the right colors."

Dad, he is pouring himself a cup of coffee and he sighs. "Well, Earl, I wish that were true, but it isn't. We killed off a whole bunch of Indians and coloreds for the same reasons."

I don't know what the hell to make of any of it, after Dad says that, 'cause now I don't know who in the hell is the good guys and who in the hell is the bad guys. When I tell Dad this, he just pats my arms and says, "Maybe we're all just a little bit of both."

Something ain't right when Dad comes home the next weekend. I can tell. He asks me how my job at the Ten Pin is going, but he ain't hardly listening when I tell him. He tells Ma that she made a fine roast for supper, and he says it's suppose to warm up next week. His words say that everything's all right, but his face don't say it. I go upstairs early and I go straight to Jimmy's room and lay down by the vent, 'cause I think Dad was waiting for me to get out of the room so he can tell Ma what's wrong.

I scratch Lucky 'til he lays down quiet, and wait for Dad to start talking.

Finally, Dad says, "I went to a town meeting in Janesville, Eileen. There was this boy there, Red Lawson. When the Japs were shuffling prisoners around from camp to camp, he got left behind somehow. He was one of the Janesville ninety-nine."

"Oh, my!" Ma says. "Did you ask him if he knew Jimmy? Did you, Hank? And Floyd? Did you ask him about Floyd?"

My heart pounds itself right up to my throat when Ma asks that question.

"Those Janesville boys are a tight-knit bunch. He knew Jimmy and Floyd, and he said that as far as he knows, they're still alive. But that was a while back, Eileen."

"Well, thank goodness you could learn at least that much!"

Dad clears his throat, but when he talks, it still sounds like he's got something in there. "Eileen, he told horrible stories about what those boys have endured. He said after Bataan fell, the Japs marched them miles in that jungle heat. They were starved and sick with malaria and dysentery and jungle sores, and the Japs wouldn't even let them have water when they came across it."

Ma, she's got both hands held over her mouth, so she ain't saying nothing. I got my hand stuck over my mouth too. Dad, he's crouched forward and he is rubbing his hands together. "They crowded them on a train then and took them to this training camp that once belonged to the Philippine soldiers. Camp O'Donnell. A lot of our boys didn't make it, Eileen."

Ma starts waving her hands. "Stop. Hank, stop! I can't hear this!" Ma, she gets up and her hands jump from her mouth to her heart, then to the hairs on the back of her neck. "Why are you telling me this? I don't want to hear this."

Dad says, "I know, Eileen, but I thought you should know. When the war ends and Jimmy comes home, well, I thought you should know what he's been through."

"That boy, he shouldn't have told those things," Ma says. "He had no right telling such things!"

That's what the government says too when them people in Janesville start writing tons of letters to Washington, harping at the government for not telling them what was happening to our boys over there. The government said Red Lawson shouldn't be telling them things. I hear Dad through the vent tell Ma that Red, he had to go to that Pentagon place, and they showed him some papers they drawed up, accusing him of telling secrets while there was a war going on. They told Red to shut his big mouth or he's gonna get locked up in prison for being a traitor. Now, Dad says, that guy, Red, he don't dare leave his house no more on accounta people keep asking him more about what happened over there and he can't say nothing.

"It's a goddamn pity what they're doing to that boy," Dad says. "The truth is the truth, and, goddammit, Washington didn't have any business keeping the truth from us in the first place, and they sure as hell don't have any business telling that boy what he can or can't say."

Next morning, when Dad and I go check up on the Skelly, Ed Fryer is there, standing by the counter, talking to Delbert. Dad gives me a Coca-Cola and tells me to go outside so he can talk to Floyd's dad. I know he is gonna talk about that Red Lawson, so I don't go over past the gas pumps and sit on the grass to wait, where Dad points for me to go. I go around the door and I stand there real quiet, while Lucky runs off to sniff things.

Dad waits a spell after Mr. Fryer says, "What's wrong, Hank?" Then Dad tells him all about Red Lawson and about what Red said at that meeting in Janesville. "It wasn't good news, Ed. After the boys surrendered, the Japs forced our boys to march through that jungle heat from Mariveles, Bataan, to San Fernando, a good fifty, sixty miles or more. They were sick and starving. Lawson said the boys that tried to get a drink when they came to a watering hole were shot or decapitated with bayonets. He said those miles were littered with empty canteens and hacked-up bodies. Lawson called it the Death March."

Mr. Fryer sighs hard, then cusses slow, "Jesus Christ."

"At the end of the march, they loaded them into boxcars. Red said there wasn't hardly any air to breathe in those cars. The sick ones, they puked and shit all over themselves, and the dead, they couldn't drop until the rest of the boys got off the train, because there wasn't any room for them to drop." My guts churn when I hear Dad say this stuff. I wanna run off far enough so I can't hear a thing, but it's like my feet is planted right there on the concrete, and I can't move.

"Red Lawson's been threatened by the government. If he says any more about what happened over there, Washington will crucify that boy.

"I hated to have to tell you this stuff, Ed, but Floyd's there, and you deserve to know what's happened to him. Oh, and Ed, just so you know. Our boys didn't surrender. Wainwright surrendered them."

Dad and Mr. Fryer and Mr. Larson, they keep talking, but I don't keep listening. I pry my feet loose from the concrete and I go where Dad told me to go and I find a patch of grass to sit on, 'cause my legs feel too wobbly to stand. I feel real scared for Jimmy and Floyd, and I feel sad too. Lucky, he comes over to me and he lays down, plunking his chin right on my leg.

Dad comes out of the Skelly, his thumbs in his belt loops, his head down. He looks sad and he looks pissed too. I think Dad feels about the government now the way I felt when I found out I'd been lied to about him being Jimmy's dad. It kinda hurts your feelings and mixes up your head when you find out that somebody you thought always telled you the truth didn't.

# Chapter 20

The Germans mighta gived up, but them Japs, they ain't ready to give up. Not until after we drop the biggest bombs ever made on their heads. We drop the first one smack-dab on a place called Hiroshima. Ma, she whacks her hand right over her heart when she hears, and she tells me that that bomb, it falled where there was women and children, and old people too. A few days later we drop another one on a place called Nagasaki. When I hear about them bombs, I'm glad, I guess, 'cause like Dad says, it'll probably make them yellow-bellies give up, but part of me is not glad. I'm hoping them kids had air drills and got practiced up good like I did so they was under a desk or a table when them bombs hit. The thought of big-ass bombs falling on the heads of little kids makes my stomach all skittery, even if they is yellow-bellies. I get to thinking about them old people, and I feel bad for them too, 'cause old people can't run real fast.

War, it's like a bonfire you make from yard crud you clean up in the spring. First, that heap just smolders. Then all of a sudden it sparks and them flames just shoot up, roaring and spitting, all cherry-red. That fire, it burns hot for a long time and it don't stop lickety-split even if you throw a couple a buckets of water on it. It just fizzles, them flames shrinking back to where they come from until there ain't nothing left but a smoking heap. That's how the war ends.

When we hear them say on the radio that the war is "officially" over, we all go nuts. People empty right outta their houses and the stores, and they dance around in the street and hug each other and laugh like it's a party. Then there ain't nothing left to do but wait for them soldiers to come home.

It takes weeks before we get a letter. When that letter comes, it's from Jimmy. He says he's in a vet hospital, and at first I think that means he's in a hospital being looked after by animal doctors. But Ma says that *vet* don't mean an animal doctor in army talk. She says it's a hospital for soldiers. Jimmy's been in a couple of them vet hospitals now, he says in his letter, but soon he'll be home. After Ma reads that letter to me, she tucks it back in the envelope and runs her fingers over the postmark. "September twenty-second, 1945," she says. Then her eyes tear up and she says, "He's been gone so long."

Mary comes into the store and she's got a letter from Floyd, so we know he's coming home too. Mary, she is worried, though. She says Floyd didn't sound good in his letter. He telled her that he ain't the same and she probably won't want to look at him no more. Ma, she don't tell Mary the things Dad telled her. She just tells Mary that he'll be all right.

Ma writes back to Jimmy, and she tells him what I ask her to tell him. She tells him I'm real glad he's coming home, and that I'm working at the Ten Pin Bowling Alley. She tells him, too, that I picked milkweed for the war so nobody would get drowned. When she's done writing that stuff, she sits there and taps the tip of her pen on the V-mailer. "Jimmy said he wrote to Molly and she hasn't answered. I don't know what to tell him about Molly." Ma lets out a sigh that's big enough to stretch from here to Ripley.

Ma, she calls Molly's mother then. She tells her that Jimmy is coming home and that Jimmy mailed Molly about it, but that she knows Molly is still in Chicago being a hatcheck girl, so could she please see that that letter gets forwarded to her. Well, Ma stops talking for a bit then, while she's listening to Molly's ma, then she says, "Excuse me?" and her eyes get all big and fat, like they is being stretched big as plates by what she's hearing. Then Ma, she gets madder than a wet hen, and she starts harping at Mrs. Franks something fierce. "What kind of a girl did you raise, anyway, Judith? She promised herself to my Jimmy!" Ma, she slams that phone down so hard it makes a ringing noise, then she rants and raves and cries 'cause Molly, she is planning to marry a guy who's almost a doctor now. They is getting married next month, and Mrs. Franks ain't gonna say nothing to Molly about Jimmy coming home. Even an idiot can figure out that a girl can't marry two guys, so I know that this means Jimmy is shit out of luck. Ma's so pissed off at the Franks that when she hears that Mr. Franks had a stroke, she don't even care one smidgen.

* * *

I can't think about nothing but Jimmy coming home. My mind, it goes wandering, thinking up every time I spent with Jimmy. I'm so busy thinking about Jimmy that I can't think about that ball rolling down the alley, and I know that by the time Jimmy gets home my legs is gonna be so whacked up that they're gonna have as many spots on 'em as them leopard cats in the *National Geographic* magazine.

Eva Leigh and the girls on the bowling teams that Ruby Leigh and her put together, they see that I ain't thinking straight, so before they crank that ball back, they shout, "Here it comes, Earwig!" but usually I forget by the time that ball reaches the pins. The girls, they is real sorry that I'm getting whacked so much, but they is real happy for me that Jimmy's coming home.

Eva Leigh, she still ain't much of a bowler, but she's better than she was when I first got hired. Mary bowls on her team too, and she laughs and shouts loud every time she, or one of the gals on her team, gets a strike. Ruby Leigh, she ain't a captain 'cause no one wanted to be on her team. She ain't a captain and she ain't on nobody's team either. I guess them ladies was afraid it would lower them to bowl with her. I tell Ruby Leigh that them ladies is nothing but a damn buncha fools for not wanting to be on her team, 'cause she's the best goddamn girl bowler I ever see'd.

Jimmy is probably gonna be home by Thanksgiving. That's what his next letter says. Soon as Ma gets that letter, she starts in making plans. "We should have a welcome-home party for Jimmy," she says. "We could rent the town hall and ask Tommy and the band to play. We could include Floyd as a guest of honor, and—" But Dad, he lifts up his hand and he tells Ma that maybe Jimmy and Floyd won't be up for a party just yet, so she'd best wait. So Ma, she starts to cleaning the house instead.

I don't know why she thinks them closets gotta be clean for Jimmy, 'cause Jimmy, he don't give a shit about clean closets or clean anything else, but Ma she does it anyway. She cleans the closets and floors, all spiffy, scrubbing and waxing and polishing 'til Dad says the whole place stinks so strong of lemons it makes him feel pukey. When Ma's done with that, she starts to scrubbing walls and washing and pressing the curtains, even though she already done them jobs in the spring. She about drives me buggy with her harping at me to take off my shoes, and don't touch the walls like that when you are wiggling on your shoes, and don't set that cup down on the clean end table without a coaster, and don't spatter Pepsodent on the bathroom mirror, and, worse of all, don't let Lucky make a mess shedding all over. I ain't got a inkling on how I'm suppose to keep Lucky from shedding, but I guess it's something I'm suppose to figure out, 'cause she keeps on saying it.

Ma bakes too. There still ain't sugar to bake with, so she can't make a buncha cookies and cakes. Instead, she bakes bread and rolls and raisin pies, and she slaps my fingers and Dad's if we even try swiping one roll while they's still warm and smelling good. "Stop that! I'm freezing those for Jimmy!" she says, and I whisper to Dad that we is gonna starve to death, and Jimmy, his ass is gonna grow to three ax handles wide if he eats all that food by hisself. Dad laughs and Ma says, "What are you two snickering about?" but we don't tell her.

I can't hardly sleep the night before Jimmy is coming home. I look at my comic books, but afterward I can't sleep. I jiggle Lucky's tail and scratch his belly, but when I'm done, I still can't sleep. Dad, he can't sleep either, 'cause I hear him down in the kitchen rooting around in the Frigidaire. I lean over the vent and ask him if I can come down by him. He says I can.

Dad makes us sandwiches from leftover chicken and raw onions. He pours us each a glass of milk.

"Son," he says. "Tomorrow when we pick up Jimmy?"

"Yeah?"

"Well, I want you to be prepared. Jimmy isn't gonna look the same. He probably won't act the same either. A lot of years have passed, Earl, and a lot of things have happened to him."

"I know," I say.

"Jimmy's been through hard times. It isn't easy for a man to be in war, son. They see and are forced to do things no man should have to see and do. And being in that camp was pretty rough on Jimmy. I just want you to be prepared."

"But he'll still be Jimmy," I say. And Dad says yes, he'll still be Jimmy.

When we take off for the bus station, big fluffy snowflakes are falling, melting right on the windshield 'til Dad swipes 'em away with the wiper blades. It's funny the way it seems like it was a hundred years ago that we was heading to the bus depot to see Jimmy and Floyd off to the National Guard—yet it seems like yesterday at the same time. I've been waiting five years for Jimmy to come home, and now that he is, I'm feeling skittery.

Ma looks into the backseat. "Earl, why are you wearing your Ten Pin shirt?" she asks as she reaches back and slaps at my hair.

"It's my uniform shirt, Ma. Jimmy and Floyd, they's gonna be wearing their uniform shirts."

"That's right," Dad says.

"Oh, look. Mary's right behind us," Ma says, and she waves to her. I turn around and wave too.

Mary is driving Floyd's car and it's making all kinds of racket. Dad says he's gonna tell Mary to bring that Ford by the shop and he's gonna fix it up for her, for free. Dad, he's gonna go back to work at the garage soon 'cause the war is over and that plant is going back to making Oldsmobiles again. There is gonna be plenty of GIs coming home who will be glad to take over his spot, he says, and the Wings' jobs too. Dad says them ladies are madder than wet hens, being told now that leaving their kids to go to work wasn't a good thing to do, after they was told it was. Dad says the husbands coming home got another think coming if they think their wives are gonna go home to cook and clean and make babies, without putting up a big fuss.

Ma, she can't hardly sit still in her seat, she's so happy about Jimmy coming home. "Eileen, don't expect too much at first," Dad reminds her. "Jimmy's been through a lot, and judging from what that Lawson boy said, he's probably been good and goddamn sick."

Ma says, "Oh, we don't even know if those things he said are true, Hank. You heard Mrs. Banks herself say that her daughter in Janesville says there's talk that that Red Lawson is just goofy in the head and that he made up those things. She said he stays locked up in the house like he's got a guilty conscience for telling fibs. Hank, if those things he said were true, don't you think the government would have told us? And don't you think he'd be able to face people?"

Dad sighs. "I was there, Eileen. I saw that boy tremble down to his boots when he talked. I looked right in his eyes. He wasn't lying."

Ma, she stops listening to Dad. She tugs on the rearview mirror and licks her fingers and dabs at a curl looped on her forehead. She pulls out her lipstick and draws herself some fresh red lips, then takes a tissue from her purse and presses her mouth on that folded tissue, making a picture of red kissing lips.

When we get to the station, it's real busy 'cause some other

GIs are coming home, and other folks are taking the bus to visit family for Thanksgiving. That whole bus station is filled with echoes 'cause them ceilings are high. When people stomp the new snow off their boots, it sounds like thumping drums.

There's a bus unloading. "Do you see them? Do you see them?" Ma and Mary, who are lots littler than me, ask. I tell 'em I don't see 'em.

"Jimmy!" Ma shouts after a bit, and Mary, she clamps her hands over her mouth and starts to bawling. Dad puts his arm around her and gives her a little shake, then Mary, she breaks free from Dad and tags after Ma, who is running through a crowd of old ladies in scarves and mas tugging along little kids in their Sunday-best clothes.

Ma and Mary, they find two soldiers, white and skimpy as ghosts, faces bony as skulls, and they start hugging and kissing on 'em like they think they is Jimmy and Floyd. The one with the dark hair, most of his arm is gone, the sleeve of his army jacket folded and tucked up and tied with twine.

Dad joins Ma and Mary, and he's slapping the backs of them ghosty guys, but me, I just stand back a ways and pick at my pants, 'cause they is kissing and hugging on guys that ain't even Jimmy and Floyd.

I move farther away. I look at the ticket man behind the barred window. I look at the wet muddy tracks smudged all over the floor. I look at a lady digging in her purse. I look everywhere but at them two.

"Earl?" It's Dad. "Earl, come say hi to Jimmy and Floyd. They're waiting."

I shake my head. "That ain't Jimmy and Floyd."

Ma, she hurries over to me and she grabs and pinches my wrist. "What's the matter with you, Earl? Go greet your brother. He's waiting." She runs back to where they is all standing, gawking over at me.

Dad leans closer to me. "I know he doesn't look the same, Earl, but that's your brother." Dad puts his hand on the middle of my back and he pushes me toward them soldiers.

When I get closer, the one, he is standing there grinning at me. His kid-skinny arm is around Ma's shoulder. That ain't Jimmy. Jimmy's got hair like yellow waves. This soldier, he's got baldy hair, dull as old straw. Jimmy got muscles like Captain Midnight, but this soldier, his uniform is hanging on him like they is hanging from a clothesline. There are tears in his eyes, eyes that are sunken back in his head and ringed like a raccoon's. "Earwig!" the guy says, and he spreads his stick arms and comes at me.

I stand stiffety-straight while he jerks me into a hug. When his arms come around me, though, that's when I know it *is* Jimmy. This guy's outsides, they don't look like Jimmy's outsides, but when he hugs me, his insides tell mine that it *is* him. I get so sad and happy at the same time that I start to bawling. Jimmy, he bawls right with me.

I'm careful not to thump his back, 'cause I'm scared I might break him. "Goddamn, it's good to see you, buddy," Jimmy says. I want to tell him that I'm glad to see him too, but I can't find no words. Not even one goddamn little word.

"Hey, Earwig," the other soldier says. I don't wanna know that that's Floyd with the snapped-off arm, but it is Floyd. I can tell 'cause he sounds like Floyd. And when he gives me a hug with that one arm, he feels like Floyd. I hug Floyd real careful-like, 'cause he feels all little and bony in my arms like he might break too.

After the hugging is done, Floyd and Jimmy, they stand close together like they is on one team and we is on another. They light cigarettes and suck on them like there ain't no air in the room, just in them cigarettes.

"Oh, you boys are so thin," Ma says, and Jimmy tells her that he is fat now compared to what he was when he got back to the States. "I was under ninety pounds when I got back, Ma. I'm up to one twenty-six now." Ma presses her gloved hand to her cheek and her eyes fill up with tears. Dad says that Ma and Mary will have 'em fattened up in no time. Then he says there ain't no use standing around talking in the bus station, and, speaking of food, why don't we go back to the house and have some of that stuff Ma's been cooking. "I hope you boys are hungry," Dad says, and they tell Dad they are.

Ma and Mary, they drag all the food Ma's cooked from the Frigidaire. When Ma opens that oven, you can smell the baked ham she left in there to stay warm while we was gone. That smell gets Jimmy and Floyd and Lucky almost drooling.

Ma and Mary work like bees, bringing bowls to the table. There's potato salad and coleslaw and bread pudding, and reheated buns and raisin pie and a plate of pickles and celery sticks and stuff like that. Jimmy and Floyd, they sit on the edges of their chairs and they smoke one cigarette after another while they wait for the ladies to set the table. Lucky is sniffing them up and down and they pat him now and then. Jimmy's and Floyd's eyes, they are darting all over the place like they is scared that a Jap is gonna spring from somewhere and hold a gun on 'em and make 'em march right back to that bad camp. Dad, he is talking away, telling them all the stuff that went on in Willowridge while they was gone. That ain't much, 'cept for who died in the war and who moved away to find work in the city.

Jimmy and Floyd, they eat like pigs, and this makes Ma and Mary real happy. Afterward, they say they feel sick, and Jimmy, he runs to the bathroom and throws up. Ma, she fusses at him when he gets back to the table, and Dad says maybe they better go light on the food 'til their bellies get used to eating again. But Jimmy don't go light. After he pukes, he comes right back to the table and he starts filling his belly up all over again.

Every now and then, Floyd, he flinches like he's in pain. Dad asks him if something's hurting him and he says that his arm is. I shit you not, he says that that arm that ain't even there is hurting him. "I've heard of that," Dad says.

Floyd and Mary, they keep making eyes at each other as we eat, and Mary, she keeps touching Floyd. This makes me feel real sad for Jimmy, who ain't got a girl no more to make goofy eyes at him. It must make Ma sad too, 'cause she says to Jimmy, "I'm sorry I had to tell you about Molly, Jimmy. I didn't want to, but I didn't want you disappointed when she wasn't waiting with us at the depot. I hope she's at least got the decency to return your ring."

"The ring doesn't matter," Jimmy says.

"I think it does," Ma says.

"Jimmy, I didn't know," Mary says, then she presses her lips together and her mouth looks all knuckly, folded over her big teeth like that. Jimmy nods.

Ma, she wants Jimmy to sit with us in the living room and listen to the radio or the phonograph after Floyd and Mary leave, but Jimmy, he says he thinks he's gonna call it a night. "I'm as weak as a baby yet, Ma," he says.

Ma nods and gets all teary-eyed again. She gets up and gives Jimmy a hug. "Oh, Jimmy," she says. Jimmy don't say nothing back to her, but he looks at me and asks me if I want to go up too.

I'm picking at my pants the whole way up the stairs, though I ain't exactly sure why. I follow Jimmy into his room, where he stands for a bit and just looks at the walls and the bed and the dresser. Lucky, he follows us, his toenails making little tippity-taps on the floor.

"It looks exactly the same as it did when I left it," Jimmy says. He walks over to the dresser and he picks up his old baseball and he tosses it around in his hands a bit. "I wanted to play for the Chicago Cubs," he said.

"Maybe you can play for the Cubs now," I say, but Jimmy, he shakes his head and puts the ball back.

Ma, she's got a pair of pajamas laid out on Jimmy's bed, so he unbuttons that army shirt and he drops it on the floor. He takes off his undershirt too, and that's when I see them marks he's got on his back and on his side, close to his belly. They is like stains on his skin, and some of 'em is puckered up too. "Them dirty Japs do that to you?" I ask. Jimmy looks down, like he's forgotten they was there, and he nods. "Some of them. Some are just scars from jungle ulcers."

"Do they hurt?" I ask, and Jimmy says yeah, sometimes they hurt.

One thing I notice is that Jimmy, he don't see real good no more. He picks up his pajama top and he thinks it's a bottom, so I gotta tell him he's got it wrong. Just like in the car coming home, when Dad pointed out something new about the factory, and Jimmy couldn't see it. "Can't you see good no more, Jimmy?"

Jimmy blinks at the shirt he's got all tangled up in his hands. "Not real good, but it's getting some better. It's from starving," he says. "Starving wrecks your eyes."

Jimmy stretches out on his bed and he smokes 'til the room is foggy. "Jeez, you got big, Earwig. You filled out, you got taller. You look like a goddamn giant." He laughs when he says this, so I laugh too. He points to my uniform shirt. "Pretty dignified there, Earwig. You like your job?"

"I sure do, Jimmy. I got friends there too. I got Slim and Skeeter and, best of all, I got Eva Leigh, and Ruby Leigh."

"Ruby Leigh?" Jimmy grins. "Well, aren't you a lucky bastard. I bet Ruby Leigh didn't ration her sweets during the war," he says, and I tell him no, Ruby Leigh wasn't on the ration board, but Dieter Pritchard was.

Then Jimmy, he stops grinning and he looks right in my eyes and he says, "I wouldn't have made it back if it weren't for you, Earwig. I just kept telling myself, every day, every hour, that I had to live through it to come home for you." The corners of my mouth feel like they is getting tugged down when he says this. I go over and I give Jimmy a hug, and I don't feel all skittery inside no more 'cause Jimmy don't look the same. "It took a long time for you to come home, Jimmy."

Funny how you can feel two things at one time, 'cause that's what I'm feeling now. I feel happy 'cause Jimmy is saying something like this, but I feel sad too, 'cause I'm thinking of how Jimmy is the best brother I ever had, yet he is only my half brother. I watch Jimmy take another puff on his cigarette, and I wonder if he knows we is only half brothers too. I want to ask him, but I can't.

The next day, Eddie comes over with a plate of warm doughnuts. "My ma said to bring these over for you, Jimmy," he says. Jimmy takes a doughnut and dunks it into the coffee he's drinking. "Thank your ma for me, Eddie." He takes one bite and halfa the doughnut disappears. "How you been, Eddie?" Jimmy asks, after he swallows.

"I'm good. My polio is all gone. How are you, Jimmy? You don't look so good."

"I'm not so good," Jimmy says. "I got pretty sick while I was over there."

"When I was sick, my ma and dad took me to Minneapolis to see Sister Kenny to get my muscles reeducated. Maybe you need something like that too, so you can get strong again like you used to be."

I get mad when Eddie says this. "Jimmy's still strong! He could still beat up anybody he wanted to!" Jimmy stops chewing. He looks at me. I know he's planning to tell me that no, he ain't strong enough to beat anybody up no more, maybe not even Eddie, but he don't got to. I already know it.

That night, Lucky wakes me up 'cause he's barking and carrying on. First I think he's just gotta piss or something, but then I hear what he's making a fuss about. Jimmy is making all kinds of racket in his room. He's screaming and groaning so loud that I can hear it right through the walls. I get out of bed, and that floor, it sure is cold on my bare feet. I hurry into Jimmy's room.

I can see Jimmy 'cause that streetlight is coming some right through his curtains, making Jimmy all glowy. Jimmy, he is batting at the air one second, then covering his head the next. He is crying and yowling, but there ain't no tears shining on his face.

I hurry to his bed and I shake him a bit. "Jimmy? Jimmy, wake up!" He grabs my arm first and squeezes it tight. Then, as I'm bending over him, trying to help him lay back down, he grabs me around the neck and he starts to choking me. I can feel his fingers digging into my neck and it hurts like hell. He's got me so hard I can't do nothing but swat at his arms and squeak. I don't want to hit at Jimmy, but I can't breathe now, and my eyes, they feel like they is gonna pop right out of my head, so I gotta swat at him.

Jimmy's eyes are open, but it's like they is seeing somebody scary, not me. I swat harder at his arm and yell at him to let me go. He blinks, then he lets go. He's shaking something fierce, and so am I. He looks around real quick, like he can't figure out where he is. Then he says, "Oh, shit. Oh, shit."

I ain't never see'd anybody that skittery. His face is so twitchy that he looks like there's bugs crawling under the skin. He jumps off the bed and he starts walking in little circles. He is breathing so hard that, I shit you not, I can see the front of his pajama shirt moving in and out from the thumping in his chest.

He reaches for a cigarette. "I'm sorry. I'm sorry," he keeps saying. "I thought you were a Jap. Shit. I'm sorry." He's pacing up and down the room, and he's stopping now and then to shake first one leg, then the other. He's rubbing the top parts of his legs too. "Your legs got the prickles in 'em from being asleep?" I ask.

Jimmy shakes his head. "They're just numb," he says.

"You have a bad dream about them dirty Japs, Jimmy?" I ask, and he says he supposes he did. I ain't sure he's all the way waked up, though, 'cause his eyes, they is skidding back and forth, and he still looks real scared. He starts thumping on his chest with his fist as he gulps for air.

"Jimmy," I say. "There ain't no Japs here." I pick up the edge of his bedspread and I hold it up and look under that bed, where there ain't even one speck of dust left after Ma's cleaning. "There ain't no Japs under your bed, Jimmy. See?" Then I go to the closet, and I open that up too, and I yank the hanged shirts and pants aside so he can see clear to the back wall. "Ain't none here in your closet either. My eyes ain't bad from starving, and I can see there ain't no Japs in here." I go to his dresser, 'cause I know Japs is little, maybe even little enough to crawl into his underwear drawer, so I open that up too and pull his underwear and balled-up socks out. "Ain't no yellow-bellies in here either, Jimmy," I say.

Jimmy's eyes are following me, and he's nodding each time I say something. I go through every goddamn place in his room that might be big enough to hide a Jap, and I show him there ain't no Japs. I sit down. Jimmy calms down some and comes to sit on the bed by me. He's still rubbing the top part of his legs some, but he ain't breathing quite so hard now.

Jimmy tells me he didn't mean to hurt me. "You gotta wake me up careful though, Earwig, 'cause when I'm sleeping, I don't know who you are."

Finally, Jimmy lays back down and he smokes, the smoke curling out of his nose 'cause his mouth ain't open enough to blow it all out. One hand is holding his Camel, and the other hand is holding his bedspread.

I don't say nothing at first, then I say, "You want Lucky to sleep by you, Jimmy? He won't let no Japs get in here. He hates Japs more than mailmen even." Jimmy, he sorta smiles, and he don't say yes or no, so I just pat the bed and Lucky, he leaps up by Jimmy. "He keeps you warm too."

After I go back to my bed, I just lay there and listen and think of what Ruby Leigh said, about how sorrows that get locked inside gotta come out or else they make you do crazy things and make your heart close up like a fist. Jimmy's got them sorrows locked up inside. Lots of them, I think. I start to thinking how sorry I am that the fever got me when I was a bitty baby, 'cause if I was smarter, I'd probably know how to help Jimmy get them sorrows out.

The next day, our regulars from the store and the Skelly, they stop in all day long and ask to say hello to Jimmy. The ladies, they bring a little something for Jimmy to eat, and the men, they shake his hand and pat his shoulder so hard Jimmy wobbles.

Jimmy and Floyd, they both come to the bowling alley to see me work. Eva Leigh, she don't know Jimmy much, so when Jimmy and Floyd come, I introduce her to 'em like they never met before. Jimmy says to Eva Leigh, "I'm sorry to hear about your husband." Floyd says he's sorry too, so I say I'm sorry, even though I already telled Eva Leigh that a long time ago. Eva Leigh thanks us, then her head dips down for a bit. When she picks it up again, she says, "I'm glad you two made it home, though." She puts one arm around my waist and leans her head on my arm for a bit. "This guy here sure was worried."

Jimmy and Floyd sit at the bar and they smoke and drink Schlitz. I watch 'em from my little triangle window. I watch 'em get drunk and I watch the ball so I can jump outta the way so they don't see me get whacked.

Ruby Leigh, she fusses over Jimmy and Floyd, making sure their glasses don't go dry, and she's licking her red lips and laughing with 'em every minute she ain't busy refilling somebody else's glass. Some of the bowlers go up and shake Jimmy and Floyd's hand, but lots more don't. They just stare at 'em when they think Jimmy and Floyd ain't looking.

When them lanes get closed, I hang up the towel I wipe my hands on when they get sweaty, and I pick up my two empty pop bottles, then me and Skeeter lock up that door. Slim, he is at the bar and he is buying Floyd and Jimmy another beer. Them two are drunk as skunks as it is, but Slim says they look like they could use another one.

Slim and Ruby Leigh and Eva Leigh start tidying up the place, but they tell me to sit at the bar with my brother and friend and to yell if we need anything. Slim pops a coin in the jukebox and he plays some tunes. Jimmy and Floyd don't know the newer songs, but they sure do like "Boogie Woogie Bugle Boy" and "Chattanooga Choo Choo." When the songs stop, Jimmy pops some more coins in the jukebox and he squints down, looking for them songs to play again, but he can't find 'em on account of he's half blind from the starving and half blind from the beers. Ruby Leigh runs to help.

When "Boogie Woogie Bugle Boy" starts playing again, Floyd starts drumming on the bar, his hand rat-a-tatting real good to the song, his head bouncing while he sings along. By the time that song is ending, though, Floyd stops making them little, quick taps and starts thumping his hand on the bar hard. *Thump, thump, thump*, hitting harder and harder 'til the noise his hand is making sounds like marching feet.

Then he starts shouting out something that is like a song, but it ain't got no singing to it, just shouting. Jimmy joins in, and together they're yelling, "*We're the battling bastards of Bataan; No mama, no papa, no Uncle Sam; No aunts, no uncles, no nephews, no nieces; No pills, no planes, no artillery pieces; And nobody gives a damn.*"

When they get done, there ain't a noise anyplace in the Ten

Pin. That is, until I say, "Good thing you didn't say no brothers or friends, 'cause I didn't forget you guys. Well, once I did for a bit—when Eddie got the polio—but other than that, I didn't forget you even for one minute. *I* always gived a damn."

When it's time to close up, me and the girls can see we got ourselves a problem. Slim's gone now, and Jimmy and Floyd, they is so drunk they can't walk. They is hanging over the bar, their heads almost scraping the ashtrays.

Eva Leigh says maybe we better call Mary to come get Floyd, so we do. Mary and one of her ugly sisters come in the Ford that ain't clunking no more since Dad fixed it. Me and Mary, we put Floyd's good arm over Mary's shoulder, and I grab him around his skinny waist and we drag him to the car. Floyd, he is bitching up a storm. "Crissakes, they hacked off my arm, not my fucking legs. I can still walk, you know." But he can't.

After we stuff Floyd into the front seat, Mary says, "Let's get Jimmy. I'll give you both a lift home." First I don't know what to do. I'm suppose to walk the girls home like I do every night, but Eva Leigh, she tells me to run along with Mary and Jimmy and that her and Ruby Leigh will be just fine.

I get Jimmy and I hoist him up in my arms 'cause he's passed out, and he don't feel no heavier than LJ when I pick him up. We don't even get a block down the street when Floyd pukes right down the front of Mary's coat. Jimmy, he don't puke 'til we get him home.

Next couple days, Jimmy is sick. Real sick. He's shaking and sweating so bad from a fever that I'm scared his brain's gonna fry. Dr. McCormick comes and he says that Jimmy's got a bout of the malaria. He says that's a sickness the soldiers get from skeeter bites over there in the jungle and that it might keep coming back for a time. He gives Ma some little white pills called quinine to give to Jimmy.

Jimmy has bad dreams most every night, but they is worse now that he's sick.

Sick with the malaria, Jimmy don't wake up when I try to shake him out of his bad dreams. And when I put Lucky on the bed to keep him company, Jimmy starts punching at him and Lucky yelps and runs back to our room.

With the fever, Jimmy don't know he's home no more. He sees them Japs wherever he looks, even when his eyes is open. I think of when me and Eddie went Jap hunting and how Eddie got scared just like that, thinking them was real Japs behind them trees. Just like Jimmy, Eddie was too scared to hear me say them Japs weren't really there. I think of how the only thing that stopped Eddie from being scared was when I put that stick rifle in his hand and told him to shoot them Japs dead. Maybe, I think, people don't stay scared of things that ain't there if they fight back to make 'em gone. So when Jimmy gets all buggy and crouches on his bed, panting like Lucky when he runs far, I run and I get my wood sword out of my closet. I put that sword in Jimmy's hand like it is a rifle, and I yell to Jimmy, "Shoot them dirty Japs dead, Jimmy! *Pow! Pow! Pow!* Shoot 'em all dead!"

Jimmy starts swinging that sword all over the place like it's a baseball bat and screaming, "Fuckers! Motherfuckers!" He whacks the lamp with his rifle and it crashes off the nightstand, the bulb and the lamp both busting up in little pieces that skip across the floor. Jimmy leaps off the bed, and he takes the sword like it is one of them bayonets, and he starts stabbing at chunks of the lamp. He is cussing worse than a sailor.

Ma and Dad come thumping up the stairs and Ma is yelling, "What's going on? Jimmy? Earl? What's going on here?"

When Ma sees the broken glass and the little red splotches left on the floor from the bottom of Jimmy's feet, her hands lift up into the air, then slap down to her legs.

Jimmy is standing on the bed again, crouched up against the wall, holding that wood sword like it's a rifle and he's looking for someone to pow. His eyes, they is shining like glass, and his face is all sweaty. Jimmy aims his rifle at Ma and screams, "Get back! Get back! You come any closer and I'll blow your fucking head off!" Ma lets out a little scream, and Dad takes Ma by the shoulders and steers her into the hall.

"Jimmy?" Dad holds up his hands. "Jimmy, it's Dad. It's okay, son. You're home now. Your ma's here. I'm here. Earl's here." Dad talks real soft as he walks closer to where Jimmy is, but Jimmy, he can't seem to hear him.

Dad tells me to stay back, but I don't. I ain't scared of Jimmy, and he ain't really scared of me. He's just scared of Japs. When Jimmy aims his sword at Dad, Dad stops, but I don't. I go to Jimmy and I say to him, loud, "It's me. Earwig. Come on, Jimmy. Lay down and I'll show you my comic books. Them Japs are gone. You killed every last one of 'em." It takes a little bit, but Jimmy, he lets me take his arm and he lays down real good. He don't look at my comic book, though. He's sicker than a poisoned pup, so he just falls back to sleep.

Ma, she goes downstairs and fetches the broom and dustpan. "Go to bed, Earl," she says as she sweeps and cries, but I tell her no. "I'm a man now, Ma, and I can make my own decisions, and I'm gonna stay right here by Jimmy."

Dad checks on Jimmy before he leaves for the garage in the morning. He pats my shoulder and tells me I'm taking good care of my brother. Dad looks at Jimmy, who's still asleep, and he takes a slow, deep breath 'til his belly blows up, then shrinks like a flat tire. "Dad," I ask. "Has Jimmy gone buggy and falled off his rocker?"

"No, son. He's just having some trouble putting it all behind him."

"Funny, ain't it, Dad, how people can still hurt from things that is gone now, like Japs and broked-off arms? And funny, ain't it, how them pictures stay in our heads for a long, long time? It was like that after I cut Mrs. Pritchard's leg. Long after that cut of hers was healed up, I could still see it in my head, all open and bloody."

"Yes, son, that's how it is when people get a bad shock."

"Dad? How does a guy get rid of that bad shock in his head and get his war sorrows out, anyway?"

"I don't know, son," Dad says. "It just takes time, I guess."

When John comes home, Jimmy and Floyd and me go to meet him. His family comes too, and so do some of their friends. That whole bus station is filled up, 'cause John ain't the only GI coming home from Europe. They got signs to hold up when the bus pulls in, welcoming the soldiers home and saying they is heroes 'cause they winned the war. I feel kinda bad when I see them signs, 'cause Jimmy and Floyd, they didn't have no signs.

One thing I'm learning quick is that people don't think the soldiers who lost the battle in Bataan are that great. It's like at baseball games. Nobody cheers when the loser team walks off the field. It ain't fair is what I think. Jimmy and Floyd, they was as brave as John, and they suffered more, seems to me. Still, nobody thinks they're heroes.

Jimmy and Floyd hug John and he tells 'em that they look like shit. Floyd says, "You don't look so great yourself, Pissfinger." John, he's gotta go home and eat 'til he's stuffed and visit with relations, but that night he comes into the Ten Pin and gets drunk with Floyd and Jimmy. Mary, she comes along around closing time without being called now, and she hangs by the counter with Eva Leigh. Even from my little window, I can see Mary's got sorrows.

After them lanes are closed up, I go by Eva Leigh and Mary. Mary's watching Floyd over there at the bar, and she ain't got even one smile or laugh in her. "I hardly know him anymore," she says. "He's not the same. He hardly talks at all and he rarely sleeps. It's like he's a bundle of nerves."

I tell her that Jimmy ain't the same either. "But he's still Jimmy," I say. "I know it when I hug him. He's just Jimmy with sorrows. When he gets them sorrows out, then he'll be more like the Jimmy he was before the war. Floyd too."

Mary, she smiles all sad-like and she says, "How'd you get so smart, Earl?" and I tell her I don't know.

Then Mary, she talks about the same thing Dad talked about at breakfast. How that army, it ain't gonna help Jimmy and Floyd. "They're trying to get out of paying them benefits," she says, "so they're saying that their hands are tied because the Japanese didn't keep any records on their prisoners."

"That's crazy," Eva Leigh says. "They know they were there because the Rangers rescued them there. How can they do this?"

Mary shakes her head. "I don't know, but they are. And the VA hospitals aren't going to help them either. They're saying they have no idea how to treat these jungle diseases, and they don't know how to help them with the shell shock either." Mary sighs. "They just don't want to help them because they're afraid they'll be paying them benefits for the rest of their lives. Floyd and Jimmy and the rest, they did their best for their country, but now their country isn't going to do the best for them. It's just so unfair."

"I don't like the government no more," I say. "First they was mean to that Red Lawson guy, then they telled Jimmy and the rest of the Janesville ninety-nine that they had better shut their mouths about what happened over there, 'cause if they don't, then that Red Lawson is gonna get the court martial and go to jail. They tell 'em to shut up, and they tell 'em they ain't helping 'em. No, it sure ain't fair."

Eva shakes her head. "How can they do that?"

Mary shrugs. "It's not like any of them are talking about what happened over there anyway. Floyd won't say a word, even when I ask him. Is Jimmy talking about what happened, Earl?"

"No, he ain't, but I ain't asked him either, 'cause I don't want Jimmy to get into trouble and go to jail."

Eva Leigh is sticking bowling shoes in the little cubbyholes. "That must be what hurts the most. They served longer than anyone, they suffered in those prison camps, and what do they get to compensate for their suffering? Not even acknowledgment for what they've been through. Not even from their own country."

Them guys, they are calling me to come have a beer with 'em. I am old enough to drink beer in the Ten Pin now, but I don't drink much 'cause I still think beer tastes like horse piss. Still, I go over there and take the glass Ruby Leigh hands me.

Jimmy, he slings his arm around my shoulder. "What do you think of this guy here, huh? A job. Money in the bank. He went and grew up on us while we were gone, boys, and turned into a mighty fine man." The guys, they lift up their beers to give me a cheer. I ain't feeling so cheery, though, and underneath their drunk, I don't think they is feeling cheery either.

Jimmy guzzles, burps, then lifts his glass again. "And here's one for our comrade, Louie." They all cheer and drain their glasses and tell Ruby Leigh to fill 'em up again.

We get to talking about Louie then, and before we know it, we is laughing. "Hey, Jimmy," I say, "remember when Louie got shockered on Floyd's electric fence when he pissed on it when you told him to?"

Floyd laughs. "No shit. What a gullible idiot."

"Yeah," John says, "the poor, pathetic bastard." John snorts a bit when he laughs, then he says, "Hey, do you suppose Louie really hosed that girl from Janesville, like he said he did?" Everybody laughs, 'cept John. "No, really. I wonder. He said he screwed her, but who to hell knows. Christ, I hope he did. Wouldn't that be the shits, getting killed before you even got any?"

"He sure didn't have any luck with the dames," Floyd says with a laugh. "Remember, Pissfinger, when you gave him a hard time about running with Preacher Michaels's daughter? The ugly, fat one?"

"Yeah," Jimmy says, and he starts yucking it up good. "Pissfinger, you told him she looked like a goddamn pig, so what does the clown do? He swipes one of the biggest sows on Larks' farm, puts a scarf around its head, props it right up on the front seat of his car, and cruises up and down Main Street."

Jimmy starts to laughing so hard he spits his beer out and Ruby Leigh's gotta sponge off her titties. "Yeah. You said to him, 'Jesus, Louie, I'm sorry I poked fun of your new girl. Seeing her in the daylight like this, I can see she ain't half as ugly as I first thought she was.' "

We laugh 'til we ain't got no more laughs left, then after we quiet down, Jimmy says, "I can't believe he's gone." And then Floyd, he says the damnedest thing. He says, "Maybe he's the lucky one."

That night, Jimmy gets them nightmares again. When I get in Jimmy's room, he's crying like a titsy baby, holding his side 'cause it hurts. He's got scars there, so I think maybe they do hurt. I go downstairs to the bathroom, and I get the Mercurochrome, and I bring it back upstairs. I paint Jimmy's side and back good with that red shit, and Jimmy, he just rocks back and forth while I do this.

I cover Jimmy up when I'm done, and he falls back to sleep. I go downstairs to put the Mercurochrome back in the medicine cabinet, and Ma comes to the door, squinting, on accounta the bathroom light is bright.

"Earl, what are you doing with the Mercurochrome?"

"I was putting it on Jimmy's marks, 'cause he was hurting."

"Oh, Earl, those wounds don't hurt anymore. They're all healed now."

I guess Ma don't know a thing about places hurting long after they look all healed up.

Ma, she don't want Dad to bitch at Jimmy, but he does anyway, though he ain't mean when he does it.

"Don't you think it's time you come back to work, Jimmy?" Jimmy, he don't even lift his head up and look at Dad, and I think it's 'cause his head is pounding from last night's beers.

"Oh, Hank, I think Jimmy needs more time. He's still weak."

Dad, he ignores Ma and says to Jimmy, "Son, I know you've been through hell and back, but the war is over, and somehow you have to get back to living. This getting drunk every night isn't helping either. You need to get back to work. You need to have a reason to get up in the morning."

Jimmy, he drops his fork onto his plate. He looks mad and sad at the same time, but he don't say a thing.

"Tomorrow morning, Jimmy, you come back to work."

Without saying no more, Dad gets up and leaves for the Skelly, and Ma hurries back to the stove to get Jimmy some more scrambled eggs that Jimmy don't eat.

# Chapter 21

When Jimmy was gone, it felt like the whole house, walls and floors and everything, was holding its breath waiting for him to come back. Now he's home, and it feels like the house is still holding its breath.

Jimmy goes back to work, but he still goes to the Ten Pin every night to get drunk. He drags me along with him on nights I ain't gotta work, and I watch out for him and Floyd and help 'em both get home. Mary, she don't come to fetch Floyd no more, 'cause she moved back home with her folks and her sisters. She says she ain't coming back 'til Floyd stops getting drunk every night.

"I think Floyd gets mean to her when he's drinking," Eva Leigh says to me real quiet-like one night at the Ten Pin.

"Floyd, he wouldn't go hitting on no girl."

"I don't think he hits her either, but I think he says mean things. And I know he's been breaking things around the house."

I look across the place at Floyd, who is singing with Jimmy and the jukebox, and I pick at my pants.

That same night, that Bottoms Conner, he starts pestering Eva Leigh. He don't grab her arm or call her bad names like he done to Ruby Leigh that time, but he keeps hanging around her counter and trying to make her laugh at his jokes about peckers and hosing. When closing time comes, I tell Jimmy I gotta walk Eva Leigh home in case that Bottoms tries following her. "Ruby Leigh is going home with that GI over there, and I don't want Eva Leigh walking home by herself," I say. Jimmy thumps me on the back and he says, "You're a good man, Earwig." Jimmy says he'll walk home with me and Eva Leigh too, even though he's so drunk I don't know if he's gonna be able to walk at all.

Floyd's daddy comes to give Floyd a lift home. He asks us if we want a ride, but Jimmy says he thinks he could use some fresh air. Floyd's skinny dad has the damnedest time getting Floyd to the car, so I give him a hand. Floyd's dad looks sad. Real sad.

Jimmy, he is wobbly, but he can still walk if I let him lean into me now and then. Outside, it feels warm for winter, them snowflakes falling softer than a whisper. There ain't a noise anywhere except the soft squishing sounds of snow under our shoes.

"Why don't you boys come up for coffee? It looks like somebody here could use some."

"You got cocoa?" I ask, after Eva pays the sitter-girl and she leaves, and Eva Leigh says she does.

Jimmy falls down on Eva Leigh's wored-out chair and lights a cigarette. He's singing a bit of "Chattanooga Choo Choo."

Eva Leigh, she gives Jimmy a cup of coffee. It's made from old grounds, she tells him, and Jimmy says, "After what I drank in the camps, this will taste like heaven to me."

"What did you drink in the camps, Jimmy?" I ask, 'cause I think that's something maybe Jimmy can talk about without getting slammed in the clink. Jimmy's hand starts shaking, and Eva Leigh takes his cup from him so he don't get burned.

"Jimmy," I say. "I'm sorry I asked. I know you ain't suppose to be talking about them camps. I shouldn't a asked you nothing."

"It's okay, Earl," Eva says. "It's not like Jimmy has to be afraid of you or me repeating anything he says." And I tell her no, sir-ree, he ain't gotta worry about that, 'cause we're both real good at keeping secrets.

Eva, she sits down on the sofa by me. Her eyes is all soft as they look at Jimmy.

Jimmy, he pulls out a cigarette, but when he goes to light it, his hands are shaking so bad that he can't strike the match. Eva leans over, and she takes the Ten Pin book of matches from him and lights it.

"Strange how that scared feeling stays with you long after the danger's gone," Eva Leigh says. Jimmy looks up at her and his eyes are red from Schlitz. He stares at Eva for a long time, right in her eyes. And then those drunken eyes, which ain't quite so sunken and raccooned anymore, they get shiny like there is tears rising up somewhere behind 'em.

"Dad says to try to get back here, but I don't know how," he says.

Eva Leigh, she's got her hands cupped around Jimmy's coffee mug. "I think you just put one foot in front of the other, Jimmy. You go through your days, scared or not, the best you can. That fear, it's like a guard dog. It's been on guard so long that it doesn't know how to not be anymore. So if you sit still and wait for that fear to settle down, you're going to be waiting your whole life. But if you keep walking through your days, doing the best you can, breathing when you forget to, and reminding yourself that things are different now, then in time that fear starts to settle down. It's simple, but it isn't easy." Eva Leigh hands his coffee cup back to him.

Jimmy nods and sips his coffee. Nobody says nothing.

Before we leave, Eva Leigh rubs the side of Jimmy's arm a little. She don't say nothing, but she smiles without showing her teeth, and Jimmy does the same.

On the way home, it's still snowing. Them teeny flakes looking almost like streaks of rain under the streetlights. Jimmy, he scoops up a handful of snow from the bank along the sidewalk and, without saying nothing, he throws it at me. That snowball crushes against my coat and falls in clumps. So I get snow and cup it into a snowball too, and I throw it back. Before you know it, me and Jimmy is running down that sidewalk throwing snowballs at each other. Jumping over the banks and ducking behind parked cars, and laughing and cussing and having a real good time.

# Chapter 22

"Well, someone sure looks spiffy tonight," Ma says when Jimmy comes to the supper table wearing Old Spice and his nice blue shirt. "You going somewhere special?"

Jimmy pulls out his chair and sits down. He don't even wait for Dad to sit down before he starts spearing them chicken pieces, looking for a thigh. "What? Can't a guy look decent when he goes to the Ten Pin with his brother?" he says. One of Ma's eyebrows lifts up as she looks at Dad, but she don't say nothing.

Jimmy and me walk to the Ten Pin. Jimmy says the walking, even that little ways, is helping his legs get stronger. We walk with our hands stuffed in our pockets and our chins tipped down into our collars 'cause the wind is whipping.

"How long have you known Eva?" Jimmy asks me.

"Long time, I guess."

"I remember Luke Leigh," Jimmy says. "A real hotheaded, arrogant son of a bitch. Never could stand him. He was mean to her, huh?"

"He sure was. She used to come into the store all banged up."

"I wonder why she didn't leave him and go back home?"

"Well, her ma said she made her bed, so she's gotta sleep in it. That's what Ruby Leigh said. I told her I woulda just stopped making the goddamn bed then, if I was Eva Leigh."

Jimmy laughs.

"Ruby Leigh, she said it didn't matter anyway. She said the home Eva Leigh come from, it weren't no better than living with Luke. She said it was worse, even."

"Does she leave with guys after work like Ruby?" Jimmy asks. He ain't smoking, but still he's got smoke puffing outta his mouth, just like me, on accounta it's so cold.

"She sure does," I tell Jimmy. "She leaves with me. Why you asking so many questions about Eva Leigh?"

"No reason," Jimmy says, but I don't believe him.

"You sweet on her?"

"Nah," he says, but I still don't believe him.

That night we walk Eva Leigh home after work. And the next night too. Both nights Eva Leigh invites us up to her apartment.

Thursday night we talk about the crazy things we did when we was kids. Friday night we talk about music, and Eva Leigh plays songs on Ruby Leigh's phonograph. When Jimmy sees she's got a Louis Prima album, he lets out a holler and puts on "Jump, Jive an' Wail." He makes Eva Leigh dance even though she ain't never done the jitterbug before. Jimmy shows both of us the steps. Eva Leigh catches on real fast, but me, my feet just tangle like fish line.

Saturday morning Ma says, "You boys sure have been coming home late. You two aren't up to any mischief, are you?"

"No, ma'am," I say, "we ain't up to no mischief. We's just been stopping over at Eva Leigh's after work. We walk her home, then we have coffee and cocoa. Jimmy taught Eva Leigh to do the jitterbug." Jimmy, he kicks me under the table so I shut up, even though I don't know why I gotta.

"Eva Leigh?" Ma's boomerang eyebrows crawl halfway up her forehead. "She's a widow. And she's got a child."

"Ma," I say, "what's wrong with girls who is left alone with a kid on accounta their man gets dead in the war? That don't mean she's the kinda girl a guy should stay away from, then, does it?"

Ma's eyes get all big and blinky. "Well, I, I . . ."

"Pass the ham there, Earl," Dad says, then he asks Ma if she remembered to renew the newspaper like he asked her to. Jimmy, he just grins down at his plate.

That night, Jimmy ain't sitting at the bar with Floyd. He's got a stool parked right up to the counter where Eva Leigh is working. "Looks like Jimmy's moving in on your girlfriend, Earwig," Skeeter says.

When I get my break, I don't go to the counter to talk to Eva Leigh like I usually do. I go to the bar and I order a Coca-Cola. Ruby Leigh, she plunks the bottle on the bar and flips her head in the direction of the rental counter. "Those two are getting pretty cozy." She almost sings them words.

"You think Eva Leigh will still be my friend, even if her and Jimmy get to be sweethearts?" I ask.

Ruby Leigh, she reaches across the bar and she taps my hand. Her hand's still damp from washing glasses. "Oh, Earwig.

Hearts aren't like glasses you can only pour so much beer into. They're as big as the sky, and a lot of people can fit into them. You're her best friend. Nothing's going to change that. You filled up the spot in her heart where a friend should be, but she's still got an empty place in her heart where Luke used to be. Jimmy's just going to fill up that spot, that's all."

That night, Ruby Leigh, she is going home with John, and me and Jimmy, we is walking Eva Leigh home. Jimmy don't say much while we is walking. "You were pretty quiet tonight, Jimmy. You all right?" Eva Leigh asks as we're rounding the barber shop.

"Sure," Jimmy says. He says it the same way he says it when Ma asks.

Eva Leigh, she sounds just like Ma too, when she says, "Maybe you're just tired. You've been keeping some pretty late hours."

Eva Leigh pours coffee into cups for her and Jimmy. She is out of cocoa, so I drink half a Coca-Cola left in the icebox, even though it ain't got no fizzles left.

I'm tired 'cause I been up late since Thursday night, so when I sit down and Eva Leigh puts on slow, quiet music, I start to slink down into the chair and my eyes go droopy.

Next thing I know my brain is waked up, but my eyes is still sleepy-shut. I can hear Jimmy and Eva Leigh talking. They is sitting on the couch. I can tell 'cause their voices are coming from over there.

"I wouldn't have asked if I didn't want to know," Eva Leigh is saying, and she sounds a little pissed, even though she ain't yelling. I think maybe she ain't yelling 'cause she don't wanna wake me up.

Jimmy, he ain't quiet when he answers, though. "Yeah, well, if you really want to know what happened, then you're the fucking first. The government, my family, folks around here, you're all the same—nobody wants to fucking hear. It's get back to work, eat, smile, strut, act like it never happened so everybody can forget and get on with their fucking lives. Nobody seems to give a shit that maybe it ain't so fucking easy for us." I ain't never heared Jimmy cuss in front of a girl before, so hearing him now makes my eyes wanna pop open and gawk at him, but I don't let 'em.

The couch squeaks, like it does when somebody gets off it, and then I hear Jimmy's feet, shuffling around like he's walking in those circles he walks in when he gets skittery. He blows cigarette smoke out hard.

I keep my eyes shut and I tell my eyeballs to stop that damn twitching or Jimmy is gonna see that my brain is waked up and that I'm listening to something I probably ain't supposed to listen to. I stay real still and try to keep from breathing hard, and I think maybe Eva Leigh is doing the same, 'cause I can't even tell she's in the room no more.

"Maybe it ain't so goddamn easy for me, because no matter how many times I wash, I still feel blood, sticky on my hands. Sure, I eat, but maybe I'm just trying to forget the taste of fucking rats and rotted fish." Jimmy is almost shouting now, his voice all hoarse and tight. He takes a few gulps of air, like he's having trouble breathing. "And let me tell you something, Eva, no matter how much perfume a girl's wearing, I still can't smell nothing but the stink of death.

"It was fucking nuts over there. One day your heart's aching from watching dying men suffer, then the next day you're kicking somebody's rotten corpse because it's stinking up the place. It turned us into fucking animals.

"Goddammit . . . grown men crying out for their mothers, to God, to anyone who might come save them. But nobody came. Nobody."

I open my eyes a teeny bit when Jimmy stops yelling. He is up against the wall, sliding his back down along it. When he reaches the floor, he wraps his arms around his legs tight, like he's trying to get warm. When Jimmy starts talking again, it's like he ain't even talking to Eva Leigh no more. It's like he ain't talking to nobody but hisself, or maybe to God. "It was so damn hard, just trying to stay alive. No wonder when the guys were on the Jap freighters and our Navy attacked because they didn't know U.S. prisoners were aboard, our guys cheered, just waiting for one of those torpedoes to blow the ship to hell, putting an end to it all.

"The sad part was that, after a time, we didn't even give a shit who died." Jimmy gets quiet, like he's thinking on this a bit. Then he says, "Well, except for Cub. It was different when it was him.

"Christ, he was just a little shit. A poor farm boy from Brodhead. His ma was dead, his dad a drunk, his little brother with no one to take care of him but an old neighbor. Cub didn't have one goddamn reason to smile, but he smiled anyway. The rest of us were walking corpses, but not Cub. Cub could still joke around. I don't know how he did it, but he did. He made us laugh, and his laugh was all we had to keep us from losing our goddamn minds.

"Floyd was holding him when he died, Cub's head on his lap. Cub was sick with jungle fever, and just the heat coming from his head was making Floyd sweat. Floyd was begging him not to die. I had his hand. I counted the seconds between his breaths. When I got up to a hundred, I stopped. I knew he wasn't going to take another one.

"Floyd, he lost it then. He started shaking Cub, cussing at him, calling him a son of a bitch for dying, leaving us in that shithole without him. I moved Cub off of Floyd and folded his hands on his chest. I had to hold Floyd off when I was moving him, because Floyd went crazy. He was swinging at Cub's dead body. He wanted to beat the shit out of him. It was crazy, but that's how it was."

I open my eyes. Jimmy's got his face tucked down behind

his knees now and he's crying, his whole body's shaking. I look over at the couch to make sure Eva Leigh's still there, 'cause I didn't hear her for a time. She's there. She's looking at Jimmy, tears running down her face like rain.

She gets up and she goes to Jimmy. She gets right down on her knees, and she wraps her arms around him and lays her cheek right on the top of his head, and she rocks him like she rocks LJ when he ain't feeling good.

She rocks him for a long time, then she gets up and she takes his hand and helps him to the sofa. She sits down and pulls him right down beside her, taking his head and tucking it right under her chin. Jimmy, he's crying and crying, and I ain't never see'd Jimmy cry like that before, so that makes my tears run like rain too.

Neither of 'em look at me, so I put my eyelids back down.

It seems like forever before Jimmy stops bawling. When he does, he starts to apologize to Eva Leigh for saying them things, but she stops him. "Jimmy, I asked. You hear me? *I asked.* I think I understand some of what you went through, because all my life, up until a year or so ago, I lived in a prison too. I know the pain of holding secrets, and I know the pain that comes with telling them. Still, those secrets have to be told or we'll never be set free."

Jimmy sniffs hard, then after a time he says, "When I was on corpse detail, carrying those bodies to the pit, I envied them because they had been set free.

"I remember once, me and Cub we were carrying this guy who died from wet beriberi to the pit. I usually took pit duty with Floyd, but he wasn't around, so I paired up with Cub.

"The ones who died of starvation or jungle fever, they were easy to carry, light as sparrows, but the ones who died from wet beriberi, they were heavy as hell, their bodies swollen up to two, three hundred pounds. Cub was getting sick from the fever and I knew he was practically on his knees, trying to keep his end of the pole up. I called back to him, 'Is this fucker heavy enough, or what?' And that crazy little Cub, he answered back, 'No shit. What to hell was this fat fuck eating, anyway?' It struck me so goddamn funny, the irony of a comment like that, that I started laughing. I couldn't help it. There were guards standing twenty feet away, but still I laughed. I laughed so goddamn hard that I went down on my knees, right along with Cub.

"The minute the body hit the ground, it split open—like they'd do if you bumped them when they were so filled up with fluid—that yellow shit spewing all over until Cub and I were soaked with it, and all we could do was laugh. Laugh and laugh until we cried."

Jimmy, he takes a big breath. When he starts talking again, he is crying, soft-like.

"After Cub died, I didn't really have anybody I was close to, except Floyd, and I didn't know if he was going to make it or not. I guess somewhere inside, I knew I would, but I wasn't sure about him. I did my best to help him get by. I told him to look up at the sky when he couldn't stand the sight of sickness and death no more."

Jimmy sighs. "I told Floyd to think of Mary, and his old man, or anything that would keep him going. That's what I did. I thought of Earwig and how he needed me. I thought of my folks having to deal with me dying. I thought about all the things I wanted to do before I died.

"I believe it was thinking about Mary and his old man that got Floyd through those first couple years . . . but then he lost his arm from a jungle ulcer." Jimmy sighs again. "Crissakes, I just can't believe this. We survived, we got back home, yet here we are, still trying to find a reason to keep living."

They is quiet for a minute, then Jimmy says maybe he should wake me up and get me home. The couch squeaks, like Jimmy's getting up, then it stops. I hear Eva Leigh say Jimmy's name, real soft.

I know them smacking noises are kisses, so I keep my eyes shut tight. I ain't suppose to gawk when Jimmy's kissing on a girl.

The smacking gets louder, and I can hear their breaths coming faster, then it stops and Eva Leigh says, "Maybe it's a good time to wake Earl."

Jimmy comes over to me and whacks my shoe, saying, "Come on, Earwig, it's time to head home."

I make myself jump a bit, like people do when they get woked up fast, and I try to act like I didn't even know Jimmy was saying them things. Jimmy, he tries to act like he wasn't saying 'em either, but not Eva Leigh. She comes over to Jimmy and she takes his arm and she turns him so he's gotta look at her. "It's okay that you told me," she says. "I mean that." For a time, Eva Leigh and Jimmy look at each other, then he reaches out and wraps his arms around her, burying his face in the loopy curls sitting on her shoulder. I can tell they wanna kiss again, but they don't.

# Chapter 23

It's a Sunday and it's spring. Eddie's coming over so we can go fetch tadpoles. Like Eddie says, getting tadpoles ain't playing. It's more like fishing, and even old men fish.

Eddie comes up the back porch. I hear his pail clunkity-clunk down the steps, then Eddie pokes his head inside. "Hey, Earwig, you in there?"

I'm in the kitchen making myself a peanut butter sandwich and trying not to slop the peanut butter all over the counter or Ma is gonna yell her fool head off. "In here, Eddie." Lucky runs to the door to meet Eddie, his paws slip-sliding across the floor. Lucky likes Eddie a lot, so he jumps all over him all the way to the kitchen.

"That's a lot of peanut butter you got on there, Earwig," Eddie says, and I tell him it sure is. I mind my manners and ask Eddie if he wants a sandwich too, but he don't. He just wants to lick the butter knife.

"Wait 'til you see what I got! You ain't gonna believe it, Earwig." Eddie scrapes the knife across his bottom teeth, then grins like nobody's business.

"What you got?" I ask, but with that peanut butter sticking my tongue to the top of my mouth, it don't sound like that's what I'm asking.

Eddie's eyeballs skitter back and forth. "Where is everybody?"

"Ma's at some party for a lady that's gonna have a baby, and Dad, he went to the garage to get a wrench to fix the sink. Jimmy's over at Eva Leigh's. Why you asking, Eddie?"

Eddie is talking in whispers. " 'Cause I don't want nobody seeing what I got, that's why. I ain't suppose to have them. If I get caught, I'm gonna get it good."

"What you got, Eddie?"

Eddie taps his ass, right over his back pocket. "Pictures, Earwig."

I start to laughing. "You got girlie pictures, Eddie? Oh, man!" I see'd girlie pictures before. Skeeter brought some to the Ten Pin and showed 'em to me. Them girls sure was something, their titties sitting there like two giant scoops of vanilla ice cream, with two big cherries sitting right on top. They had their legs open too, but you couldn't see much of what they had there, on accounta they had that fuzzy hair covering that place up.

"Nope. I got something better than girlie pictures."

"There ain't nothing better than girlie pictures, Eddie."

"Wanna bet?" Eddie picks up the Skippy jar and twirls the butter knife around the inside to get some more. Lucky wants a sandwich, but Eddie's hogging up the last of the peanut butter, so Lucky's gotta have just plain bread.

"Well, let's see 'em, Eddie."

"Just a minute." He sets the licked-shiny knife on the counter and pokes his finger in the jar to rub out the last of the peanut butter. Eddie don't put down that jar 'til there ain't a bit left.

Eddie bends over and looks in the living room to check for somebody who might give him a lickin', then he wipes his smeary fingers on the sides of his shirt. "Okay, Earwig, but you gotta promise you're not going to tell nobody that I showed them to you."

Eddie digs in his pocket and pulls out a mess of pictures. "You know my uncle Mike?" I tell him I sure don't know his uncle Mike. "Well, he's my ma's brother. He's from up north. He went to the Pacific to fight in '43, and he took pictures and sent some to Dad. I snuck them out of Dad's drawer."

Eddie spreads them pictures on the table, lining 'em up neat as church windows, while I put away the bread so Ma don't harp. "These are pictures of real live dead Japs, Earwig."

Lucky must not want to see no pictures of dead Japs, 'cause he crawls under the table and lays down.

I go to the table to take a look. I pick one up. Eddie stands so close to me I can feel his breathing on my arm, and it's warm and smells all peanutty. That picture is something awful. So awful it about makes me get the dizzies. Them dead soldiers are all tangled up with each other, their guts all spilled out. But there ain't a Jap in that picture. Not a one.

"Ain't that something, Earwig? Their guts are all blown apart. Must be a hundred dead yellow-bellies slung across that field."

"What to hell you talking about, Eddie?" I say. "There ain't no Japs in this picture."

"What do you mean?" Eddie takes his finger and zigzags it across the photograph. "Jeez, Earwig, there's dead Japs all over the place. You go blind, or what?"

"These are dead Japs?" I ask.

"Sure they are, Earwig."

My breath gets hung up on my Adam's apple. Them Japs, they ain't nothing but men. Just men. Men just like me and Jimmy and Floyd and John. And some of 'em ain't even men at all, but boys just like Eddie. Even in black-and-white pictures, I can see they ain't yellow either. Not even their bellies that are naked, their shirts flung up to show the holes in their guts. Their bellies is the same shade of gray as their faces.

Eddie slaps another picture over the one I'm holding. "Look at this one, Earwig. It's a close-up. You can see the dead guy's face real good." That guy's eyes, they are wide open and so is his mouth. He's got a big dent where the rest of his head should be, and dark blood is soaked down the front of his shirt.

Not me or Eddie or Lucky hear Dad come into the house. Just all of a sudden he's there, standing in the kitchen. Eddie says, "Oh, boy" under his breath.

"What do you boys got there?"

Eddie, he backs his ass up against the cupboard, like maybe he thinks Dad is gonna take a swat at it.

Dad sets his wrench on the table and picks up a picture. He holds it out far as his arm stretches, on accounta his eyes ain't what they used to be.

"They is just like us," I say to Dad, and my voice is girlie-soft. "Everybody said they weren't. They talked about 'em like they was dirty, mean hornets or something, but all them Japs is is guys. Guys just like us." Dad picks up a couple more, looks at 'em quick, then tosses 'em back on the table.

"Nobody told me they was guys like us," I say. My eyes feel

all stingy and my belly ain't feeling so good. I'm hoping I don't start bawling in front of Eddie.

Dad looks at me for a time, then he turns away. "I guess that's something we can't think about too hard when we've got a war to fight."

"Why?" I ask.

Dad chews on his lip a bit, then he says, "Well, I guess we couldn't kill them if we thought of that, Earl. So we tell ourselves they're different, so we can hate them enough to kill them. That's the goddamn shame of war, Earl. Each side having to hate so they don't have to admit they are killing human beings just like them. Sometimes, though, people gotta lie to themselves so they can do what's gotta be done. This had to be done, Earl."

I look down at my feet. I blink hard and try to suck the tears back up into my eyeballs. "They ain't even got yellow bellies, do they?"

Dad's shoulders look all droopy. "That's just a name for someone who's a coward, Earl. That's all."

Dad scoops all the pictures up into a pile and holds 'em out to Eddie. "Where'd you get these, son?" I butt in and tell Dad they come from Eddie's dad's drawer, 'cause Eddie looks too scared to tell him anything. "I think you better take these home, Eddie, and put them back where you found them."

Eddie, he forgets all about getting tadpoles. He scoops up the pictures and runs out of the house. I can see him out the window, running so fast no one would ever know that he used to be crippled up from the polio.

After he's gone I get his pail that is tipped over at the bottom of the steps and I set it down on the porch, real gentle-like.

# Chapter 24

Mary is gonna have a baby. That's what she tells us when she stops by after supper while we is listening to *Fibber McGee and Molly*. She ain't looking so good, with her face all peaked and her eyes all red from crying. "Oh, honey," Ma says. She moves to the couch and sits down by Mary and takes her hand. Dad turns the radio off, and now I'll never know where Fibber is really going when he tells Molly that he's taking night classes when he ain't.

"I just don't know what to do anymore, Mrs. Gunderman."

"Does Floyd know?" Dad asks.

Mary nods. "He told me to divorce him now, before the baby is born. He said it's better for me and for the baby."

"Jimmy . . ." Ma says, like she expects him to say something that will make Mary stop crying.

Jimmy lights a cigarette. He don't say nothing 'til he's got all that smoke blowed out of his mouth. "Floyd's a mess. And it seems to me he's getting worse."

"Can't you talk some sense into him?" Ma asks.

Jimmy, he's dumped out lots of sorrows. I know this 'cause he ain't having them nightmares so much anymore, and during the day his step, sometimes it's got something a little bouncy put back into it. But Floyd, it's like he ain't got nothing happy left in him. I know this 'cause four times now Ruby Leigh or Slim had to tell Floyd to leave the Ten Pin 'cause he was getting real mean with the customers and talking crazy.

Jimmy tells Mary that he'll do what he can, but he ain't promising it will do any good. Mary smiles, even though she's crying. She thanks Jimmy and says, "I don't want to lose him, Jimmy."

"Maybe she's already lost him," Jimmy says once we get to the Ten Pin, when he tells Eva Leigh what happened. "Maybe we all have."

"It's so sad," Eva Leigh says as she looks over to where Floyd is sitting, staring at nothing, his cigarette ash long and fuzzy as a caterpillar. "Are you going to try to talk to him, Jimmy?"

Jimmy nods. "For all the good it'll do."

Jimmy picks up his Coca-Cola, which he is drinking most times now 'cause he says that beer is bothering his guts. He goes over to Floyd and pats his back and sits down on the stool next to him.

Most of the bowling lanes are empty 'cause it ain't a bowling-league night, plus, Tommy and the Toe Tappers are playing over at the town hall. I stay behind my triangle window and watch Jimmy sitting with Floyd.

Floyd, he keeps telling Ruby Leigh to fill up his glass. He shouts it to her even when she's way over on the other side of the bar taking care of somebody else. He is being so loud that a couple old guys at the bar turn their heads to stare at him. Floyd looks at them and yells, "What the fuck you looking at?" Slim, who is over by Eva Leigh giving her some change for her drawer, he looks up and I know he's thinking that it's almost time for Floyd to go home.

Jimmy leans his head over like he's trying to get Floyd to look at him. I can't hear nothing Jimmy is saying, 'cause he ain't yelling. Floyd, he don't pay no attention to Jimmy, not 'til Jimmy puts his hand on Floyd's broked-off arm. Floyd gets so pissed his face turns red. He jerks his stump away from Jimmy and gets off his stool. Jimmy's got his hands held up, his arms spread, and he's talking, but Floyd keeps backing up.

"Listen, you prick," Floyd shouts. "I don't need you or anybody else telling me what the fuck I should or shouldn't do! Get the fuck outta my way."

Slim, he hears Floyd and starts heading over to the bar. Floyd sees Slim and he shouts, "Save your breath, old man. I'm leaving."

Floyd circles around Jimmy and walks all wobbly-like to the door. Jimmy starts to follow. When Floyd gets to the door he turns around. He looks like a top that's winding down. "Get fucked, Gunderman! I don't need your shit. You hear me?" He opens the door and stops for a second like he's gonna say more, but Slim, he yells at Floyd to keep walking.

Mary ends up moving back with Floyd 'cause her ma and dad say she's gotta now that she's gonna have a baby. This scares the dickens out of Eva Leigh. Whenever Mary comes into the store I look good at her puffy face to see if it's got yellow and purple on it. It don't, but like Eva Leigh says, some hurts don't leave bruises you can see on the outside.

When Floyd stops coming to the Ten Pin, Jimmy gets worried. One morning when Jimmy runs home from the Skelly to fetch a hacksaw Dad left in the basement, he stops Mary as I'm carrying her groceries to her car. He asks her how Floyd is doing.

"Oh, Jimmy," Mary says. "He doesn't even leave his chair anymore, except to go to the bathroom or get another beer. He won't eat anything either. He's acting so strange that I'm afraid to leave him home alone, even to run here or to my doctor appointments."

Jimmy don't say nothing as he watches Mary drive away, but he sure does look worried.

It's a Sunday, so Jimmy ain't gotta work in the garage and I ain't gotta work in the store. I gotta clean the dog shit out of the yard, though, 'cause the winter snow's melted now and them turd piles is strung all over. Jimmy is helping. It's a good brother who will help you clean up dog shit when he don't even gotta.

Jimmy picks up a gob of dried turds with his rake and he shouts, "Think fast, Earwig," and he flings them turds right at me. I jump fast, but one of 'em hits me right in the leg anyway. "You son of a bitch!" I yell. Jimmy laughs.

So I scoop turds on my rake, and I'm just about ready to give 'em a heave when Mary runs up from the alley. Mary's got a pooch of a belly, and that would be the baby. She's got a hand over that baby and her eyes are all buggy. "Jimmy! Jimmy!" She can't hardly talk 'cause she lost her wind while she was running.

Jimmy drops his rake and hurries to her. "What's wrong, Mary?"

"Floyd. He's got his rifle out and it's loaded. He's just sitting there holding it. Oh, God, Jimmy, it's like he can't even hear me!"

"Earwig, you take Mary inside." Then Jimmy takes off running down the alley, which is quicker to Floyd and Mary's place than taking the sidewalk or even the car. Ma, she comes out on the porch and she asks what's wrong. She sees Mary carrying on and she hurries to her. I take off after Jimmy, Lucky barking at me from his chain.

My heart is beating in my ears as I run up the apartment steps. The door, it's open a little, but I don't go inside at first. I'm scared that Floyd is gonna be dead in there, his guts ripped open or his head half blowed off like the guys in Eddie's pictures. I lean my ear right to that crack and I listen. I can hear Jimmy talking, but I can't make out what he's saying. Jimmy wouldn't be talking to no dead guy, I don't think, so I go inside.

There is a kitchen first. I pass the table, where there's a bowl and baking stuff out like Mary was fixing to make biscuits or something, then I go through the living room. There is beer bottles on the end table next to a big chair. I peer down a short hall and I can see the bedroom down there. I can tell it's a bedroom 'cause I can see a dresser with a couple shirts sitting on top, folded pin-neat. Jimmy is standing in there. I can see his back parts through the doorway. It don't seem like Jimmy notices I'm here. "Floyd, talk to me. Come on, buddy. Put the gun down and talk to me."

"Leave me alone, Gunderman," Floyd finally says. "I mean it. Get the hell out of here and leave me alone." His voice don't sound mad, though. It just sounds tired.

"I'm not leaving. If you're gonna blow your brains out you're gonna have to do it in front of me, 'cause I'm not leaving."

Floyd laughs then and his laugh is too loud, too hard. "Why?

You want to watch the one-armed wonder try to figure out how to get a rifle up to his goddamn head?"

"Floyd, come on. Think of Mary. Think of your kid. Jesus Christ. She waited for you. You owe her something, don't you?"

"It's no good, Jimmy!" Floyd says, and he is coming close to crying now. "She waited for someone else, not some fucking lopped-off lunatic who can't even get it up no more. Jesus Christ, Jimmy, I can't even sleep through the night without crying like a goddamn baby. She's better off without me. So is the kid."

"So you're gonna let the Japs win, is that it? You didn't let those bastards break you then, but you're gonna let them break you now. Crissakes, Floyd. Think about it."

I scoot closer to the door. I can see most of Floyd, who is sitting on the bed, where sheets and blankets are dripped to the floor. He's got the gun in his hand. Floyd ain't looking so good. His face is white as his knuckles and he ain't shaved. His eyes is so raccooned that anybody can see he ain't slept in a long time.

Floyd, he moves his hand so his finger is right on that trigger. I get scared for a minute, thinking maybe he's gonna shoot Jimmy, but then my head tells me that he ain't wanting to shoot nobody but hisself.

"I can't take it anymore, Jimmy. I'm good as dead inside anyway. I can't feel nothing. I can't taste nothing. I can't see nothing but that place, and it won't get out of my head. I'm not here anymore, Jimmy. I'm still in that fucking hole and I can't get out." Floyd, his voice sounds like it's got tears in it, but he ain't got none on his face.

Jimmy's shoulders fall some then. "I know, Floyd. It was the same for me for a long time. Still is, some days."

"Jimmy, I don't know how to make it stop. Either I'm feeling nothing, or else I'm feeling so goddamn much rage that I want to rip the whole fucking world to shreds."

Jimmy sits down on the bed, careful-like, right by Floyd. "I know, Floyd. I know."

Floyd finally says, "I killed one of us." Floyd sounds like he's choking on them words. "On the Hell Ship. When I volunteered for work duty. You told me not to go, remember? But I did anyway, because I had to get to hell out of that goddamn shithole before I lost my mind.

"You remember that look the guys would get a couple hours or a couple days before they died, like their fucking souls already left, even while they were still breathing? Every time I'd catch myself staring off into the distance, not a fucking thought in my head, I'd think I was getting that death stare, and I'd get so scared I'd almost piss myself.

"They put us down in the hold. We were down there for five days, maybe six. We were packed like rats, and there wasn't enough air to breathe. A couple guys, they went nuts down there. They couldn't take it anymore and they just went nuts. God, Jimmy, you know what guys are like when they go nuts. They don't cry or scream. They howl. They howl like goddamn wounded animals."

Jimmy, he don't say nothing.

"The Japs, you know how scared they were of nuts. The first time, they stuck a couple rifles down into the hold and fired. The second time, they threatened to shut off our air vents. I didn't want to suffocate. I didn't want to die down there in a puddle of my own shit and piss. So me and a couple other guys, we choked those howling, nutty bastards. We choked them so they'd shut the fuck up. Our own guys."

"Floyd," Jimmy says. "Those guys were already gone. There wasn't anything you could have done to save them. Maybe what you did was the only kind thing to do."

"I didn't do it to be kind!" Floyd shouts. "I did it to save my own fucking ass! Just like when I tried to get Cub to hang on. I didn't give a shit if he lived for his sake, I wanted him to live for mine!"

I move closer until I'm standing right inside the room. Jimmy looks up at me. He looks pissed that I'm here. Floyd, he don't look up, 'cause now he's bawling so hard that he probably can't see me.

Floyd's head rolls back. "I did it to save my own fucking ass!"

Jimmy talks loud so Floyd can hear him. "That's what war is, Floyd, fighting to save your own ass. I don't know about the rest of you guys, but it took one shot close to my head to destroy any notions I had about being a goddamn hero. From then on, I was fighting to save my ass. Nothing more. I think we all were."

I don't think Floyd can hear nothing Jimmy's saying, on accounta he's still bawling. The gun slips outta his hand and clunks to the floor.

Jimmy, he starts to tell Floyd to "Shhhhhh," and I go all the way inside the room and I shake my head.

"He's gotta get his sorrows out, Jimmy."

Jimmy scoots the rifle away from Floyd's bare foot, using his boot to move it. Floyd's bawling like his guts is getting ripped apart, and it's a pitiful sound for sure.

It's a long time before Floyd stops howling. Then his guts heave, like them tears is trying to puke out the rest of the sorrows that the howls left behind.

"I don't know how to do this," Floyd finally says. He's got strings of spit from his top lip to his bottom. "I don't know how to live here anymore."

Then Jimmy, he says, "You just gotta keep putting one foot in front of the other, Floyd. Walking through your days the best you can until you walk far enough away from those hard times to be able to live again. That's what I'm doing.

"And you have to find something good to cling to, Floyd. Remember how good you felt when you stepped off the bus and saw Mary waiting for you? You said, 'Crissakes, Gunderman, look at that. She's looking at me like I'm Humphrey Bogart.' You remember that when the horror pictures start, Floyd."

"Mary . . ." Floyd says when his guts stop heaving and he can talk a bit better. "She deserves better than this. So does my kid. He deserves a dad who can hold him with two arms, for godssakes."

I clear my throat 'cause it's got some snot in it from the tears I'm crying. I take a couple steps so I'm closer to the bed. "My dad, Floyd, he don't ever hold me with two arms. He puts one arm around me, just like this," and I show him by putting my arm across his shoulders. "And that one arm, it's enough to hold my scared down. That's all a dad's gotta do to help, Floyd. Just use one arm."

Floyd, he looks up at me like it's the first time he notices me. He smiles, even though his eyes are still sad.

"You just walk through your days, Floyd," Jimmy says, and he's got teary eyes too. "And when you feel like you're going to fall on your ass again, you just grab tight to the first person that's nearby and you hold on until you steady yourself enough to take another step."

The front door creaks open and I can hear a lady's shoes clacking down the hall. Then Mary is in the doorway, her eyes all puffy from crying. She sees Floyd and brings her shaky hand over the top of her big titties. "Oh, Floyd," she says. And Floyd, he gets up and he hugs Mary with his good arm and she cries like a baby.

Jimmy tugs my arm and we leave. We walk home real slow, neither of us saying nothing. Jimmy, he wraps his arm around my neck and gives me a few little punches in the belly. When we reach our yard Jimmy lights a cigarette and leaves it between his teeth as he grabs his rake. I grab my rake too and drag another pile of dog turds toward the pile we already made. Shit sure does pile up over the winter.

# Chapter 25

We is going to the Founders Day Picnic tomorrow! That's the picnic they used to have a long time ago, before that Depression and the war come along. Folks in town say it's time to put them bad times behind us and have ourselves a little fun now, so that's what we're gonna do. This picnic, it is for some guy whose name was Henry something-or-other, but they called him "Willow" instead. He ain't coming, though, on account of he's been dead for a long time now.

Ma is all busy baking cinnamon rolls and pies for the baking contest, and me and Jimmy and LJ, we is in the garage making a kite for LJ to fly in the little kids' kite-flying contest. The kid with the kite that flies the highest wins. LJ is all happy 'cause

Jimmy's making him an army kite, just like he wants. Jimmy says it's gonna be the biggest goddamn kite there, but Jimmy don't say "goddamn" in front of LJ, 'cause LJ's got a cussing problem, so Eva Leigh says nobody can cuss around him no more.

Jimmy makes the kite shaped like a Stuart tank 'cause LJ likes army tanks. He don't paint the tank with the sides falled off, though. I cut the sticks first, right where Jimmy telled me to, and now I am ripping up stuff for the tail while Jimmy paints the kite. He paints a big-ass red V right over the tank, then he starts painting words inside that V. I know what the words say too, 'cause while he's painting 'em, he reads 'em out loud. That kite, it says, *Remember the Janesville 99* in blue paint, and under that, it says, *The Battling Bastards of Bataan.* He writes them words in red, and he says that's for Red Lawson.

"This kite here is gonna be the best goddamn kite at that picnic, LJ. You're gonna win a blue ribbon, for sure!"

The next day, Dad's eyes are rolling in his head when Ma gets to harping while he's trying to put them pies and rolls she baked for the contest in the backseat just right.

"Hank, that apple pie is going to slip right off the seat if you leave it there! Tuck it over alongside the rolls. No, not like that! Oh, for crying out loud. Move, Hank, I'll do it myself." All her fussing makes me damn glad I'm gonna ride to the picnic with Jimmy, Eva Leigh, and LJ.

"Those pies and rolls look and smell delicious, Mrs. Gunderman," Eva Leigh says, after Ma gets everything lined up perfect-like on the seat. "You'll win first prize in both categories, I'll bet."

Ma, she's got the nerves. "Well, I can only hope, but Edna Pritchard has won both categories for as long as I can remember."

That picnic is right at the park that sits smack-dab alongside of Spring Lake. When we get there the road is already lined up with cars and there is folks all over the place, carrying blankets and baskets and stuff.

"Hey, Earwig," Jimmy says. "How about you and me signing up for the three-legged race?"

I think my eyes is gonna pop right outta my head when Jimmy says that. "You ain't gonna run it with Dad like you used to, Jimmy?"

Dad laughs. "I think this old fart better stick to contests he can win. Like the pie-eating contest." I tell him maybe that's a good idea.

That three-legged race, that's when two guys tie their inside legs with a rope so it looks like they has got three legs altogether, instead of four. Then they gotta run like hell to that finish line. I ain't never runned the three-legged race before, but I'm gonna now, and Ma and Dad and Eva Leigh and LJ and Eddie and a whole buncha other folks is gonna watch.

Jimmy, he's shorter than me, so our knees ain't in the same place, but Jimmy says that don't matter. As Jimmy ties the rope tight around our legs, Eddie tells us to watch out for the Banks boys, 'cause they run like the wind.

When Jimmy gets our legs tied up so tight that the rope is pinching, we hop on over to the start line. We is stuck together so tight that we gotta hold each other around the waist or we can't move. Sam from the barber shop, he's the guy who's gonna tell us when to go.

"Don't pay attention to the guys behind us or on the side of us, Earwig," Jimmy says, talking real fast so he can finish saying what he's gotta say before Sam starts the race. "Just keep your eyes on the finish line and run like a jackrabbit."

Sam, he steps up to where us guys is standing on the line, and he shouts, "Okay, gentlemen, good luck! On your mark. Get ready . . ." Then Sam, he lifts a pistol from his side, and, *pow!* That gun goes off, and so does the crowd, hooting and hollering like we's got a pack of coyotes on our asses.

I move my legs soon as I hear the shot, but Jimmy don't. That leg of his, it just stands straight like a fence post stuck in the ground.

I look down at Jimmy as I'm dragging him along, but I can't see nothing but the top of his head. I don't need to see his face, though, to know that his legs got the freezes. The rest of his body don't, though. I can feel it shaking like it's a freeze-your-ass-off winter day, instead of a hot summer one.

"Jimmy!" I yell, but it's like he ain't hearing me. I'm moving best I can, but I can tell Jimmy's loose leg is just scuffing across the ground, slowing us down.

There ain't nothing I can do then 'cept take the arm I got wrapped around his waist and yank so that his leg that's dragging behind comes up offa the ground. I lean all tipped to the side, my hip poked out like Eva Leigh's used to be when she carried LJ, and I run like a jackrabbit, just like Jimmy telled me to.

There is five pairs of racers ahead of us. Two of 'em is Skeeter Banks and his brother, Charlie, and they is way out in front of the rest of us guys. That Skeeter, he turns his head around, sees me and Jimmy lagging behind, and he gives me a grin. That little bastard. I know he's gonna tease the shit outta me at work if he wins, so I run all the harder.

Out the corner of my eye I can see Eddie and LJ running right alongside us, egging us on. "Faster, Earwig! Faster!" So I run faster.

Jimmy, he's still freezed up, and he's still shaking. I yell down to him, "Run, Jimmy, run!" I get us right up next to Skeeter and Charlie when I feel Jimmy start to thaw. Then I lean up straighter so his other foot can get back on the ground, and Jimmy, he starts running hard too.

Skeeter and Charlie Banks cuss up a storm when we pass

'em. That crowd is just going nuts. I see Ruby Leigh standing there in her tight red dress, and I know damn well she's gonna give me a hug if we win, squishing her pointy titties right up against me. I grunt real loud and that grunt goes right down into my legs, making them move even faster. When that happens, me and Jimmy, we get across that finish line first!

I am panting and laughing at the same time when people start swarming us like bees, banging on our backs and buzzing about how damn good I runned. And just like I thought, Ruby Leigh, she gives me a big-titty squeeze.

I'm so goddamn happy it takes me a little while to figure out that Jimmy is leaned over, grabbing at the rope that is strung around our legs like that rope is on fire and he's gonna fry if he don't get it off.

Not paying any mind to the guys who is slapping my back now, I brush Jimmy's fumbly-jumbly fingers out of the way and untie the rope. Jimmy shakes his leg out of the loops and disappears into the crowd. Eva Leigh, who's standing nearby, she sees Jimmy leave and she disappears too.

Jimmy ain't around when Sam starts handing out the ribbons. Sam takes the blue ribbon first and hands it to me, and I know that means me and Jimmy are the number-one guys.

I'm showing Ma and Dad the ribbon when I see Jimmy and Eva Leigh disappear into a clump of trees at the end of the park. "You did a damn fine job," Dad says, but Ma, she don't say nothing 'cept, "Earl, is your brother okay?"

I wait by the quilt stand 'til Jimmy and Eva Leigh step out into the park. Jimmy's got his arm wrapped around Eva Leigh's waist and she's resting her head on his shoulder.

I hold up the ribbon and wave it as I run it over to Jimmy.

Jimmy takes the ribbon and looks down at it, then he looks at me and smiles a bit. "Well, you did it, Earwig. You won yourself a blue ribbon."

"We won it, Jimmy. Not just me. Our two legs, they was tied together like two halfa legs put together to make one whole leg. We was a team, Jimmy, and we winned it together."

I don't hardly even get them words out when a thought pops into my head. That's what me and Jimmy is! We is half brothers, tied together so tight that we make whole brothers. And ain't that something!

"That ribbon sure is going to look fine hanging in your room," Jimmy says, and I tell him I'll hang it in my room for a time, then he can hang it in his. "We'll take turns keeping it, Jimmy, 'cause this ribbon is for both of us."

Jimmy, he pats me on the back then and he laughs and says, "Who's stronger, Captain Midnight or Superman?"

"You are, Jimmy," I say.

And Jimmy says, "No, Earwig. You are."

We don't even get to where all the people are when LJ and Eddie come running up. "It's time for the kite contest, Jimmy! Hurry, get my kite. The kids are lining up already!"

"Then we'd better get our butts moving," Jimmy says. Jimmy and Eva Leigh give each other a little smile, then Jimmy drops his arm from her and runs off with LJ and Eddie to get the kite out of his car.

Me and Eddie and Jimmy and Eva Leigh, we go right over to where the people is lined up along the rope and we wait for Dieter Pritchard, who is judging the kite-flying contest, to tell the kids they can start.

Some of them little kids, they can't even get their kites off the ground, even though the wind is kicking up plenty good. They run and jerk their strings, but them kites just hop across the grass and plop over like they is drunk. There is mas and dads screaming all over the place, telling the little kids what to do, but lots of them littler ones can't do much of anything but bawl and stomp. But not LJ and the bigger kids. Their kites take off like rockets, filling the sky.

LJ, he is doing real good—leastways 'til that kite gets up real, real high. Then you can see he's got a problem. His feet are popping right off the ground, 'til only the toes of his sneakers is skimming the grass. "Whoa!" LJ yells.

"Holy shit," I say, "LJ's gonna get sucked right up into the sky!" And Eddie, he starts to laughing so hard he doubles over.

"Hang on there, LJ!" Jimmy shouts. "I'm coming!"

Them people, they are all laughing 'til they sound like a flock of geese when Jimmy kneels down and takes ahold of LJ's ankles. Jimmy holds on 'til that kite is flying so high that there ain't nobody but God who can read them words Jimmy wrote.

After a long time, Dieter Pritchard, he looks at his pocket watch and yells, "Time's up!" Me and Eddie and Ruby Leigh, we start cheering good 'cause we know that LJ's kite is flying the highest.

Dieter Pritchard, he goes out to where the kids are and he holds his hand up against the sun and gawks and gawks, 'cause it's him who's gotta say who won first and second and third. It takes him so long that after a while some other guys go out to help him gawk. I think it's a whole lotta fuss for nothing, 'cause anybody who ain't blind from starving can see that LJ's kite is flying the highest—and I'm pretty damn sure that Dieter Pritchard ain't starving.

We all think LJ's won that kite-flying contest, sure as shit, but that ain't what Dieter Pritchard thinks. When he gives out them ribbons he gives the blue one to Sally Banks, even though her goddamn kite didn't get nearly as high as LJ's. Then he gives them other two ribbons to two boys who is big as men.

"Hey!" Ruby Leigh shouts out. "LJ Leigh's kite flew the highest, you asshole!"

Mr. Pritchard, he is wearing a grin that don't look nice at all. "LJ here was disqualified, miss. The rules say the children have to fly their kites themselves, and LJ here, well, he had a little help."

"But LJ flied that kite fair and square, Mr. Pritchard," I shout. "And that blue ribbon oughta be his. Jimmy didn't even touch the string. He just kept ahold of LJ's feet so he wouldn't get sucked up into the sky!" This makes everybody snicker louder.

Ma comes over to me and she pinches my arm, and that means I gotta shut up.

LJ sure is bawling up a storm when them kids that won ribbons run past him, their ribbons flapping like flags. Pritchard is yammering about what time this starts and what time that starts. He is so busy flapping his gums that he don't seem to notice that LJ has breaked out of Eva Leigh's hold and is charging at him. "You dirty, lying son of a bitch! I won first place fair and square!" LJ starts kicking Mr. Pritchard in the shin. "Where's my blue ribbon? I want my goddamn ribbon!"

"LJ, you get back here!" Eva Leigh yells.

Mr. Pritchard plunks his hand down on LJ's head, trying to hold him back, but it ain't helping much 'cause LJ's legs is stretching like rubber bands. Before Jimmy can get through the people to get a hold of LJ, LJ hauls off and kicks Pritchard right in the nut sack. Dieter Pritchard grabs his balls and flops on the ground, moaning and groaning like he's dying.

"Oh, grab him, Jimmy," Eva Leigh yells.

Most of the ladies gasp, but some of them guys drinking beers, they start to laughing 'til they're howling. LJ gets one good kick to Pritchard's ass before Jimmy picks LJ up and slings him up over his shoulder. Eva Leigh and me follow Jimmy, and poor Eva Leigh looks like she wants to cry, with everybody staring at her boy like they is.

We walk over by the trees where there ain't no people. LJ

ain't kicking no more, so Jimmy sets him down. He rubs the top of LJ's head. "It'll be okay, little buddy. We know you won." LJ grinds his fists into his eyes.

Eva Leigh leans over and yanks LJ by the arm so he's gotta look at her when she yells at him for swearing and for what he done to Mr. Pritchard. "I don't care what happened, you can't go kicking people like that, LJ." Then she hugs him.

I feel bad for LJ. Even if he does got the orneries like his daddy, he *did* win that contest fair and square, and he oughta have a blue ribbon to show for it. I look down at the blue ribbon that is flapping against my shirt. I unwind the cord I got strung around my button, and I hand me and Jimmy's blue ribbon to LJ. "Here, LJ," I say. "You winned a blue ribbon fair and square."

LJ looks up at me and sniffles his snot back up his nose.

"Go on, LJ," I say. "You winned it, fair and square."

Eva Leigh looks like she's gonna cry when LJ snatches that ribbon and holds it right to his nose to look at how shiny and pretty it is. She reaches up and gives me a kiss, right on the cheek, and whispers a thank you in my ear. Jimmy, he slaps me on the back, and he looks so proud that I don't hardly care that I ain't got a blue ribbon no more.

# Chapter 26

It ain't more than a night later when Molly Franks comes into the Ten Pin before the teams start bowling. I can't hardly believe my eyes when I see it's her everybody is staring at, 'cause she's dressed up like a movie star.

She stands just inside the door, takes off her hat, and looks around like she's looking for somebody. It don't take no smart guy to figure out who she's looking for.

Eva Leigh looks over at the door to see what I'm gawking at.

"It's Molly Franks," I say. At first that name don't seem to clank no bell in Eva Leigh's head, but then must be it does,

’cause all of a sudden her face droops. She looks over at the bar where she thinks Jimmy is, but he ain’t there.

Molly goes up to Bottoms Conner and asks him something. Bottoms looks around a bit, shrugs, then points over to where I’m standing.

I get the nerves when Molly starts walking over to me. She is still tiny and cute like a piece of candy.

“Hi, Earl,” she says, and when she smiles a little I can see that her teeth is still lined up in a neat row like buttons. Eva Leigh, she is busy renting out shoes to the Texaco team, but I can see she’s watching us outta the corner of her eye. I want to say hi to Molly, but I don’t want Eva Leigh thinking I’m a two-timey friend.

“My, I just can’t get over how much you’ve grown. You were a boy when I moved to Chicago, but now look at you. How are you, Earl?”

I don’t wanna say nothing, but Molly, she just stands there waiting for me to answer, so finally I say, “I’m okay.”

Molly looks around a bit. She’s biting her pink lip. “Earl, I was hoping Jimmy would be here. Do you know where he is?”

I ain’t even got time to think up a lie, ’cause Jimmy, he steps out of the shitter right then. Molly sees him too, and her breath sucks in like a wind has caught her in the face. Jimmy goes straight to the counter and picks up the three pop bottles Ruby Leigh’s set out for him. He starts heading our way, then stops all of a sudden and goes back to the bar.

“Excuse me, Earl,” Molly says. And then that two-timer, she marches right over to the bar and puts her hand on Jimmy’s arm.

I wanna say something to Eva Leigh, ’cause she’s standing there looking at me like she don’t know what to do next, but I don’t know what to say, so I don’t say nothing. I go over to the bar and I sit myself right down on the stool next to Jimmy’s.

Ruby Leigh, she is looking like maybe she wants to dig Molly's eyes right out of her head.

Jimmy is fumbling in his shirt pocket. He pulls out his Camels and matches and calls to Ruby Leigh to bring him a beer. Ruby Leigh, she pours Jimmy a beer and plops it down so hard that some slops down the outside of the glass. She looks at Molly and says, "You want something?" Molly shakes her head and says no.

"I'll bet," Ruby Leigh says. She goes to the other side of the bar and lights a cigarette. She watches Molly and Jimmy through squinty eyes.

"You look good, Jimmy," Molly says. But Jimmy, he don't look so good to me. His face is turning red, and you can see his heart beating in his neck.

Molly is holding a tiny purse that's got beads stuck all over it. She starts picking at 'em while she waits for Jimmy to say something.

"What are you doing here, Molly?" Jimmy finally says.

"I came back to help my mother with my father. You heard he had a stroke, didn't you?"

"No, I mean, what are you doing *here*?"

Molly looks ready to cry 'cause Jimmy's voice sounds mad. I can't help feeling a little sorry for her, even if she is a two-timer.

"Is there someplace we can talk?"

"Isn't that what we're doing?"

"Jimmy, please. You know what I mean."

I take a swig from one of them bottles of Coca-Cola Jimmy's got sitting in front of him, 'cause my throat has got the nerves. I look over at Eva Leigh's counter.

Jimmy takes a swig of his beer. "I don't see that there's anything to talk about."

"I just want to explain some things, Jimmy. Please."

Jimmy takes a suck off his cigarette. He sits there a minute, then he turns right to Molly and looks her square in the eyes. "Let me get this straight. I went off to fight, got stuck in that hellhole for almost four fucking years, and while I was gone, you ran off to Chicago to marry some rich asshole. And now you want to explain? What the fuck is there to explain?"

Molly's eyes are watery. "I'm not married, Jimmy. I called off the wedding when Dad had his stroke. I told everyone I wanted to wait until Dad got well enough to walk me down the aisle, but that wasn't the real reason. Jimmy, I never loved Peter."

Jimmy grinds his cigarette out in the ashtray. He puts his hand up, the same way Dad does when he wants Ma to shut up. "You can stop right there, Molly."

Molly, she gives me a quick look. "If we could just talk for a minute."

I cross my arms right across my chest. Now I'm getting pissed, 'cause I know what Molly's up to. Ma says women who try to break up a couple, they is nothing but troublemakers. I used to like Molly, but I don't like her so much no more. She breaked Jimmy's heart, that's what she did, and now she wants to break Eva Leigh's heart too.

Molly breaks out in big baby tears. "Jimmy, I'm sorry. I was scared and lonely."

"And I wasn't?"

"I thought you were dead! For godssakes. I was young and scared and—"

"Oh, Jesus Christ," Jimmy says, and Molly stops talking. She stands there for a minute, them tears pouring outta her eyes fast now. She digs in her purse and takes out that little ring Jimmy gived her and sets it down on the bar.

Jimmy looks at the ring for a minute. He picks it up, real slow-like, and rolls it around with his fingertips. Then all of a sudden he jumps up and whips that sucker so hard you can't even tell where it go'd. Jimmy picks up his beer and one of them bottles of Coca-Cola and heads to Eva Leigh's counter.

Molly, she looks over at me then, and her eyes sure is smeared up from tears. I don't even wanna look at her.

Molly stands there for a bit after Jimmy leaves, then she says, "I'm sorry, Earl. I really am."

I get up to go over by Jimmy and Eva Leigh, but Ruby Leigh tells me it's time for me to get to work. Skeeter's already back in our room and the Texaco team is lined up to bowl, so I gotta hurry to lane one and lane two.

I lean up to my little window and I take a peek over by Eva Leigh's counter. Eva Leigh is busy handing out shoes to bowlers, and damn if she don't look like a wilted flower again. And Jimmy, he's just sitting there, drinking his beer, and looking at nothing. Next time I get a chance to take a peek over there, Eva Leigh is just standing there, like she don't know what to do next, and Jimmy is gone.

"I told Eva Leigh to go on home, that you and I would close up," Ruby Leigh says after we get the lanes closed up. I get the broom and, while I'm sweeping, I see Molly's sparkly ring laying on the floor under a table. That ring was suppose to be a promise but, shit, turned out it weren't a promise at all. I sweep that ring up with the rest of the dirt and throw it away.

# Chapter 27

Next morning, I got a screwdriver and I'm fixing a shelf that come loose on one end. I got a bunch of canned goods waiting on the floor 'til I get the shelf back up. Mrs. Pritchard, she is walking right past me to get to the stool. "Be careful there, Mrs. Pritchard," I say. "I got canned goods all over the floor and if you ain't careful you're gonna trip on 'em." I tell her this 'cause I don't want her falling on me, squashing me like a bug.

"I think she can see that, Earl," Ma says. I am on the floor looking up at Mrs. Pritchard. I can't see her face, just her wiggly belly and her hangy-down tits. I know damn well that if I can't see her face then it ain't real likely she can see me. "No, Ma," I say. "I don't think she can."

Mrs. Pritchard sits down with a big whoosh. "How are you today, Eileen?" Ma say's she's got a bit of a headache, but she's okay.

Mrs. Pritchard opens her purse, takes out a hankie, and dabs at the sweat puddles under her eyes. "Well, it sure was nice having our Founders Day picnic back again, wasn't it?" Mrs. Pritchard gets a grin on her face. "I couldn't believe that I took first place in every baking category I entered, but, as so many have said, there isn't a better baker than me this side of Ripley."

Ma gets the dishrag out and wipes the counter, even though it looks plenty clean to me.

"You know, Eileen, you'd have done better if your rolls were more uniform in size. You have to watch where you set your dough to rise, dear, or sure enough, some won't rise as high as the rest."

"Thanks for the tip, Edna," Ma says, but she don't sound grateful at all.

"Eileen, I hesitated coming here. I knew you'd feel a little jealous of losing out to me, but I didn't come to gloat. I came as a friend to give you that little baking tip and to give you another little piece of advice."

Ma, she stops washing the counter. "Oh?" she says.

"You know, Eileen, I've raised four boys myself, so I know how boys can be when they're sowing their wild oats. Still, my boys always made sure to use discretion and never conducted themselves in public in ways that would stimulate gossip."

"What are you getting at, Edna?" Ma says.

"Well, dear, I'm talking about Jimmy taking off into the woods with Eva Leigh, the way he did at the picnic. People noticed, Eileen. And they *are* talking.

"Now, I'm not much for catering to gossip, but I did hear that Molly showed up at the bowling alley last night to talk to Jimmy, then left in tears. How desperate that girl must have been to go into an establishment like that, unescorted no less. She still loves your boy, Eileen. Even Judith admits that. And although Judith doesn't exactly approve, she realizes she can't live Molly's life for her. I hope Jimmy realizes what he could have with Molly. Granted, young men often let their heads turn when a willing girl like Eva Leigh comes along, but in the end it's the good girls they want to marry, or it *should* be.

"Don't get me wrong, Eileen. Eva Leigh has always been friendly to me, and I don't have a thing against her personally, but she *is* a Leigh, and I don't suppose one person at the picnic forgot that for a second. It was bad enough when that son of hers behaved the way he did to my Dieter. The icing on the cake, however, was when Eva Leigh was bold enough to sneak off into the woods with Jimmy right in broad daylight in front of everyone in town."

It's funny how them mean thoughts are. It ain't like you get the notion to have a mean thought, then work hard to think one up. It's more like one minute you're just fixing on a shelf and feeling fine, then some fat lady starts talking bad about your brother and your friends, and that mean thought just slices through your head like an ax through fat. I gotta press my lips together tight to keep myself from saying the mean things I'm thinking.

Mrs. Pritchard starts to say something else, but Ma cuts her off. "Eva Leigh is a wonderful person. And as mean as that husband of hers was, she stayed true to him while he was in the war. That's more than I can say about Molly Franks."

"Well," Mrs. Pritchard huffs, "Molly thought your Jimmy was dead. You must admit, Eileen, that there were times when you wondered the same thing yourself."

"Edna." Ma slaps her rag down hard. "I think it's best we end this conversation right now."

"Good heavens, Eileen. I don't see why you're getting so huffy. I came here to talk to you as a friend about your son's future and his reputation and to give you a baking tip. If you don't care that people are gossiping about your son, then I guess I shouldn't care either. Perhaps I judged you wrong, Eileen."

Boy, I'm having lots of mean thoughts now, and them mean thoughts, they bubble up out of me so hot there ain't nothing I can do to stop 'em. I scramble to my feet.

"I shoulda axed that big mouth of yours while I had the chance!" I say. "There ain't nothing that comes outta your mouth that's nice!" Mrs. Pritchard gasps so loud it sounds like she's gonna choke on her tongue.

"I don't appreciate you talking about Jimmy and my friends, Mrs. Pritchard. Eva Leigh, she's good as anybody, and Ruby Leigh, she might be the town whore all right but she's got a heart of gold, just like Eva Leigh says." Ma is gasping now too, and I know I should shut my big mouth, but I am so pissed off I can't stop.

I lift my fist and start shaking it at Pritchard. Her eyes about bug out of her head when they look at the screwdriver I'm still holding. I can tell Pritchard thinks I'm gonna poke her with it, but I ain't, so I drop it.

"You ain't got no business saying you see'd Jimmy and Eva Leigh going off into the woods, like they was going off there to do something bad, when they weren't. But even if they was, you ain't suppose to repeat them kinda things. You don't hear me repeating what I see at the Ten Pin, 'cause Ma says hurting people's feelings by repeating what you see ain't nice. Them guys that come into the Ten Pin to get some free milk from Ruby Leigh, most of 'em is married, so I don't say nothing 'cause I don't wanna make their wives feel bad. Yep, I coulda telled you lots a times that I see'd your mister sneaking a feel from Ruby Leigh, but I don't say it 'cause I don't wanna make you feel bad, even though you make people feel bad all the time."

Mrs. Pritchard chokes out, "Eileen! Did you hear what your son just said to me?"

For a minute, Ma looks back and forth between Pritchard and me, like a deer in the road that don't know which way to run.

I don't wait for the good bitching and cuffing I know is coming. I run out the back door and down the street, going like a bat out of hell. Lucky sees me leaving without him, and he jerks so hard on his chain that he snaps it and catches up to me. I don't know where to hell I'm going, but I know I ain't going back to that store. Not ever!

Near midnight, Jimmy finds me down by the millpond, sitting on a rock by the water, getting chewed to shit by skeeters. He says Ma is worried sick.

"I ain't going back there, Jimmy. And if you know'd what I said to Pritchard, you'd know why I can't."

Jimmy slaps me on the back and sits down. He starts to laughing. "Oh, I know what you said to Pritchard, all right. Ma told Dad and me at supper. Shit, Earwig, she was laughing so hard I thought she'd piss her pants! She kept saying, 'I know I shouldn't be laughing, but, oh, did that old bat have it coming!' "

I can't hardly believe my ears. "That right, Jimmy?"

"Yep," he says, and he slaps me on the back again.

"I didn't mean to say them things, Jimmy. But that fat-ass sure did have it coming, talking bad about you an' Eva Leigh and Ruby Leigh like she was and bragging up that Molly like she is something special."

Jimmy lights a cigarette, and his smoke floats out on the water.

"Jimmy, I know why you and Eva Leigh went off into the woods like that. It weren't to sneak a feel or to do some hosing. It was 'cause you got skittery from that starter's gun going off. Ain't that right? You had to get away from people 'cause you got skittery, just like I gotta get away from people when I get skittery. I know'd Eva Leigh was just helping you, like Dad helps me sometimes."

"Don't worry about what people think, Earwig. Long as you know what's true, that's all that matters."

"Jimmy? Eva Leigh, she done being upset about Molly showing up at the Ten Pin?"

Jimmy blows more smoke across the water. "She wants me to take a few days away from her, Earwig. She said she knows it wasn't my idea to break things off with Molly, and now that Molly wants me back, she thinks I need some time to sort out my feelings."

This makes me scared. "You told her you didn't need no time to do any sorting, didn't you, Jimmy?"

Jimmy, he don't answer, so I ask all over again.

"Earwig, Eva thinks maybe I turned to her just because she was there when Molly wasn't."

"But you telled her that wasn't true, didn't you?"

Jimmy don't say nothing.

"Jimmy, that ain't true, is it?"

Jimmy flicks his cigarette into the swirling water. "I don't think so, Earwig. I just don't know."

I feel a lump of sad drop into my guts when Jimmy says that. I always liked Molly 'cause she smiled pretty, but Eva Leigh, there's something extra special about her. It's like she knows how you feel and she always makes sure to let you know that you ain't dumb for feeling it.

"Hey, I got a couple beers in the car. You want one, Earwig? I know I sure could use one." I tell him I want one, even though I don't.

Jimmy gets the beers and hands me one as he sits down. "Sometimes I think I'm just as fucked up from the war as Floyd is."

"You ain't fucked up as Floyd, Jimmy."

"Yeah, I am. Some days, I want to take that loan the bank says they'll give me, buy a decent car, put a down payment on the Williams place, and marry Eva Leigh and raise a family. The next minute, though, I just wanna get in my car and drive just as far as I can go, never looking back.

"When Molly showed up at the Ten Pin, there was a second there when all I wanted was to take her in my arms and go back to the way things were before. The war has me all fucked up. I don't know what I want anymore."

"Jimmy?" I say, after we sit awhile.

"Yeah?"

"Is Floyd gonna be okay?"

"I hope so. He's messed up in the head right now, but he's doing all right. He's had a lot a shit to deal with in his life, with his ma dying, and his dad being a drunk all those years. He's got a lot of shit to deal with from the war, and new responsibilities on top of it. Still, he's trying, Earwig. He's doing the best he can."

"Jimmy?" I say again, even though I know I'm being a real earwig, asking so many questions.

"Yeah?" Jimmy says.

"When you was in that war, did you shoot some Japs?"

"Yeah."

"How many Japs?"

"I don't know. Dozens, I suppose."

"Was it hard doing that, Jimmy? Killing them guys that was just people like us?"

"At first, yeah. Then after a time it wasn't no harder than killing a deer."

"That right?"

"Well, no, it probably ain't right, Earwig. But that's how it was."

Jimmy flips his head back and downs the rest of his beer, then he tosses the empty bottle far into the water.

"I see'd dead Japs in some pictures Eddie swiped outta his dad's drawer. Some guy took 'em and sent 'em to Eddie's dad. I thought them Japs was different. You know, like not people or somethin'. Their eyes are different, I could see that on the one picture where the guy was staring, even though he was dead, but that's all I could see that was different. They ain't really no different than us, though, are they, Jimmy?"

Jimmy scrapes his hand over the ground, scooping up a handful of little rocks, and he starts tossing 'em into the water, one at a time. For a while, he don't say nothing, then he says, "When I was at O'Donnell, this Jap guard handed me the rest of his cigarette. I didn't know what in hell to think at first. I thought maybe it was some sort of trick, so I wasn't going to take it. Then I looked him in the eye and I saw he wasn't up to anything. He was just being a decent human being, and I realized that him and I were nothing more than little pawns in a big game."

Jimmy gets up and brushes off the back of his ass. "Come on. We'd better get back before Ma puts together a posse to go looking for you."

We just get pulled in the driveway when a car comes off the street and pulls in behind us. I turn around and look, wondering who in the hell's coming this time of night, and hoping to hell it ain't got nothing to do with Floyd wanting to blow his head off so I gotta hear some more screaming and howling. I twist around and look out the back window. It ain't nobody saying somebody's gonna blow their head off, but I think maybe there's gonna be some screaming and bawling anyway, 'cause it's Molly.

I look at Jimmy soon as we step out of the car. He don't look like he's gonna be doing no screaming, though. He just looks tired. Jimmy tells me to go on in the house, but I tell him I gotta wait for Lucky to take a piss before I can take him in.

Lucky is barking at Molly, probably 'cause he don't like two-timers either, and Jimmy tells Lucky to shut up. Lucky takes a leak on Jimmy's tire, then runs off to the backyard and starts sniffing around, running in them little circles he always makes when he's looking for a good place to take a shit. Jimmy tells me to go on inside and he'll let Lucky in when he's done, but I don't. I circle 'round the back of the house, go up them three porch steps, then stand flat against the house, hoping I can hear something. I don't hear nothing, though. When I lean over to take a peek to make sure they're still there, Jimmy tells me again to go inside. "If I do that, Ma's gonna be poking her nose out here," I say, so Jimmy says I should just wait on the porch.

I don't stay on the porch, though. I go in the backyard where Lucky is, his butt crouched, taking his crap. I'm so mad at that two-timer, I'm wishing I could pick up a turd and throw it at her.

That Molly, she's talking so soft a guy can't hear her, and Jimmy, he ain't talking at all. He's leaned up against his car, his ankles crossed, his head down while he smokes. They don't talk long, then Jimmy crushes out his cigarette and pulls his butt off the car like he's gonna leave. Then Molly, that troublemaker, she puts her hand on his chest and leans over and gives him a kiss right on his lips. Jimmy keeps his hands in his pockets, and he don't even move when Molly does that. Molly hurries to her car, and Jimmy, he heads to the house. I wanna chase after him and find out what that two-timer said, but Lucky won't come in. By the time I get that damn dog inside, there ain't no Jimmy downstairs, just Ma, and I gotta sit down and listen to her harp at me about how I better never run off like that again.

I can't run off, but Jimmy's gonna. That's what he tells me when he wakes me up a couple hours later. "Where you going, Jimmy?" I am up on my elbows and my eyes ain't hardly open yet, but my ears sure as hell are.

"I don't know. I just need to get away for a few days to think."

"About Molly and Eva Leigh?"

"About everything. Tell Ma and Dad not to worry, and don't you worry either. I'll be fine."

Jimmy gives me a pat and tells me to go back to sleep, but I don't. I lay there long after Jimmy leaves, thinking and thinking and thinking, and wondering why in the hell Jimmy can't think at home if I can.

Next morning, I tell Ma and Dad that Jimmy's gone off for a few days. Ma, she looks at Dad like she's expecting him to explain, even though I just did.

Dad says, "Don't worry, Eileen. He just needs some time to himself."

Ma gets huffy. "It's that Franks girl, I'll bet. I wish she'd never come back here!"

Dad shakes his head. "It's not Molly. It's the war."

When I go back to the Ten Pin, I gotta tell Eva Leigh that Jimmy's gone off. Eva Leigh nods. She looks tired, like maybe she ain't got no trouble thinking at home either.

Eva Leigh, she plays with the bottom of her blouse, picking at a thread that's dangling there. "Earl, I feel awful asking you this, but do you know if Jimmy's seen Molly since she was here the other night?" Eva Leigh don't hardly get that question out, when her head and hands start making little shakes. "No, no, don't answer that, Earl. It was unfair of me to ask."

For days Ruby Leigh bitches about Molly. She calls her a two-timing bitch, and she talks about how Molly was born with a silver spoon stuck up her ass, which is something I never even knowed could happen to a baby.

A few days later, I'm at the bar, bringing back the empties Skeeter left in the pinsetters' room, when Ruby Leigh says, "Ah, Earl, just look at her over there. It's like her heart's been torn out and stomped on. She deserves someone who treats her good, you know? She's busted up right now, yet all she talks about is how she hopes that Jimmy can find some peace and happiness. Shit, if that were me I'd be kicking him in the balls and ripping Molly Franks's hair out, curl by pretty curl. Eva Leigh's a bigger person than that, though."

I don't see Eva Leigh smile the whole time Jimmy's gone, 'cept for when she comes into the store for some milk and Ma takes both her hands and says, "Jimmy will come home to you, Eva. Don't you worry. I know my boy, and I know he'll realize that you're the best thing that's ever happened to him."

# Chapter 28

I guess Ma does know her boy, 'cause after eight days Jimmy comes into the Ten Pin while the women's league is bowling, and right there, with everybody gawking on and me watching from my little window, he gets right down on his knee and tells Eva Leigh that he loves her and wants to marry her. Good thing everybody stopped what they was doing to watch, or I woulda gotten the shit whacked out of my legs for sure.

Eva Leigh, she can't do more than nod her head and cry and laugh, all at the same time. Jimmy picks her up and twirls her around, and Ruby Leigh, who is all girlie-crying too, she lifts a glass and shouts, "Drink up, everybody. The next one's on the house!"

Jimmy don't come home 'til early the next morning. I hear his car pull in and I go to his room to wait for him to take a piss and get upstairs. When he comes up, I shake his hand, like you're suppose to do when somebody says they is getting married.

"Hey, Jimmy," I say, "you remember how you said after you get married, I get to live with you?" Jimmy peels off his shirt. His hair is a mess. He throws his shirt at me and it smells like Eva Leigh.

"Sure I remember, Earwig. I even thought to talk it over with Eva tonight. She said she'd love having you with us. And LJ, well, you know he'd love it. You're his best buddy."

"Well, Jimmy," I say, "I ain't gonna move in with you and Eva Leigh and LJ. Me and Lucky, we is gonna move in to our own place." Jimmy's undoing his pants, but he stops and squints at me.

"Me and Ruby Leigh, we was talking it over tonight after we closed up the place. She telled me that she is gonna move to Milwaukee after the wedding and start herself a new life. That got me to thinking then about how maybe I should start a new life too.

"Ruby Leigh, she said, 'Why don't you move into our place after we move out?' So Jimmy, that's what I'm planning to do, if Sam don't mind. Slim telled me before he left tonight that he ordered them automatic pinsetting machines that they is using in the cities now and that I ain't gonna be a pinsetter no more. At first I thought he was telling me I was shit-canned, but instead he telled me he's too old and tired to spend so much time at the Ten Pin anymore, and he asked me if I can be the custodian. That means I'm gonna keep the place cleaned and fixed up. I gotta boot the drunks out too, if they get too mouthy."

"Jesus, Earwig."

"Ruby Leigh, she figured it out for me on paper. With the money I'm gonna make at the Ten Pin, working six nights a week now, and what Ma pays me for helping in the store, plus the money I got saved up, I got more than enough to live on my own, Ruby Leigh says."

"Earwig, you sure about this? 'Cause, like I told you, Eva said she'd be glad to have you move in with us. There'll be plenty of room, if that's what you're worried about."

"No, Jimmy, I ain't worried about that. It's just that I'm all growed up now, and I want to live like I am."

"You'll get lonely all by yourself."

"I ain't gonna be all by myself, Jimmy. I got Lucky. And Eddie, he'll come by to see me pert' near every day. We is gonna play checkers and eat candy bars and drink Coca-Cola and look at comic books and stuff. And you and Eva Leigh and LJ, you can come by to see me now and then, and so can Ma and Dad. I can ride my bike and see you guys sometimes too. I'm gonna buy me a radio and listen to it even when I'm busy, and I might even save up for one of them television sets so I can see the pictures that go with them stories. Won't that be something!"

Jimmy, his mouth is smiling, but his eyes, they look a little sad.

# Chapter 29

Me and Jimmy, we start packing up our stuff a few days before Jimmy's wedding, 'cause the day after, we is moving out to start our new lifes. We dig out our closets and we both find a lot of good junk. Jimmy, he don't want most of his good junk, so he gives the stuff to me, and I put it in the boxes lined in the hall that got a big E writ on the side.

Ma, she fusses over our boxes every time she comes upstairs, taking clothes out and folding 'em up again, and taking out shoes and boots and tying the laces together so they pair up. "Earl, you're not taking those silly bottle caps with you, are you?" she says when her and Dad come upstairs to see how we're doing.

"I sure am," I say, and Dad tells me he thinks that's a good idea.

Ma asks if I have enough socks and underwear, and she tells me she don't want me going without nothing, and all I gotta do is ask if I run out of things like toilet paper or milk. She tells Jimmy the same. Dad laughs a little. "Eileen, stop fussing. It's not like they're moving across the ocean, for crissakes. Jimmy's just moving outside of town, and Earl is just going down the street. They'll be fine."

Ma, she gets all teary-eyed. "It's silly of me, I know," she says, dabbing her eyes with the corner of her apron. "But this house is going to feel so empty with you two gone." Jimmy, he goes to Ma and puts his arm around her shoulder, so I go and put my arm around her other shoulder, right over the top of Jimmy's. Ma looks up at Jimmy, then she looks at me. "My boys," she says. "Where did the time go?"

The night before Jimmy and Eva Leigh's wedding, we don't hardly get to sleep when Lucky zips down them stairs, lickety-split, and wakes up the whole house with his barking, 'cause somebody's pounding on the door. Dad's the first one to the door. By the time I can get down the stairs, Floyd's standing there, and boy, does he got the nerves!

"It's Mary. The baby's coming, Mr. Gunderman! I need to use your phone to call Dr. McCormick. Mary says she'll never make it to the hospital in Ripley."

Dad pulls Floyd into the house. "Settle down there, son."

"Hank, what is it?" Ma says as she's coming into the room.

"The baby's coming, Eileen, and Mary doesn't think she can make it to Ripley. Call Dr. McCormick, will you?"

"Oh, dear!" Ma says. She hurries to the kitchen.

"Holy shit," Jimmy says, as he comes down the stairs.

"Settle down, boys," Dad says. "Ma will get Dr. McCormick

on the phone and he'll come and take care of Mary just fine. Women have been having babies at home a hell of a lot longer than they've been having them in hospitals. Everything will be fine, Floyd."

Dad is smiling, but he stops when Ma comes back into the living room and says that Dr. McCormick went out on a call and that Mrs. McCormick, she weren't awake enough to hear where he said he was going. "She said she'll send him over as soon as he gets back."

"Oh, shit! Oh, shit!" Floyd says.

Dad rubs his chin a bit, then he says, "Floyd, you head home and tell Mary not to worry. We'll be right over, as soon as we pick up Mrs. Lark."

"Mrs. Lark?" Ma yells. "She delivers calves, Hank, not babies!"

"Well, there can't be that much difference, can there?" Dad says. "Floyd, you go home and put some water on to boil, and get some clean towels together, and you keep Mary calm. We'll be right along." Ma hurries off to put on some clothes.

"Okay, okay," Floyd says. He's so skittery that the empty sleeve he's usually got tied up is flapping like a white flag. "I keep Mary calm and get together some towels, and boil some water. Shit, what am I boiling water for again?"

"I don't know exactly, Floyd, but I know you have to boil some," Dad says. "Now, go. Hurry."

"I'll go with you, Floyd," Jimmy says, slipping on his shoes, even though he ain't got any socks on.

"Me too," I say. I almost pop poor Lucky's head off shutting the door when I don't see him trying to squeeze out behind me. I shove his head back inside and run to catch up with Jimmy.

We run like jackrabbits down the alley, stirring up them sleeping dogs until the whole neighborhood is filled with barks. My heart is beating right in my ears. I ain't never been around no lady having a baby before, but I heared they scream like they's getting killed.

Mary ain't screaming when we get there, though. Least not 'til Floyd tells her that Dr. McCormick ain't coming, just Mrs. Lark. *"What?"* she bellers. "*Mrs. Lark?* Oh, my God!" Then, just when I think Mary ain't gonna scream and carry on, she doubles over as much as she can with that big belly and screams like she's got a sword stabbing through her.

Floyd hurries to catch her so she don't fall over, then Jimmy and Floyd help get her down the hall to the bed.

Mary, she holds her fat belly as they lower her down. She's got two wet spots over her titties, like she dipped 'em in a sink of dishwater by accident.

"Oh, God, Floyd," Mary says, after that pain lets up a bit. She reaches for his hand and squeezes it tight. "I'm scared," she says, then she starts screaming again and that pain makes her close up like a jackknife.

When Ma and Dad show up with Mrs. Lark, me and Jimmy and Floyd gotta wait in the living room with Dad. Ma and Mrs. Lark go into the bedroom and shut the door behind 'em.

"The water," Dad says. "We gotta boil the water." Now Dad is as shook up as Jimmy and Floyd and me.

We look for a pan, but we ain't got a goddamn clue if we is suppose to boil lots of water or just a little bit. So we get out a big pan, a middle-sized pan, and a little pan, and we boil water in all three of 'em.

Us guys sure is a mess. Jimmy and Floyd smoke and walk in little circles, and Dad, he walks in a long loop, his thumbs stringed through his belt. I don't even know I'm picking at my pants 'til I feel my fingers pinch some of my skin.

"Women have babies all the time," Dad says. "We've got to remember that. Childbirth is as natural as taking a shit." Mary lets out a big-ass holler and we all stop, our ears perked up like Lucky's when he hears a loud noise.

"Jesus," Floyd says, when that scream quiets some. "Some women die having babies, don't they?" And Dad tells him yes, but that ain't gonna happen to Mary.

Floyd sits down on the couch and blows his breath out, hard. "I wish my ma was here." He rubs his leg a bit with the only hand he's got. "Ma would have liked Mary, and she sure would have liked having a grandkid."

Dad goes over to Floyd and squeezes Floyd's shoulder. "I know, son. I know."

Then, just like that, we hear Mrs. Lark yell, "Push, Mary! Push!"

Mary's scream sounds like a siren, only that scream don't fall down, it just keeps rising and rising. Floyd leaps up. "Jesus Christ!" he says, and he looks like he's gonna jump right outta his skin.

Mary's scream stops, lickety-split, and I listen hard, thinking she keeled right over and died. Then I hear it, little squeaks that turn into the screeching of a baby. I know the rest of 'em hear it too, 'cause they start to laughing.

Floyd runs down the hall, me and Dad and Jimmy running right behind him.

Floyd throws open the door. I can see right over the top of Jimmy and Dad's heads, and boy, I'm sorry I can! There is Mary, her legs spread like chicken wings, and on the bloody sheets, right between her legs, is a gray blob that looks like a gut pile.

"Holy shit!" I say. It don't look like no baby I ever see'd before, but sure enough, it's gotta be the baby, 'cause I can hear it crying.

"Get out of here!" Mrs. Lark yells, and Ma runs to push us out the door.

"Mary! Mary!" Floyd is yelling.

"It's a girl, Floyd! A little girl!" Mary yells back.

That didn't look like no baby girl I ever see'd before, and I hope to hell I ain't gotta tell Floyd he's got a cute baby there, 'cause that sure would be a lie.

We is standing around like fools when Ma comes to get the water. Soon as she steps out of the hall and sees that foggy air swirling, her boomerang eyebrows scrinch down. She hurries to the stove and peers into the pans. "What on earth were you boys doing here? Boiling water for a bath? Good grief, couldn't you smell this little pan scorching?" She shakes her head, opens a drawer and grabs a pair of scissors, and tells us all to go sit down and stay out of the way.

Floyd, he can't go sit down, though, on accounta he's gotta puke 'cause he's got the nerves, even though all the screaming is over. While he's off puking, I tell Dad that I hope that baby don't stay as ugly as she looked when she comed out, all gray and flubbery like that.

Dad laughs, and so does Jimmy. "That wasn't the baby, Earl. That was the afterbirth. The sack the baby was growing in." I sure am relieved to hear that, 'cause Floyd probably woulda puked all over again, if that had been the baby.

Mary is sitting up, propped on pillows, when they finally let us in. She's wearing a pretty pink nightie, and that baby's wrapped up in pink too. Mary's got tears in her eyes, but she's smiling big.

Floyd hurries to the bed and kisses her. Mary pulls back the baby's blanket, so we can see all of her. That bitty baby is kicking and clawing like a turtle that's flipped over on its back. I'm real glad to see she ain't got no silver spoon sticking out of her ass.

I move closer to the bed so I can see her better. When she stops all that fussing, she looks kinda cute, even though she's wrinkled like a raisin, and her mouth is all bald inside. Floyd reaches down and takes her little fist, which ain't no bigger than a plum pit, and gives it a few bounces.

That baby, she opens her eyes while I'm bending over taking

a look, and she turns them teeny button eyes right to me. "She's looking at me! She's looking right at me!" I say.

"That's your uncle Earwig," Floyd tells her, and that gets me to laughing.

"I want to name her Kathleen," Mary says to Floyd. "After your mom." This makes Floyd get all choked up, and it makes them ladies drop tears all over the place.

We is so busy looking at the new baby that it takes awhile before any of us figure out that somebody's knocking on the door.

Ma goes to open it and comes back with Dr. McCormick. He sets his doctor's bag down on the dresser and takes off his jacket. "I'm sorry I'm late, Mrs. Fryer. But it looks like you were in good hands." He looks for a place to put his jacket, then he looks at us guys and frowns. "What are you men doing in here? You aren't supposed to be around the baby this soon. Come on, now, all of you, out. That means you too, Daddy."

Ma comes out a couple minutes later, and she tells us that Mary and the baby's gotta go over to the hospital in Ripley. When Floyd gets skittery, Ma touches his arm. "Nothing's wrong, Floyd. The doctor just wants to make sure both Mary and the baby are looked after properly for a few days."

Dad puts the bag Ma packed with Mary's things into Dr. McCormick's front seat while Floyd helps Mary into the back-seat. Once Mary's got her legs in, Ma hands her the little bundle of blankets that would be Kathleen.

"You get some sleep tonight, Floyd," Mary says. "You've got an important event to attend tomorrow." Mary looks over to Jimmy. "I'm sorry I'm going to miss your wedding, Jimmy. Give Eva my best, though." Mary thanks Ma and Mrs. Lark for helping, then Dr. McCormick says it's time to go. Floyd reaches in and gives Mary a kiss, then he kisses the blanket that's folded over Kathleen's head.

After the doctor's car's gone, Dad says, "Well, I'll get you ladies home now. Jimmy? Earl? You want a lift?"

"Nah," Jimmy says. "I'm gonna hang around with Floyd for a while."

"Me too," I say.

"I'd appreciate that. I'm still a wreck."

Before Dad leaves, Floyd asks him to stop off at the farm and tell his dad that the baby comed. Dad says he sure can, and I tell Dad to watch out for them goats 'cause they'll butt you in the ass if you ain't watching. Dad laughs and Ma tells me to watch my language.

# Chapter 30

After Dad's car leaves, Floyd and Jimmy light cigarettes. "Whew! I sure could use a beer right about now," Floyd says. Jimmy says he could too and that he's got a couple bottles in his car, so we head back to our place.

When we get home, Lucky starts in barking 'cause he wants to come out with me.

"Maybe we should go for a little drive," Jimmy says, "or this damn yapping dog is gonna have Ma up yapping."

Jimmy sneaks in the house and gets his car keys while I untie Lucky so he can go with us. "Where should we go?" Jimmy asks once we are in the car.

Floyd shrugs first, then he says, "Ah, let's go down to the millpond. It'll be like old times."

We get almost to Millpond Road when Jimmy turns the car around. "Where you going, Jimmy?" I ask.

"To roll Pissfinger's ass out of bed. If we have to stay up all night and look like shit tomorrow, then Pissfinger has to too. Besides, he's got a case of beer."

While we is banging on the door, John cusses and asks us what to hell we think we're doing, waking him up in the middle of the night. "Come on," Jimmy says. "We're celebrating. Floyd here became a daddy tonight, and I'm getting married tomorrow. Get your dead ass out of bed and come have some beers with us."

John opens the door, and we gotta wait while he gets dressed. As we is walking through his porch, Jimmy picks up the case of beer John's got sitting there and swings it up on his shoulder.

"You asshole," John says. "No wonder you came to get me."

We pass right by Louie's house that's all dark inside, the drapes pulled tight. I glance down the driveway, thinking for a minute that I'm gonna see Louie waiting there, his hair all lit up like fire, but Louie, he ain't there, and neither is his car.

"Hey, look," I yell as we bounce down the road that goes to the millpond, "there's a titty moon out tonight!"

When we get to the millpond and get out of the car, John stretches and yawns and Floyd stands real still, looking at the water that is full of swirly sparkles. "Now, ain't that a sight for sore eyes," he says.

Jimmy tosses me the car keys and tells me to get the beer. "You got your can opener on you?" he asks me.

"I sure do, Jimmy," I say, and I tap at my belt loop to show him. Jimmy grins, then him and John go off to find sticks for a fire.

I open the trunk and yell over to Floyd, "Hey, we ain't got no bucket to put the beers in." Floyd, he just shrugs and says he guesses not.

I carry the loose Schlitz bottles first, then I go get the case and bring it over to where Jimmy's standing, dumping some little sticks he finded for kindling on the ground. "We ain't got no bucket, and now our beers are gonna be warm as piss," I say.

Jimmy tells me not to worry about it, but still I worry. When John comes out of the woods carrying an armload of bigger wood, I tell him we ain't got no bucket too. John says, "Hmm. I thought I saw an old bucket out there in that clump of elm. Just a few feet in." He points off to where the woods are thick and dark. "Why don't you go see if you can find it?

"What's the matter, Earwig?" John says when I don't move. "You aren't too scared to go into the woods by yourself, are you?"

I shake my head. "I ain't scared of the woods!" I say, and that's the God's honest truth. What I'm scared of is the goddamn bears.

I call to Lucky, knowing damn well if a bear comes along, Lucky's gonna chase that big bastard off. I call, but Lucky, he's busy sniffing a dead fish over by the water, and he don't come.

"Ah, Earwig, don't be such a girl. We're all right here." Floyd laughs a bit, but Jimmy don't, 'cause he's bent over trying to blow them sparks into flames.

I know goddamn well John is gonna start teasing me bad about being a girl if I don't go, so I give another call to Lucky, trying to make it sound like I'm just asking him to go along to be polite, but that damn dog, he ain't gonna come, so I head into the woods by myself.

I don't take more than a few steps before I can't see where I'm going 'cause it's so dark. I am bent over, my hands waving through the brush, feeling for metal, 'cause that would be the bucket.

"A little farther in, Earwig!" John calls.

"You sure?" I yell back. It's helping me not be so scared if I can hear him yelling back.

"Yep, I'm sure."

I'm feeling all over the place. I feel sticks, and damp leaves, and some fuzzy moss, but I don't feel no bucket.

"I guess it's a little farther, Earwig. Go in a few more yards."

Just then I hear some rustling a ways back in the woods. "Hey, you guys," I call. "That beer probably ain't all that warm, huh?" But Floyd, he calls back that nobody wants piss-warm beer, so I should keep looking.

I walk a few more yards in. I stop and tip my head back, looking for that moon. I don't see it, though. I don't see nothing but black trees, trees so tall they gotta be tickling God's ass.

"Farther, Earwig. Just a little farther and you should come right to it," John shouts. I am crouched over when I lift my boot to take a step, then I stop. I'm hearing it again. That rustling, only this time it's louder. I got the freezes. I can hear that bear good, snapping sticks as he comes closer.

"I'm hearing a bear, Jimmy!" I yell, then I wait to hear Jimmy yell back that it ain't nothing but the wind, but he don't. Instead, it's John who calls back, "Bear, Earwig. Run!"

I pop up so fast that I whack my head on a branch thick as Pritchard's thigh. "Where?! Where?!" I yell.

"Behind you!" John yells. "Run!"

"Holy shit!" I scream, and I start dancing around in circles on accounta I don't know which way to run. I'm screaming like I'm gonna piss myself.

Just when I think I'm a dead duck 'cause I can almost feel that bear breathing down my ass, I make another circle and see the orange flames of the campfire showing between the trees. I ball up my fists and run, the brush whacking me good.

When I get close enough to the clearing, I dive right between two trees and roll outta the woods like a bowling ball. I jump to my feet, ready to make a beeline for Jimmy's car, when I see that them guys ain't running at all. They is just sitting there by the fire, slapping their legs and laughing. John is laughing so hard he's tipped over.

Just then, Lucky runs out of the woods behind me, leaping at the back of my legs. "There's your bear, Earwig," Floyd says.

"You bastards!" I say. "I bet there weren't no bucket either!"

Them guys are laughing it up good. I sit down by the fire and rub the top of my head, where that egg is throbbing. "That weren't even funny, Pissfinger. I almost died from the fright."

John stops laughing and makes his eyes get all big and buggy. He cocks his head to the side. "What did you just call me, Earwig?" Floyd and Jimmy are laughing so hard now that they is almost choking.

"Pissfinger," I say.

"You called me *what?*"

"Crissakes," I say, "you go deaf or what? I called you Pissfinger."

Floyd lets out a long whistle.

"You gutsy little asshole!" John says. "Get over here!" He jumps to his feet and hurdles right over the fire, not even minding that them flames are high enough to cook his balls.

I get up fast, and I start to running. I know I'm in a heap of trouble now, but I'm laughing anyway.

"Get over here, you mouthy bastard!" John yells behind me. "When I'm through with you, you're gonna *wish* a bear had gotten to you first!"

"Pissfinger! Pissfinger! Pissfinger!" I yell. Lucky, he runs with us, yipping to high heaven, while Floyd and Jimmy crack up over by the fire.

I think I'm real smart when I ditch for Jimmy's car, thinking that if I reach it, I can run circles around it and keep John away from me, but I ain't so smart, 'cause I don't figure out that all a smart guy's gotta do then is spring over the hood of the car and he's got me. That's just what John does.

He grabs me around the head and starts rubbing his knuckles over the top of my head so fast and hard it feels like my head's on fire. Still, I'm laughing. "Take it back, Earwig!" he says, but all's I say back is "Pissfinger! Pissfinger!"

John lets go of my head just long enough for me to wiggle out of his hold. I don't get more than a foot away, though, when John grabs my belt in the back and starts tugging me by my ass to the water. I'm laughing so hard I ain't got the strength to fight him off.

John, he gives me a twirl and then a shove, and I ain't nothing but a shooting star going into the water.

John is pissed, but not so pissed he wants me dead, 'cause he only throwed me in the shallow part. Still, that water's cold as shit even at this time of year, and my breath gets sucked right outta me.

"I hope your balls freeze off!"

I spit water out of my mouth and lie, "The water ain't even cold. Not for a real man, anyway, but for pissfingers like you, it might be cold enough to make you scream like a girl!"

John, he growls like a bear, then that nutty bastard, he starts hopping around trying to get his shoes off. He pulls his pants down and turns while he's hopping and shakes his bare ass at me. "Take this, Earwig!" he says, and I tell him no, sirree, I wouldn't want to take that ugly ass with me anywhere. We is all laughing up a storm now.

John gets his clothes off and jumps into the deeper part of the water, then splashes over to me and dunks me under.

"A little cold, boys?" I hear Jimmy call, once I'm back up and got the water drained outta my ears. John's got water dripping down his head. He gives me a wink and says to Jimmy, "Nah, Earwig was right. It ain't even cold. You girls gonna come in?"

Jimmy strips off his clothes, then whoops as he jumps in. A big-ass splash swallows him, then spits him back up. Jimmy's screaming up a storm. "Jesus! You lying bastards!" He splashes at me and John, then yells to Floyd to come on in.

It takes Floyd awhile to get his britches off with only one hand to work with, but he does it. He pauses a bit when his hand reaches his shirt buttons, like maybe he don't want us to see that lopped-off arm of his, but then he strips his shirt off anyway. He lifts his good arm and his stub into the air, then whoops as he jumps in.

My shoes, they is feeling all slippy-sloppy on my feet, so I climb out and take 'em off, then jump in butt-naked too.

We play like we is little kids. Splashing and dunking and calling each other names like fart-sniffer and ass-sucker. We tease each other about whose pecker is shrunked up the littlest from the cold water.

We stay in the water 'til our teeth are clinking, then we pull ourselves out and hurry to our clothes. Mine is sopping wet, so it don't feel no warmer once I got 'em on. Jimmy says he's got a dirty work shirt in his car, so he runs to fetch it for me.

"Hey, Earwig, open us a beer, will you?" John says once we're all sitting around the fire.

I crack open the first Schlitz, but I don't know who I'm suppose to give it to.

"Give it to the new daddy," Jimmy says.

Floyd, he looks at the beer I'm holding, like he wants to snatch it right out of my hand, but instead he takes a breath and looks away. "Nah, give it to your brother. It's his last night as a single man, so he's gonna need all the beers he can get." John laughs, and Jimmy shakes his head.

"I say Earwig gets the first beer tonight," John says. "Any

earwig who's got the balls to call me Pissfinger is the number-one guy in my book." Jimmy and Floyd say that's true and tell me I get the first one.

"What to hell you doing there, Earwig?" Floyd says, when I set the first beer down on the empty spot next to me.

John laughs. "Hell, he's so proud of earning that first beer that he's gonna set it there for a while just so he can admire it. Ain't that right, Earwig?"

"Nah," I say. "That beer there is for Louie. He's the number-one guy tonight." John looks away, but Floyd and Jimmy, they look right at me and nod. We is all quiet as I open four more beers and pass 'em out. When we all got our beers, Jimmy holds his up and says, "To Louie," and we all lift our beers to the sky too and say, "To Louie."

We quiet down and stretch out on the ground.

"I used to dream of this place when I was at O'Donnell," Floyd says, and nobody says nothing. I guess they, like me, is thinking about all the things that happened since we was here last. It seems like forever ago, yet it seems like yesterday too. "I never thought I'd see this place again, but here I am. Married, and a dad to boot. And tomorrow Jimmy gets married, and Earwig here moves in to his own place. And Pissfinger . . . well, he'll still just be a pissfinger." Floyd laughs and John throws a stick at him.

Floyd sighs then. "God, I hope I don't fuck up."

And Jimmy says, "I hope I don't fuck up either."

I look over at Floyd, and then at John, who's laying next to him. Then I look at Jimmy. Ain't a one of 'em that's all better yet. I can tell by the way they get skittery when they hear a loud noise or see something move fast out of the corner of their eye. I can tell by the faraway look they get sometimes when they is suppose to be listening, and by how quick they get pissed when some itty-bitty thing goes wrong.

Dad said that he thinks the goddamn shame of war is having

to forget you're fighting people just like you, so you can hate 'em enough to kill 'em. I think, though, that another shame of war is that when it's over, a soldier don't get to leave it behind where he fought it. He's gotta carry it right back home with him, in his head, and in his heart. I don't know for sure how long Jimmy and Floyd and John gotta carry that war around, but I hope to hell it ain't forever.

I curl my arm under my head and look back at the sky. Louie is up there. I can feel him looking right down on us. And feeling him there makes it seem like we is all together again, just like the old days.

It's the best night ever, with that titty moon shining over us as we warm our feet by the fire and drink beers until morning. And simpleminded or not, I know that even if these good days don't last, a guy don't have to give his right nut to get 'em back. All he's gotta do is put one foot in front of the other and keep going. And I shit you not, he'll walk right into some more good days again.

# Acknowledgments

My thanks to Mr. C., for helping me discover the magic in books; to Jim L., who taught me the power of storytelling; and to Shirley L., who helped me realize the power of my own story.

My love and thanks to my family, who supported me in one way or another as I learned to write. To Kerry, who made it possible for me to do the work I love. To my daughter Shannon, who proved my words true even before I believed them myself—that we can realize our dreams if we work hard and believe even harder. To my son, Neil, who shared the computer with me with little complaint. To my daughter Natalie, who is the best editor a writer could have and diligently plucks commas from my manuscripts and fearlessly gives me her honest opinion. And to my brothers, who understand more than anyone what a challenge this climb was for me.

And thank you to my cherished friends. To Lynn, who taught me to stay resolute, and especially to Gerta and Vikas, who held on to my dream for me during periods in my life when I could not.

To Sophey, my littlest angel, whose name the wind will whisper to me until we meet again.

And last, but by no means least, thank you to my dear, supportive agent, Catherine Fowler, the gentle soul who lovingly took Earwig by the hand and led him to the warm heart of Jackie Cantor, an incredible editor in every respect. Many thanks to Jackie, to my publisher, Nita Taublib, and to all those at Bantam Dell who took Earwig and caringly tucked him between covers.

My heartfelt appreciation to all of you for helping me make my dream come true.

# About the Author

SANDRA KRING lives in the north woods of Wisconsin. She has run support groups and workshops for adult survivors of trauma. *Carry Me Home* is her first novel.